PRIZE of MY HEART

Books by Lisa Norato

From Bethany House Publishers

Prize of My Heart

Also by Lisa Norato

Where Eagles Fly
I Only Want to Be with You

PRIZE of MY HEART

A NOVEL

LISA NORATO

BETHANY HOUSE PUBLISHERS
a division of Baker Publishing Group
Minneapolis, Minnesota

© 2012 by Lisa Norato

Published by Bethany House Publishers
11400 Hampshire Avenue South
Bloomington, Minnesota 55438
www.bethanyhouse.com

Bethany House Publishers is a division of
Baker Publishing Group, Grand Rapids, Michigan

Printed in the United States of America

Library of Congress Cataloging-in-Publication Data
Norato, Lisa.
    Prize of my heart / Lisa Norato.
       p.   cm.
    ISBN 978-0-7642-0942-0 (pbk.)
    1. Family secrets—Fiction. 2. Massachusetts—History—1775–1865—
Fiction. I. Title.
PS3614.O7P75 2012
813'.6—dc23   2011040776

Scripture quotations are from the King James Version of the Bible.

This is a work of historical reconstruction; the appearances of certain historical figures are therefore inevitable. All other characters, however, are products of the author's imagination, and any resemblance to actual persons, living or dead, is coincidental.

Cover design by Dan Thornberg, Design Source Creative Services

Author is represented by The Seymour Agency

12   13   14   15   16   17   18   7   6   5   4   3   2   1

To my father, Richard Norato, with love.
A man of strong faith who leads the way as a good
Christian example to his family.

DUXBORO, MASSACHUSETTS, 1815

Captain Brogan Talvis was rounding the stern of his newly constructed square-rigged ship when, from across the shipyard, the sight of a young woman took him aback.

He'd ventured out for an early private inspection—his first sight of the 880-ton merchantman—and what a beauty she was! Soon she would be christened the *Yankee Heart*. Until then, she rested complete and ready to be launched on a pair of stocks that sloped down the bank into the Bluefish River.

All he'd wanted was a few solitary moments alone with his precious ship. An opportunity to reflect on all that had brought him to this seaside town on the south shore of Massachusetts and the mission that still lay ahead.

Brogan had fully expected the yard to be deserted at this early hour—only moments ago he'd caught his first glimmer of the sun behind a horizon of bay inlets and calm waters—but there, in the flat stretch of marshland beyond, among the tall, gently swaying grass, sat the girl on a broad, flat rock.

He found it odd that she should be alone in such a place. Her legs were drawn up, spine curved in a long, slim arc with her forehead resting on her knees, her face concealed from view. Lengthy whorls of ginger-brown hair escaped a white cotton kerchief knotted atop her head. She wore a checked gingham dress the color of mustard seed relish and Boston brown bread. From beneath its ruffled hem, the toes of a pair of serviceable shoes pointed toward the river.

Brogan stepped forward, the soles of his black leather Hessians crackling over a clutter of wood chips—golden new chips scattered and heaped over faded aged ones. A summer breeze stirred the air, hinting of salt and carrying the fragrances of fresh lumber and pine tar.

As he looked more closely, he noticed the girl's muslin apron stained with spots of a deep berry red. A kitchen maid, no doubt, but what business had she idling about a shipyard at this hour of the morning? Her presence annoyed him.

Why should he feel so drawn, so curious about her, when a matter of far weightier import occupied his head and heart?

For this was a pivotal day in the life of Captain Brogan Talvis. It marked the inception of his plan to reclaim the son who'd been lost to him three years ago, when his wife abandoned their child to strangers and refused to reveal where she had disposed of the boy.

What could have caused Abigail to do such a horrible thing?

The question tortured him. Brogan would not rest until he learned the mystery behind her cruel deceit and uncovered

8

anyone else's involvement, for surely, Abigail could not have acted alone. But oh! He had since discovered the whereabouts of his son. It was Nathaniel Huntley, one of New England's most notable shipbuilders, who had possession of Ben.

Thoughts of Benjamin had haunted him the entire three years he'd captained a privateer in the War of 1812. Never a day passed when Brogan didn't miss him, when his heart didn't break and pine with love for his lost son. At the most inopportune times, he'd felt torn between a desire to return and search for Ben and a duty to defend America against England's oppression.

At last, both his search and the war were over.

Ben's name had been changed. He lived under a new identity, residing in a home of wealth and comfort, but in the end, who could be trusted to love and care for the lad, strangers or Ben's own flesh-and-blood father? Why would a prominent shipbuilder secretly accept another's child as his own? To raise as a servant? During his own youth, Brogan had suffered firsthand the exploitation of innocents.

He turned his attention to the *Yankee Heart*, admiring her full apple-round hull, supported by live oak, twenty-two inches thick. He raked his gaze upward to the rise of her stern. Her beautifully carved arch board with its graceful moldings and pilasters surrounded her quarter gallery like a framed picture. She would play a vital role in rescuing his son.

Even so, it was another woman altogether who called to him now. Brogan found he could not walk away from the maid without inquiry, could not ignore her no matter how much he'd prefer to. She had intruded upon his privacy, and he would have turned without a backward glance to return to his lodgings on Washington Street for a hearty breakfast and a hot bath, but something about her intrigued him.

Her stillness. She remained frozen in place, so much so that he wondered after her welfare. Could this young miss be in distress? Was her head bowed in tears or perhaps in mourning? Did she suffer some malady?

He would inquire. Perhaps he could be of assistance. And if the maid worked for the Huntley estate, as reason would suggest she did, perhaps she could be of assistance to him.

Dawn arrived in timid rays of soft pewter light. It rose off the horizon like an aura, while the rolling echo of the surf washed over the sandy shoreline of the Bluefish River with a sound as rhythmic as a man's breathing. Each wave returned to the briny blue with a deep, satisfied sigh.

In quiet, solitary moments such as these, the still, small voice of the Lord spoke to her heart. Resting her head on her bent knees, Lorena Huntley closed her eyes. She needed to hear.

Why this foreboding, this uneasiness of late? She understood it to be God's way of alerting her spirit, but as to what she seemed unable to discern. Had it to do with Drew? With Papa? Perhaps even George?

No, this warning was more immediate to family than the unfortunate business of George. She'd come out to her favorite spot to pray, but hours of baking in the summer kitchen had left her sleepy, and she fell into a doze only to be awakened by an unnatural stillness in the air.

She flashed open her eyes, a gasp of surprise escaping her even before she lifted her head to glance up.

Above her stood a goliath of a man.

Shoulders as broad and square as a doorframe, he towered above her, his boots planted in a wide stance that looked for all the world like even the strongest northeaster couldn't shake his timbers.

He grinned, and were he not already intimidating in stature and bearing, Lorena might have been stricken speechless at his handsomeness alone.

He wore no hat, no coat; no neckerchief adorned the collar of his white linen shirt. Simply a pair of suspenders looped over the shirt's full, dropped shoulders, its sleeves rolled up to reveal forearms corded with sinew and as tight as yarn hemp. His bisque trousers were tucked into a pair of shiny black knee boots, and at his side hung fists the size of a plow horse's hoof.

He had a hawkish nose with chiseled features, a squared jaw, and longish sandy-blond hair, parted slightly to one side. A lush stray lock spilled onto his forehead. Long side whiskers grew down in front of his ears. His was not the milky complexion of gentlefolk, but the bronzed, healthy glow of a man who obviously spent his days out-of-doors. His masculinity unnerved her, and gazing up at him, Lorena grew irritated for the ease with which she had allowed this giant to take her unawares.

She considered making a dash for home, but surmised him more than capable of outrunning her. She could scream, but no one would hear. Her father's shipwrights and yard workers would shortly be arriving for work, but until then, there was nothing she could do but stand her ground and refuse to show fear.

She met his gaze boldly, and as they regarded each other, he tipped his head in greeting. "Good morning to you, miss."

Disarmed, Lorena scrambled to her feet on top of the rock and, shaking out her skirts, straightened to her full height of five and six, until they stood face-to-face. She eyed him warily and gave a nod.

"My apologies for awakening you, but I wondered why you were so still."

She narrowed her eyes suspiciously. "You've been watching me?"

He took thorough inspection of her, from kerchief to leather shoelaces. "Aye, and a more fetching sight I've yet to see in all Duxborotown. What are you doing out here? All alone."

What was *she* doing here? Whatever was *he* doing here? And how dare he trespass on her father's property? Who was he anyway? she wanted to ask. But this man had the most arresting, melancholy eyes of china blue. They pinned her with a stare that sealed her lips as tightly as a caulker's mallet drove oakum in the seam between two planks.

"N . . . nothing." And then Lorena thought better of her answer and added, "Nothing of your concern, anyway."

"Oh?" His brows lifted in mock surprise. "Nothing to do, eh? And what, pray, would your employer think, not only of your idle hands but to find you asleep on the job?"

She could tell by the grin on his handsome face that he was toying with her, purposely trying to make her feel vulnerable. She would have none of it, however.

"I find you unmannerly, sir," she spat.

"Unmannerly?" He chuckled at that. "As though I had committed an offense in wishing you good morning."

Lorena waved an arm to indicate the surrounding area with its strewn timbers and storage sheds. "This land is the property of Nathaniel Huntley. These are his yards. What business have you to stroll through uninvited?"

"Bold words for a kitchen maid. But I see. I've disturbed you, haven't I?"

"Disturbing me is the least of your offenses." She jumped from her rock, bringing them into closer proximity, which was not her intent. "Now please step aside to let me pass."

Even with her own generous height, this man stood head and shoulders taller than she. When he did not move, it was like facing an impenetrable wall of fieldstone and granite. Only this stone wall had a pulse. She watched a vein throb in his neck.

She sidestepped to walk around him. He moved into her path. "In due time, girl. All in due time. Now, what did you say your name was?"

"I did not say." Lorena swallowed despite the lump of trepidation wedged in her throat.

As she glanced about the lonely, deserted shipyard, her gaze traveled straight through the exposed ribs of a small sloop to an enormous completed ship in the distance. Between them, no smoke emitted from the brick boiler's chimney, no steam from the long wooden steam box. The area she was accustomed to seeing ablaze with activity lay quiet in the gray light of dawn.

Her heart raced. She was alone with this stranger.

"I wish to return home," she repeated, this time more forcefully. "My family will be expecting me. I must insist again that you remove yourself from my path."

Andrew Benjamin Huntley crouched low in the marsh grass. He was quiet. Quiet as a mouse. It was easy to be a mouse when you were only five years old and too small to reach the cranberry tarts cooling on the summer kitchen's breadboard table without standing on tiptoe.

Lorena liked to bake him tarts and he liked to eat them. She said he was every mother's dream with his angel's halo of fat buttercream curls and two glowing cherub cheeks, the pearly pink of a seashell. He didn't have a real mama, but Lorena was as real as a mama could be, when she scolded in a loud voice that his behavior did not match his angelic appearance.

Drew—everyone called him Drew, because it had the same *d-d-d* sound as David, like in King David—was glad for the times he did not behave as an angel. Sometimes a man needed to be a man. He viewed the world shrewdly through eyes the peacock blue of cloudless August skies, and what they saw this morning made him angry.

He must save Lorena from the giant.

He could see she was frightened and clenched a pudgy fist around the smooth stone in his right hand. He thought about what he would do and slowly unclenched the fist. His palm was sweaty.

He looked at the stone. It was his finest, saved for an occasion such as this. He set it in his sling. Lorena had gifted him with the sling and taught him how to use it. Drew had learned well.

When Lorena was nowhere to be found this morning, Drew made certain to carry them with him when he went looking for her. He knew, of course, where to find her, but he never expected a giant.

He recalled again King David, who also carried a sling. If David could slay a giant when he was just a boy, then so could Drew. Drew twirled the sling round and round, forcing the weapon to gather speed and force. He took aim and let the stone fly, watching as it sailed through the air, waiting for it to hit its target, for the giant to fall upon his face to the earth.

The man began to chuckle softly. "All of a sudden you're anxious to return to your duties, are you? My apologies, for it seems I've frightened you."

When Lorena refused to share in his amusement, he presented her with an exaggerated frown. "What? Not even a smile will you grant me? Ah, very well then, girl, since you won't tell me your name, and you're obviously not in any sort of distress, I suppose I shall have to let you pass, but first it is my desire—"

The squared jaw dropped. Those sharp blue eyes lost their focus as they rolled back in his head. He swayed on his feet, and Lorena shrieked, sprinting from his path as he staggered, then fell facedown in the grass with a force that shook the ground beneath her feet.

Stunned, she leaned forward to inquire, "Sir? Sir, are you all right?"

He seemed not.

"Yeeooowee, I got him. Are you hurt, Lorena?"

Drew leapt out from the grasses, his rugged child's body clothed in knee breeches dyed an emerald green to hide the grass stains, shoes but no stockings, and a striped red-and-white waistcoat as gay as the grin on his round, pink face.

As Lorena watched him advance, she struggled to understand what had just happened.

At her feet lay a mountain of a man, unconscious.

"Drew, what have you done?"

Hands planted squarely on hips, the child squinted up at her as though she were a simpleton. "I slew the giant, Lorena. Like David. Just as you showed me. I saved you." Losing all patience with her, he turned away to search the tall grass. "I must find my stone. I might need it again someday."

"You naughty, naughty boy. I gave you that sling so you'd take more interest in your Sunday school lessons. How many times must I explain, it is only to be used when we pretend Goliath is a tree. We do not aim stones at living creatures. And what is that red smudge on your cheek? Oh, tell me you haven't been eating my cranberry tarts. Papa's client is dining with us this evening, and now what shall I serve him? Listen to me, prattling on about cranberry tarts, while this poor fellow lies . . ."

Lorena knelt beside the body. Grass stuck up around the stranger's form like the staves of an unfinished basket. Warily, she leaned closer to listen for his breathing. Her hand trembled, suspended over his rugged face with its darker blond side whiskers. She was tempted to reach out and touch him as a sense of destiny moved fleetingly through her spirit.

Drew pulled a dirt-stained finger from his mouth. "We should get away, Lorena. Before he wakes. He is a dangerous giant. I can tell by the looks of him."

Lorena snatched back her hand. The clever mite did have a point. He was an exceptionally astute child, she was proud to admit, although she felt none too proud of this latest show of his abilities.

Straightening, she released the breath she'd been holding. "Yes, we should be gone. He is not seriously injured, only stunned, thank goodness. He'll fare well enough, although I do despise the thought of leaving an unconscious man unattended," she went on, as much to herself as to Drew, "but Papa's workmen shall be arriving any moment now. They'll find him and revive him, if he hasn't already done so himself."

Then, hopefully, this man, whoever he was, would continue on his way, go back to wherever it was he'd come from and forget the whole incident.

Or perhaps his employer would happen by and find him asleep on the job.

Oh, Lorena, how can you jest? She was a Christian woman, but she wasn't stupid enough to wait around until he woke and face a possible wrathful confrontation between this colossus and a small boy, who had clobbered him with a well-aimed stone.

And then it occurred to her that Drew indeed had saved her, for this man's last words were "But first it is my desire . . ." What had been his desire? she wondered. A kiss?

She glanced at the unshaven face and blushed to the roots of her heavy cloud of curls.

"When we get home, Lorena, will you read to me again of David?"

Lorena smiled down at the precious golden child God had placed in her care to love and protect. She'd deal with Drew's misconduct later, but right now her heart couldn't help but fill to bursting at her little misguided hero. She leaned forward, hands on knees, and addressed him sweetly. "If you wish to hear more of King David, we shall read his psalms. You need to learn David's wisdom before you mimic his actions, or the next thing I know you'll be trotting off to slay a bear. Tonight we'll start with—"

A loud groan erupted from the stranger sprawled on the thick carpet of marsh turf. For a moment they both froze as the man stirred.

Lorena grabbed Drew's hand, and they ran like Elisha fleeing the wrath of Queen Jezebel.

2

"I've already told you, Jabez, I don't know what happened. I was about to inform the girl she could expect to receive me this evening by saying, 'It is my desire to know what you shall be serving for supper,' when the next thing I knew, I was sprawled on the grass with the worst headache of my life."

Brogan angled his face in his handheld traveling mirror as he shaved. "But you can be certain I intend on finding that skinny slip of a scullery maid and discovering whaaa . . . ahhhhhk . . . enough of this contemptible blade!"

Blood pooled on his chin as he flung the straight-edged razor into a porcelain bowl with such disgust that soapy water splashed over the rim onto the night table and dripped to the floor.

Then, for no other reason than because the fellow happened to be standing nearby, Brogan directed his aggravation at his chief mate, who was presently leaning against the doorjamb of the room they'd taken at the inn. "Shall I interpret that smirk to mean you're about to laugh, Mr. Smith? If so, pray, let me caution you. Do not give in to it."

Jabez Smith shook off the threat with a shrug of his brawny shoulders while across his densely freckled face stretched a grin that deepened the creases at the corners of his dark blue eyes. "I find it so unlike ye, Cap'n," he bellowed in a voice deep and resounding enough to be heard over a strong quartering wind. "In all our years together—and they've been many—I've never known ye to be careless."

He uncrossed burly arms from over a thick barrel of a chest and stepped forward into a pool of warm sunlight slanting in from the open window. He smelled of the sea, and in the glaring brightness his coarse head of coppery curls and bushy side whiskers came ablaze with glowing tints of orange and gilt.

"Carelessness is unthought of in privateering if a man values his life. A privateer has to have skill, courage, and endurance. But most of all, a privateer has to stay alert. And you, sir, were one of the greatest American privateer captains in the War of 1812. And here I see this brave, daring master of the sea seated on the edge of a bed, whining over a sore head and a razor nick on his chin."

Brogan curled his lips in a soundless growl.

"Well, what did ye expect?" the mate raved on. "Why must ye be such an arrogant fellow? Flaunting yerself before a good girl on Nathaniel Huntley's land? It ain't polite to go up to some unfamiliar woman and force yer acquaintance without so much as a 'how d'ye do.'"

Brogan checked his reflection for damage to his face, but saw only his scowl and a slow drip of blood from his chin. He blotted the spot with a towel. "I was only having a little fun.

I meant no harm, and if in the process I managed to glean a bit of useful information about the Huntley household, all well and good, but the girl was not the least cooperative. Anyway, I do recall wishing her a good morning."

"Well, a good morning it turned out to be indeed. Someone did not like yer idea of fun, and do ye wonder maybe it wasn't one of the blessed Savior's angels, come to knock ye over the head for the deed ye hope to carry out?"

"Don't be a fool, Jabez. The Almighty does not send out angels to knock men over the head." The ache in the back of his skull had begun to throb again. Brogan swung his long legs onto the coverlet of faded blue-checkered linen and leaned back against the goose-down pillows. "I can assure you, He hasn't the time to bother about the doings of my life." From beneath the straw-filled ticking, the bedstead ropes groaned as he stretched out.

"No, Mr. Smith, there is only one thing I have ever received from your blessed Savior, and that is indifference."

Jabez winced, giving Brogan pause with regard to his choice of words. His troubled relationship with the Lord was not for lack of his friend sharing his faith.

Raised by his devout Christian grandmother, Jabez Smith had a gift for zeroing in on people in need of his guidance. Brogan had been no more than six when Jabez rescued him from the gutters of Boston Harbor, procuring him employment as a cabin boy on the vessel he sailed with. Until then, Brogan had been a scrawny waif on the run from an orphan asylum, where he was repeatedly forced to wear a tag labeling him as *Bad*. He'd been told that God would see the tag and ignore his prayers, for God wanted no part of baseborn orphans.

To his credit, Jabez had tried to dispel the belief. He procured a pocket Bible from a local Bible society to use as text for Brogan's reading and writing lessons in the same manner other children were taught at Sunday school. Brogan discovered a passion for learning and the focus to comprehend even the complicated mathematics of navigation. He made certain to be in attendance each time their generous and fair captain held school for any interested crewmen. He sought to better himself, but more, he sought truth, though he continued to feel unworthy of that truth.

He took that Bible with him on every ship he sailed with. He carried it in his ditty bag through manhood and into the war. Before long, it would hold a place of honor on the bookshelf of the great cabin aboard the ship *Yankee Heart*. The odd thing was, Brogan could not recall the last time he'd so much as opened the cover.

Jabez cleared his throat and the sound returned Brogan's attention to the issue at hand. "Well then, aren't ye at least concerned the boy may not come willingly to a father he does not remember? Benjamin may resent being taken from the only life he's ever known."

Brogan raised himself on one elbow. "I will not allow a son of mine to be raised an orphan, believing he has no one in the world he truly belongs to, when he has a father who loves him. I know the pain in that. Benjamin is very young; he'll recover. On the other hand, I must be gentle yet swift in gaining his affections. I don't wish him hurt. I intend to restore my relationship with my son during the time I remain in Duxboro. I shall convince Nathaniel Huntley to allow me to take the boy for a short cruise on my new merchantman, and then we three shall sail off, never to return."

"A ship's deck makes for a queer playground. Maybe the boy needs more than a life at sea."

Brogan mulled the comment with one raised brow. "The sea has been good and fair to the pair of us. And he'll have a parent who loves him looking after his welfare. God rest her soul, we both recall what little care Benjamin's mother had for her own child, don't we?"

The look on Jabez's face was answer enough. "Very well, then," the mate conceded. "Aren't ye intimidated by Huntley's wealth and influence? What if he decides to pursue us? And I am willing to bet he will. What will we do then?"

"Mr. Smith, have you ever met a man who could outsail me on the high seas?" Jabez shook his head, whereupon Brogan added, "If I were one to believe in the honesty of others, I would confess the truth in good faith to Nathaniel Huntley, asking that he release the boy to his natural father. But the day Abigail informed me I'd never find my son still burns in my memory. She told me to forget Benjamin in a tone she may as well have been using to refer to a castoff sock."

Brogan rose off the bed to pace the small confines of the room. "You see, Jabez, I believe there was more to Abigail's abandoning Benjamin than a desire to wash her hands of me and my son. She wanted Ben and me separated. Why, I do not know. But Huntley had to have been involved in her scheme. And with Abigail dead, who shall confirm my paternity? Who shall speak that I am the boy's father as I claim to be? Something evil is at work; I can feel it. Deceit is afoot. For if it were merely a case of Huntley caring for the boy on Abigail's behalf, then what purpose was served in changing his identity? He has been hiding the boy, just as

Abigail insinuated to me that Ben was well hidden. You have to agree the whole state of affairs is not right."

He ceased his agitated pacing and turned to wait upon his friend for a reaction.

Jabez bowed his head to contemplate a ray of sunlight streaking across the dusty floor. "Aye, Cap'n. Something is not right."

"And Ben is caught in the middle of it. So shall I risk a long and scandalous legal battle with a powerful, affluent fellow like Nathaniel Huntley for the right to my own son? If so, what assurance do I have of success? Me, a man some repute to be of a nefarious sort. A legalized pirate, as privateers have been called. I also worry what effect such a course would have on Ben. I want him freed and unscathed, living with his natural father. So you can understand, Jabez, why I feel the need to steal back my son, just as he was stolen away from me."

The Huntley estate occupied a hundred acres on the north bank of the Bluefish River and stood at the head of the bay in an area known as Powder Point.

Jabez at his side, Brogan walked the coastal road from town, which years ago had been named Squire Huntley Road by the town's citizens in honor of Nathaniel's father, due to the magnitude of his Duxboro holdings.

Squire Huntley Road followed the bay, then rounded a sharp bend as one neared the large black-and-white Federal house. This morning it resonated with the sounds of working men and animals, of blacksmiths and horses and carpenters, the clattering of a wagon, the jingle of a harness, and the echo of the sea.

Brogan took his first full breath of that sea, and as it filled his lungs, the salt and rugged air penetrated his body to cleanse every pore. After the stale confines of the inn's lodgings, the sunlight and fresh wind revived his senses.

As they started up the brick walkway toward the beautiful two-story dwelling, Brogan paused to glance back across the road at the waterfront. Several outbuildings surrounded a fitting dock that extended into the bay. Here, he knew, Huntley vessels were rigged, their finishing touches added.

For a moment he wondered whether it might be selfish to deprive a child of such a grand place to live. Then he thought better. Selfish to believe a son should be with his father? The ease with which orphans fell victim to families in need of cheap labor was common knowledge. Homeless young boys, raised to feel too unworthy to deserve better, could provide a lifetime of servitude, helping to secure that family's inheritance for its heirs. Nay! No amount of riches or beauty could compare to the worth of a father's love.

His heart raced knowing he'd soon confront young Ben for the first time in three years. Ofttimes in his seafaring career, Brogan had faced danger. He'd shortened sail ninety feet above a swaying deck with the wind lashing at his back, many times in the darkness of night. The violence of the waves could snatch a man from the deck and hurl him into the sea, but the prospect of failure had not been as daunting as the task at hand.

What if he were unsuccessful in regaining his son's affection?

"Cap'n? Something wrong?" Jabez asked.

Brogan proceeded without comment up the hedge-lined walkway to the large black lacquered door.

He banged the brass knocker, and moments later the door

was opened by a young servant girl, not the girl Brogan had met in the shipyard earlier but one of a more robust figure, at least half a foot shorter and a few years younger. Beneath her little white cap, her hair shone a light butter toffee brown. Her hazel-green eyes stared up at him, round and curious; yet as large as they were, they widened at the sight of two beefy fellows come to call.

Brogan doffed his beaver top hat and bid, "Good day. We have an appointment with Mr. Huntley."

"Good day, sir." She blushed shyly and glanced down at his tall black Hessians. "What name shall I say, sir?"

"Captain Brogan Talvis and Mr. Jabez Smith."

She welcomed them into the hall, which Brogan could see ran the full length of the house. As she hurried off to fetch her employer, he searched for any sign of Ben—a small chair perhaps, a child's toy, the echo of boyish laughter from a distant doorway, a voice, a noise . . .

Noise. He heard it at the top of the stairs, the padding of tiny feet, and immediately looked up to see a barefoot child with plump pink toes descend the stairs. The lad's hair was a shock of curls, as pale and as fine as corn silk, just as Brogan's had been at that age. His sturdy body was brightly clothed in emerald knee breeches and a striped waistcoat. One chubby hand clutched a sling, the other a carved, painted sailboat.

He bounded down and, in his haste, remained unaware of the visitors below. Brogan preferred to believe it was due to the bond they shared that suddenly the lad realized he was being watched. The boy stopped, as hypnotized by what he saw as Brogan was himself.

The blood rushed to Brogan's head, leaving him dizzy with excitement, while the moment etched itself in his memory.

Staring back at him was an innocent version of Abigail's eyes, and how vividly he remembered them. They had haunted his dreams these three years. Exotic blue eyes reminiscent of the tropics.

"Ben," he hailed, his voice no louder than a hoarse rasp. He moved as though to mount the staircase and pronounced more clearly, "How fare you, Ben?"

The boy's mouth dropped open; his eyes rounded in fright. An iron grip fastened around Brogan's arm to hold him steady, as the deep, low voice of Jabez Smith cautioned in his ear, "Not now, Cap'n. Ye've scared the lad."

"Ah, Drew, there you are. Come here and meet— Drew? Drew!"

The voice was Nathaniel Huntley's, and as the shipbuilder strode into the hall, the boy backtracked up the stairs and disappeared around a corner as though the devil himself were hot on his heels. It was then Brogan realized his blunder in using the boy's true given name and not the one he now answered to.

"Ah, Drew . . ." With a chuckle, Nathaniel Huntley threw up his hands and turned to his guests. "Do forgive the boy's lack of hospitality, gentlemen. I believe he must have jumped out of bed this morning before his manners had a chance to follow. I often find myself inquiring, 'Drew, have you left your manners under your pillow?'" Again the man chuckled, tickled by his own humor, and extended a hand to Brogan. "Captain Talvis, I am most pleased to see you again."

As Brogan gripped Nathaniel Huntley's hand, the shipbuilder clasped his left palm over the back of Brogan's own hand to firmly seal the handshake, then pumped with a lively vigor.

His face was full and jolly. Deep laugh lines bracketed a well-defined mouth, and his brown eyes shone with a gentility that seemed to radiate from even the crinkles at their corners. When he laughed, the stripes of his silk waistcoat bounced gently over a protruding belly that strained at the buttonholes. His side whiskers had turned to white; his hair had worn to a soft gray brown and was left a tad longish behind the ears, where it feathered outward like the tips of angels' wings.

The shipbuilder's good cheer was infectious, and Brogan's smile widened in response. "Thank you for your generous welcome, sir. And I return your enthusiasm. In fact, I have thought of nothing but this visit for months. Please allow me to introduce my chief mate, Jabez Smith."

Huntley offered his hand. "So pleased to meet you, Mr. Smith."

"Aye, and you, Mr. Huntley."

"Am I to assume you are as anxious as the captain to proceed with this new venture?"

Brogan noticed a moment's hesitation before Jabez answered, "Aye, that I am."

Huntley clasped his hands together, lips firmly pressed as he inhaled and then expelled a deep breath of pleasure. "Well, gentlemen, this brings me great satisfaction. Do excuse my pridefulness when I tell you this merchantman is my finest achievement to date. My daughter, Lorena, is seeing to the arrangements for the launching ceremony. I should very much like to make an introduction this evening. I thought we might discuss the details then. I do hope you gentlemen still plan on joining my family and me for supper?"

Before Brogan could respond, Jabez elbowed him in the

ribs, an imperceptible nudge that told Brogan the mate was wondering the same as he. How was it that their plan should unfold so neatly? Too neatly, as though the angel Jabez had spoken of earlier had come to aid and not to thwart. Quickly, lest Huntley think he was having second thoughts, Brogan nodded acceptance of the offer and said, "Thank you for your trouble, sir. You have gone out of your way to please me, for which I am extremely grateful. We accept your invitation and welcome the opportunity to meet your children."

"Good, gentlemen, good," Nathaniel Huntley chanted. "But I offer simple hospitality, that is all, as I expect we shall enjoy each other's company for some time. It's going to take at least two weeks, Captain, to haul your merchantman into the deep waters of the bay, not including the time afterwards when her masts and spars will be rigged."

"Two weeks? Isn't that an unusually long time to launch a vessel?" Jabez inquired of the shipbuilder.

"I'm afraid so, Mr. Smith, but you see, our Bluefish River is quite shallow, too shallow to accommodate a ship of this magnitude. My men will only be able to move her a few yards with each new tide. But not to worry." With his next words, Huntley included Brogan, saying, "When you see her, you'll agree she's well worth the wait."

Brogan refrained from telling the man he already had, as the dull ache in the back of his head well reminded him. "I have every confidence in you, sir."

Nathaniel Huntley grinned, motioning to the rear of the house. "And now, if you'll follow me, I won't keep you waiting any longer. We shall step out through the back, and I shall take you straightaway to the shipyard so you may have a look for yourselves. Then we'll stop by my carpentry shop.

I wish to introduce you to George Louder, the talented master shipwright who designed your merchantman."

Brogan followed, his thoughts not so much on his ship as on all the possibilities two weeks could hold. For that matter, an evening could hold, because tonight he'd be dining with his son.

Standing before the looking glass of her two-tiered Sheraton dressing table, Lorena worried her bottom lip as she tried to contain two handfuls of tight spice-brown ringlets that seemed to overtake her head the way English ivy overran a brick wall.

"No, Drew, you mustn't" came Temperance's voice from just outside her bedroom door. "A gentleman never intrudes upon a lady's bedchamber. If you wish to see Lorena, you must wait until she is ready to receive you."

"Oh, she won't mind."

Lorena dropped her hands, releasing the unbound coils that spilled to her waist, and then opened the door in time to see Temperance narrow her eyes at the rebellious little scamp. "I saw how rudely you behaved to Papa Huntley's guests, and won't you be embarrassed when you greet them for supper?"

She didn't pause for Drew's response, but marched past the boy, only to have him squeeze by her into the bedroom before she could finish closing the door in his face.

"I've seen him, Lorena."

"He's come!"

They spoke at once, both Temperance and Drew rushing to her side. Lorena raised a hand to ward them off. "Please, one at a time. Of whom do you speak?"

"Captain Talvis."

"The giant!"

Again, they spoke at the same time, and it was all Lorena could do to still her racing heart long enough for reason to assure her they could not possibly be referring to the same man.

Temperance scrunched her nose at Drew as if he were something green and slippery that had crawled out of the root cellar. "The giant. What giant?"

Drew stuck his tongue out at the girl.

"Wait for me in your room, would you, Drew?" Lorena directed. "I'll join you in a few minutes." The giant . . . well, nothing could be more urgent than the giant, but Lorena needed to dismiss Temperance first. The giant was a most private and embarrassing matter.

"But—"

"No argument. Be a good boy and go to your room." She eyed him sternly to end further protest.

Her astute little man got the message. He turned and walked out the door, practicing with his sling.

With an inward sigh of relief, Lorena turned to the fourteen-year-old servant girl she mentored like a sister. Both Temperance Culliford and her mother, Wealthea, had been fixtures in the Huntley household these seven years. Long ago, Temperance's father vanished at sea amidst rumors he'd been impressed by the British, and Papa, being the good Christian man he was, had taken compassion by offering Mrs. Culliford employment as the family housekeeper. This included not only a steady income, but a cozy home within walking distance from Lorena's own residence. Temperance and her mother were treated with the fondness and consideration of family members.

Lorena pulled a long piece of straw out from under the small ruffled cap hugging the top of Temperance's head. "I thought I smelled horse," she teased.

In the early morning hours, if either of them were nowhere to be found inside the house, just as everyone knew to look for Lorena in the summer kitchen, so too could they be assured of finding Temperance in the stables.

She was a spirited girl, and though some might look upon her equestrian pursuits as unladylike, Papa did not believe in discouraging an impassioned heart. And Temperance's passion was for horses. For several years now he had turned a blind eye to her daily visits to the stable. He pretended not to notice the occasional absences from her duties. No one complained when there were no carrots to be found in the garden for dinner because they'd been fed to the horses earlier. Anyone could see they thrived under Temperance's love and attention. They were God's creatures. And Papa considered she was doing him a service in helping to groom and exercise his horses, for as long as the girl promised to be careful, he did not forbid her to ride them.

Sometimes he even brought her along riding with him for the company.

Lorena handed her back the piece of straw. "Now, Temperance, what of Captain Talvis? Has there been a change of plans about his joining us for supper?"

"Oh no, nothing like that." Temperance claimed the white ribbon Lorena held and turned her to face the mirror. As she combed her fingers through Lorena's long brown ringlets, she said, "But Mother would like to know which sweet you plan on preparing for this evening's dessert."

Lorena waved the girl's hands away. "And what of my

cranberry tarts? I was up at five this morning baking them."
As she whirled to confront Temperance, her hair tumbled
once again down her back. "What's become of them?"

"Drew ate two, dropped one on the floor, and stuck his
fingers in another. There's only a few left to serve with tea."

Lorena didn't dispute it was true, but four missing tarts
was not cause to bake a whole new dessert. "And?" she prod-
ded, suspecting more than Temperance was telling. "How
many did you eat?"

"Only two. Mr. Huntley said I could, after he took four
for his own breakfast and made me promise not to tell."

Temperance lowered her lashes, twisting the white fillet
ribbon around her finger in a show of conscience. A show,
Lorena knew, because not a moment passed before Temperance's frown curled into a grin.

"Oh, Lorena, it will be little bother for you. All of Duxboro knows how much you enjoy baking sweets. Of course,
Mother is the house cook. She could easily prepare something, but you told her you wished to do the baking for
dinner guests."

Lorena had no argument, and with a roll of her eyes admitted, "Yes, yes. I did say that. Very well, Temperance. I had
hoped to avoid the heat of the summer kitchen at midday,
but I suppose I'll have to change back into my work dress
and bake a gingerbread."

Temperance's face dropped in disappointment. "Gingerbread? For a guest like Captain Talvis? Oh no, Lorena, your
father would not be pleased. I suggest you make your chocolate custards."

"Chocolate custards require a great deal of preparation. I
have too much on my mind at present to bother with chocolate

custards." She started for the door before Drew got restless and came looking for her, but Temperance blocked her path.

"Lorena, I have come to tell you something more. I have come to advise you to choose your garments carefully this evening."

"And why is that, pray tell?"

"Because the captain . . . Captain Talvis, that is . . . oh, his eyes, they're beautifully . . . haunting. You will need to see for yourself to understand, but he bears quite a singular and striking appearance."

Lorena was already haunted by a pair of eyes from earlier that morning; she had no interest in another's. For a brief instant she regretted to think she'd never behold them again, and she was quite horrified to discover some obscure part of her maintained even the slightest interest in a second encounter with that arrogant stranger.

She shook it off, and as she brushed past, Temperance chimed in a little birdy voice as though expounding some great prophecy, "I suspect Captain Talvis will be capturing the attention of all the marriageable young ladies in Duxboro."

"Hurrah for Captain Talvis and the unmarried ladies of Duxborotown. I am going to see about Drew."

"You know, Lorena, at nineteen years of age, with no husband and no suitable prospect for one, you should pay more attention to a man like Captain Talvis," Temperance called after her from the bedroom doorway. "Unless you've changed your mind and plan on marrying George. Have you? Changed your mind, that is?"

This was not a subject Lorena wished to discuss shouting across the hall, but neither could she let the question go unanswered. She spun around. "I seek a better future for myself than marriage to a man I do not love. But if you had your way, Temperance, you'd have me betrothed to every unattached fellow who strolls through our door."

Temperance approached to brush a thick fall of gingery curls off Lorena's shoulder. "No, not every fellow," she said, "but why not a handsome, smart fellow like George? You did seem to favor him well enough once. Has he done something to displease you?" She picked at the pristine lace edging on one of Lorena's short puffy sleeves, her voice dropping to a soft, wistful tone. "Or do you refuse George because he is sailing for England, and you would not wish to be separated from us?"

"Temperance, if ever in my foolish youth I imagined affection for George Louder, I can assure you, I have long since grown to feel otherwise. England, bah. Under no circumstance would I wish to abandon my family." And then Lorena remembered to add, "And in referring to family, you know I include your mother and yourself?"

Words Temperance had been waiting to hear, for the corners of her mouth curled into her full cheeks, widening into a smile that fairly reached her ears.

Then, as though seeking further reassurance, Temperance narrowed her hazel-green eyes in a keen, assessing stare. "George hasn't done something to upset you, has he, Lorena? You wouldn't keep secrets from me?"

Lorena dismissed the notion with a giggle. "Temperance, I do not have a secret," she assured and did not lie, because thanks to this morning's misadventure, she had two.

Temperance grinned, content to let the matter drop. "In that case, Lorena, I beg you to make your chocolate custards. Shall I tell Mother you'll join her in the summer kitchen?"

Lorena summoned what little patience she had in reserve. "Very well. Chocolate custards. Though not for the sake of Captain Talvis. I am doing this for my father."

Temperance gave no reply, save for a smile and the prim satisfaction on her face. She'd gotten exactly what she'd come for and excused herself with a nod.

As Temperance bounded down the staircase, Lorena admonished herself for being so easily persuaded and continued on to Drew's room. As quickly as she stepped inside, however, the boy was upon her.

He threw his arms about her legs and mumbled incoherently into her skirts.

"I cannot understand you, Drew."

The child lifted his face. "The giant is come. Come to get us."

Lorena refused to get unnecessarily alarmed. She took Drew's chubby hands and held them tightly in her own as she leaned forward to search his face. "You're telling me you've seen the man from the shipyard again?"

He nodded.

"Where, Drew?"

The boy stomped his foot angrily on the carpet. "He is here."

"Here. Here in our house? You've seen that man in our house?"

Drew nodded, vigorously this time, as shock washed over her. Lorena could barely think straight. First in the shipyard, now in her home. Who was this giant? she wondered, knowing full well he was no giant, but a man.

The same striking figure of a man who had impressed Temperance, with eyes she could not describe, and as Lorena feared, her papa's client—Captain Talvis.

"He is a dangerous giant," Drew warned. "I can tell by the looks of him."

"Did he speak to you?"

"He smiled like it was Christmas and he had found a present under the tree. He tried to get me, but I ran away."

Get him? Lorena hardly thought so—not in their home, surely. Doing her best to hide her confusion, she squatted level with the boy. She braved him a smile and ran her fingers through his soft white-gold curls. "No one is going to get you, I promise. We needn't fear the giant. He is our papa's client, Captain Talvis. Remember your papa Huntley telling us about him? He's master and owner of the largest ship built in our yards."

Drew considered her words carefully. "Captain Talvis?"

"Yes. I imagine the captain was anxious for a look at his finished ship. That would explain his presence in the shipyard this morning."

Where I had the misfortune of meeting up with him, Lorena thought wryly.

She gave the child her most serious face. "Drew, if anyone were to find out about what happened in the shipyard this morning, the captain would be embarrassed. I think it best if we do not mention the giant to anyone."

Pressing a finger to her lips, she made a soft shushing sound. "We must refer to him only by name. Captain Talvis. And not as the giant. Do you understand?"

He stared back with that precious, innocent face she loved so well. He did not fully comprehend, Lorena could tell, but he would do as she asked.

"Yes, ma'am."

"At a convenient time, I will apologize to him in private.

Meanwhile, you are not to hurt the captain again. No sling, no stones, not even a cross word. Promise me."

He avoided her gaze, stubbornly refusing to answer.

"Drew . . ."

"I promise."

"There's my good boy." Lorena kissed his soft cheek with a loud smack.

"He called me Ben," Drew blurted.

Lorena pulled away, startled and speechless. Benjamin had been Drew's name before he came to them. Why would Captain Talvis call Drew by his former name? How would he even know of it?

A chill of foreboding stole up her spine, rattling her composure until her hands shook. She clasped them behind her back, before Drew noticed how shaken she was. This innocent child had no idea of the dark secret that surrounded him.

But Lorena knew the secret. It smoldered bitterly in her heart.

Except for Papa and herself, no one knew about *Ben*.

No one who was still alive.

3

Her father asked that she wait in the east parlor, but Lorena brought Drew across the hall to the more feminine west parlor, where she would be better situated to hear her dinner guests arrive.

Butterflies flittered nervously in her stomach, making her wonder whether it wasn't the anticipation of receiving her papa's client that had her pacing the floor or the inevitability of another face-to-face encounter with Captain Talvis.

He'd never seen his attacker in the shipyard, and since Drew had reclaimed his stone, Lorena doubted the captain even realized what had hit him.

She feared his reaction. Would her identity shock him? And once revealed, would that identity as the lady of the house, rather than a servant, diffuse any anger he might be inclined to vent for the way she'd left him lying in the marsh?

The blame was not all hers to bear. By all accounts, the captain should have made a proper introduction. It would have explained his presence in the shipyard. Lorena could have welcomed him to Duxboro and might now be looking forward to his stay in town with pleasure instead of dread.

More than the sort of nervousness a woman in her situation might be expected to feel, she felt disquiet.

Benjamin was Drew's middle name. Andrew Benjamin Huntley, named for her paternal grandfather, Squire Andrew Josiah Huntley, whose portrait hung over the mantel in her father's study and who had founded the shipbuilding empire he later passed on to his eldest son. Had Captain Talvis mistakenly transposed Drew's first and middle names? Was it that simple? Had she overreacted, or was there good reason to remain leery of the man?

In any case, this was her home, and she would not allow him to take her at a disadvantage again. No, not as he had this morning, approaching her unawares, bullying her with muscle and arrogance, with haughty smiles and deep, arresting stares.

She peered out one of the front windows, but the dark, moonless night saturated the glass so thoroughly, Lorena saw only her reflection and the parlor's interior.

Hand-blocked French wallpaper depicted a mural of well-dressed ladies and gentlemen at a lakeside picnic. The tall case clock ticked five past the hour. Chinese porcelain vases sat atop the fireplace mantel adjacent to a yellow and ivory silk damask sofa, where her gaze came to rest.

She whirled about. "Don't slouch, Drew, or your clothes will get rumpled."

The child half sat, half reclined on the sofa, head propped against the back with his chin pressed to his chest in a way that concealed his pout in the lacy ruffles of a cravat. He wore a pistachio waistcoat that did marvelous things for bringing out the peacock blue of his eyes.

Yet perhaps it wasn't the waistcoat at all but the angry defiance blazing through those eyes that intensified their color.

Lorena marched over for a seat beside him, leaning closer when he made no visible acknowledgment of her. "Listen to me, sweetheart. Papa Huntley is entertaining a very important client this evening. Think how rude it would be for Captain Briggs to sit on the table while you carried on a conversation with him none of us could share in. You'll be together with Captain Briggs soon enough. In the meantime, give me a smile and be a good boy for your papa Huntley. Think of all the nice things he does for you. Why, just the other day he took you for a ride in the chaise to Timmy Baker's farm and let you chase the baby pigs through the mud. And didn't he say you could have one of Taffy's puppies once they've been weaned?"

Drew turned his head and mumbled something about a stupid giant, his body slumped in a manner that reminded Lorena of the cloth doll he pined for. Captain Briggs wore a tiny sea captain's uniform in honor of the father he believed had perished at sea. Drew and Captain Briggs had joined the household as a pair. Young and disoriented in his new home, the frequency with which Drew had awakened during the night came as no surprise, but Captain Briggs, tucked under the quilt beside him, never failed to ease the child back to sleep.

It brought to mind a certain Boston townhouse during the war. Heavy fringed draperies hung at the windows, blocking the sunlight but not the sound of soldiers drilling or the constant beat of their drum. Vessels sat anchored up and down the coast with British men-of-war standing guard over them in the harbor.

The voluptuous blond woman showed no emotion as she delivered the baby called Benjamin into Papa's arms. Papa bounced the pudgy towhead on his hip, but Ben squirmed against a stranger's embrace. He searched pitifully about the foyer, and when he didn't find whom he was looking for, he screwed up his little face and cried out, "Papa?"

Lorena thought it terribly tragic he didn't call for his mama, but the closest the woman came to compassion was to shove a tiny sea captain's doll she referred to as Captain Briggs into Lorena's hands. She addressed her only child for the last time, saying, "That silly doll is the last you'll ever see of that papa of yours." The murderous look in her eyes sent a chill up Lorena's spine.

She shook off the unpleasant memory and grew stern. "Drew, this morning I promised I'd read aloud to you from David's psalms. Remember I said you needed to learn David's wisdom? Well, young man, this sulking is very unwise. Tonight of all nights. And if it does not stop, I shall be forced to put you to bed with no stories of David for a week—"

"No!" he barked, blue eyes blazing and in a voice far too demanding. One look at Lorena's sharp, disapproving glare, however, and he quieted. The color rose high on his cherub cheeks, his golden lashes lowering ashamedly as he murmured, "I . . . I'll be good."

With a little assistance he wriggled to an upright position and not a moment too soon. Footsteps thudded down the hall. Lorena straightened his cravat and wiped the drool from his chin. Outside in the foyer the footsteps halted, then thumped back across the corridor toward the west parlor.

"I don't understand where they've gotten off to." It was her father's voice. "I thought they'd be waiting. . . ." Papa appeared in the doorway. His eyes twinkled at her while he addressed the gentlemen behind him. "Ah, here they are," he said, chuckling. And to his daughter, "For a moment I thought I'd misplaced you."

"Sorry, Papa." Lorena rose to greet her guests. Her white lace shawl slipped off one shoulder to ruffle in the crook of her arm. Its silky fringe dangled from her elbow as she anxiously watched her father enter. He was followed by a rusty-haired fellow, heavily freckled, with long side whiskers as coarse and wild as a boar's-hair brush, and a chest so thick it seemed to overpower the lower half of his body.

Then suddenly he was before her. The guest of honor strode through the door like the giant he was, looking all the more so standing inside Lorena's dainty parlor.

With the exception of his unkempt, shaggy hairstyle, he made quite the fashionable figure in a single-breasted jacket of midnight blue, cut straight at the waist with knee-deep tails. His waistcoat was yellow silk brocade, his trousers dove gray and tucked neatly into the same black knee boots of this morning. The points of both his starched white shirt and jacket collars were turned up to flank his lean cheeks and parallel the edges of his long side whiskers. Beneath the determined set of his jaw lay a white neckerchief tied in a meticulous bow.

Lorena could not tear her gaze from the imposing sight of him. There was something about his confidence . . . something in the firm set of his jaw and the steadiness of his expression . . . something in his look of fierce determination that made her wonder whether he'd come with a purpose more substantial than supping with her family.

She regretted her presumptuousness in thinking she could

remain in complete control, fearful at any moment he might unleash his anger, blanching against the riot of butterflies in her stomach, only to watch his gaze pass idly by, as though she had blended into the wallpaper.

He looked instead at Drew.

"Gentlemen, may I introduce my daughter, Lorena, and my young son, Drew. Children, meet our guests. Captain Brogan Talvis and his chief mate, Mr. Jabez Smith."

At Nathaniel Huntley's introduction, Brogan held back and left Jabez to exchange pleasantries while he indulged in the sight of his son, dressed in the attire of a little man.

My, how the lad had grown these three years of their separation. His heart swelled with pride, so much so that he remained barely aware of Huntley's daughter, until the boy scooted off the sofa to stand beside her and take her hand.

Watching, a pain stabbed Brogan's heart. He felt excluded. His gaze rose from the girl's white satin slippers to their ribbon laces wound around her trim ankles and peeking out from beneath a shortened hemline that displayed the lace edge of a petticoat. The gown was of Empire fashion, in a shade somewhere between that of spring lilacs and a ripe plum. Its satiny fabric shimmered in the glow of the oil lamps the way a pool of water captured the reflection of a rainbow.

When at last Brogan looked into that delicate face framed by ginger ringlets, he found her regarding him with chocolaty brown eyes he recognized at once.

His breath caught.

That morning he had mistaken her for a servant, but she hardly fit the part now, did she, dressed in finery with her hair bound at her crown and silver earrings dangling from her ears?

In kerchief and soiled work clothes, she had been fetching. This evening, however, with her beauty displayed to full advantage, she stole all logical reason from his mind. He'd been certain nothing could distract him from his course of action, but suddenly all his long-awaited plans were swept away in a wave of attraction, and he was conscious of nothing save the blood pumping beneath his skin.

Brogan deepened his shallow breathing until his heart slowed to normal, and when at last he could breathe freely again, his anger had increased tenfold.

So the skinny scullery maid was not a maid at all. Nay, she was a rich shipbuilder's daughter, but did that give her license to bash a man over the head and then leave him rotting in the wet marsh, while nasty midge flies flew up his nose and gnawed on his flesh? His jaw clenched, tightening the surrounding muscle and straining the cords of his neck, until Brogan felt his head might explode. Were it not for the others present, he would demand she explain what trickery she'd used to knock him out cold.

But he refused to say a word. Aye, she owed him an explanation, but to mention the incident now would only heap embarrassment upon himself.

And she did have pretty ankles. Thinking of them made it possible to smile in the face of his displeasure. Brogan bridged the distance between them with a few strides and bowed.

As he reached out, she placed slender fingers in his broad, callused palm and greeted, "Welcome to our home, Captain. I hope this evening finds you faring in the best of health."

"Thank you for your hospitality, Miss Huntley, and good

evening. I am well, aye. However, I did have the earlier mis-fortune of having been struck with a headache. It came upon me suddenly and with great force."

It was an odd greeting for the lady of the house, to which she paled, her smile waning into an expression of remorse. She reclaimed the hand, but not before Brogan felt her tremble, and moved in a manner to block Drew from his view with the shimmery folds of her gown, much in the manner of a mother hen hiding her chick beneath a wing.

"I am very sorry to hear it, sir," she said.

Brogan dismissed the apology with a silent *harrumph* and leaned toward his son. "How fare you, Drew? We would have met earlier, but I think perhaps I may have frightened you on the stairs this morning."

The little fellow stepped out from hiding, but instead of accepting the hand Brogan offered, he pointed a finger at his father and shouted, "I do not fear giants. George says you're a pirate. Are you a pirate?" He narrowed his eyes sus-piciously, running his gaze over Brogan's person. "Where is your sword?"

The only sound in the room was that of Jabez's deep, husky chuckle.

Huntley's daughter colored with embarrassment. "Perhaps you misunderstood George," she told the boy. "We shall ask him later, but regardless, that is not a polite question for our guest."

"It is a fair question," Brogan countered. "I wish to answer the boy."

Brogan saw the surprise on her face, but Miss Huntley merely conceded with a graceful nod. "As you wish, Captain."

Turning from her, he braced a hand on each thigh as he

bent to address the child. "Drew, I was granted a letter of marque signed by the president to serve as a privateer during the war. I am not a pirate. There is a difference."

"George says there is no difference."

Brogan straightened. He did not know this George, though the name did ring familiar. As for Drew, his son had pluck for such a wee one. It filled him with pride, and in response, his smile was one of love and patience. "Oh, does he now? Well, you can assure George there is a considerable difference. Would you like to know what that difference is?"

The lad stuck a finger in his mouth and mumbled something that, as far as Brogan could decipher, sounded like, "Uh-huh."

"Then I shall tell you." Clasping his hands behind his back in a wide-legged stance as though he were once again braced for balance on the schooner *Black Eagle*, Brogan explained, "A pirate acts out of greed, but a privateer serves his country. Take for instance this war past. Our American navy amounted to a paltry seven frigates and fifteen armed sloops. England faced us with eight hundred war vessels, almost two hundred of which were ships of the line. Now, Drew, how would you propose to defend your country in such an instance?"

Brogan bowed lower in anticipation of an answer, but all he received was a gaping stare.

He answered his own question. "Utilize the talents of thousands of Americans who have been trained exclusively for the sea and send out privateers to strike England where she is likely to suffer the most—that is, her merchant fleet. In so doing we drive the price of British goods to the sky and let all England know they cannot infringe on our rights to free trade, nor impress our men."

Brogan frowned, concerned his zealous views may have exceeded the comprehension of a five-year-old. "Have I confused you, son?"

"George says stealing is wrong!"

Brogan gazed down upon his son's sweet, scowling face, and then squatted before the lad, his own expression just as intent, yet longingly so. He ached to hold him. Instead, he searched the boy's eyes, fully aware of the significance of what he would say next and spoke from his heart, heedless of the others in the room. "Drew, taking back what is yours by right is not stealing."

Jabez cleared his throat, a hoarse warning, or merely an expression of his disapproval. No matter, for Brogan doubted he had disclosed any secrets with just those few words. What he didn't expect, however, was for Miss Huntley to draw further attention to the remark.

"I find that a rather queer statement, Captain. I mean, I do understand the strategy of our American defense system in sponsoring privateers, but I fail to see how you can justify . . . stealing . . . by claiming . . ."

Her words dwindled to a soft, inaudible whisper that dissolved on her tongue as Lorena watched Brogan Talvis straighten to his full height. He stood with his back to her father, blocking her from Papa's view, and fired her a condescending glare that dared her to continue.

She didn't, of course, but her reaction was borne more of shock than fear.

Jabez Smith intervened. "Please do not mistake the cap'n's meaning, Miss Huntley," he implored, his expression apologetic. "He is a zealous man and was merely defending a cause he believes in. I can assure ye, the cap'n esteems justice and honor and loyalty like the true patriot he is and meant no offense."

"And certainly none was taken," her father quickly assured before Lorena could answer for herself. Then, with a lift of his thick graying brows, he added, "Children, we are talkative this evening."

She bristled at the rebuke. Did Papa think because she was a woman she did not understand conversation about war? Or perhaps, more accurately, he thought so highly of Captain Talvis that he believed the man to be above reproach. She clearly heard the captain claim that the goods of the British merchant fleet rightfully belonged to the United States.

Lorena did not wish to be unsympathetic, prejudiced, or quick to judge. She knew the realities of war and its hardships. She realized there were times men found themselves in circumstances where no alternative seemed right. Still, that didn't release him from bearing responsibility for his actions, and as a future man, Drew needed to understand he could not justify taking what was not his to take.

But apparently, any lessons were best taught in private and not before guests, so Lorena swallowed her indignation while her father announced, "Gentlemen, I believe supper is waiting. Shall we proceed to the dining room?"

The diners gathered around a long oval table in a room lit by candlelight, where they were greeted with the clean aroma of bayberry and a heartier one of fresh-baked cornmeal-and-molasses bread.

A warm piece of the loaf had been wrapped inside each individual napkin and left in a tidy bundle on the porcelain dinner plates. Bayberry tapers burned on pewter holders scattered across the mantel, from a tiered silver epergne on the sideboard and in a pair of silver candlesticks on the table. Their flames cast flickering shadows on the white linen cloth, magnifying the three-tined forks to the size of pitchforks.

After a first course of lobster stew, the entrees were brought out: stuffed and roasted pigeons, buttered and sprinkled with crackers and seasoned with sweet marjoram; boiled leg of mutton garnished with Brussels sprouts; a whole cod fish, baked inside a pastry crust and stuffed with lobster and oysters; and roast pork with spiced apple sauce and cranberry relish. There was sage-and-onion pie, boiled carrots, a salad of cabbage, and creamed potatoes.

And mashed turnips. Drew thought they tasted like the worm he ate that afternoon. The oysters resembled it. Captain Briggs liked oysters, because they were slippery going down and didn't need to be chewed.

If Drew were king, he would let Captain Briggs eat at his table every night, and no giants. Giants ate like the pigs at Timmy's farm. Like they couldn't get enough food into their bellies.

But what really bothered Drew was the way the giant stared. Drew didn't like being stared at. He couldn't understand why the giant's eyes looked sad. It was like when Timmy had moved to Duxboro with his family. On Sunday mornings he'd stand alone in the meetinghouse courtyard, watching Drew and the other boys play, wanting to join in, but too bashful to make new friends until Drew made the first move.

Drew knew the giant wasn't bashful, but he wondered if he had friends. He had Mr. Smith, but maybe he scared everyone else away because he was so big.

Drew liked Mr. Smith. He liked the way Mr. Smith raised the food to his mouth on the rounded edge of his knife blade instead of using a fork. Drew had tried to do the same, but Lorena squealed when she saw him and snatched the knife away before he'd gotten the oysters halfway to his mouth.

Mr. Smith had a drawing of the Savior nailed on the cross pricked into his arm. "Done with India ink from China," said he. It could never be washed off. He let Drew touch the picture, but all Drew felt were the bristly hairs on Mr. Smith's arm.

Mr. Smith also made exaggerated faces and told scary stories, like the one about how the giant had once killed a shark with his bare hands. Drew thought it would be fun to have a friend who could kill a shark with his hands. But then he remembered he was still angry, because it was the giant's fault Captain Briggs could not come to the table.

Dessert arrived. Chocolate custards, sweet and rich, served on blue-and-white Staffordshire china. They looked wonderfully patriotic, Lorena proudly observed, garnished with white swirls of fresh cream, ripe blueberries, and red raspberries.

Just the thing to serve an American privateer captain who believed in justice and honor and loyalty.

She had not forgotten the scornful glare Captain Talvis bestowed on her earlier. They weren't off to an amiable start. Lorena remained hesitant to join in the dinner table conversation. Not that it interested her. Papa monopolized his guests with talk of ships and the merchant trade, trying to impress the captain with his ability to turn the sea into profit in hopes of interesting him in a new business venture.

"Something troubling you, dear?" Mrs. Culliford leaned in to whisper as she placed a serving of custard before her. "You seem far away."

"I have a lot on my mind, Mrs. Culliford."

The dear woman gave Lorena's shoulder a squeeze of motherly affection. "I insist on helping with arrangements for the launching ceremony," she promised before moving on to serve the captain.

Lorena heartened at the kindness. She picked up her dessert spoon as a custard was placed before the captain and paused for his reaction.

The process of making chocolate custards was no easy chore, but an exercise in precision and care, from boiling the milk to measuring each ingredient to simmering the custard at just the right temperature and then stirring, stirring, stirring in only one direction. But not a moment did Captain Talvis spare the artistry of her labors or savor its decadent, visual appeal. No matter that he'd been eating heartily of the savory dishes, he attacked her dessert with all the impatience of a man who hadn't enjoyed a decent meal in weeks.

Lorena had been observing him, stealing glances through coyly lowered lashes as she endeavored to gain a better understanding of the privateersman. She took note of frivolous things like the pleasing arrangement of his sharp, masculine features. They lent him a formidable air while at the same time she found something about Captain Talvis to be curiously sentimental.

He seemed taken with Drew, although what interest a hand-some bachelor sea captain had in a small boy, Lorena could not imagine. She might have been disturbed if not for the sincerity of his gaze. The captain's countenance was just as Drew described. As a man beholding a gift, a rare jewel, a treasure beyond imagining . . . a prize.

She found him full of contradictions. And the more time Lorena spent in his presence, the more mysterious he grew.

"May I offer you another, Captain? I daresay, chocolate cus-tards must be your favorite sweet," Papa remarked, motion-ing for Mrs. Culliford to bring the captain another portion.

Lorena spooned a cream-dipped raspberry into her mouth. She hadn't believed Mr. Smith's sea yarn for a moment, but if ever there were a man who could rip a shark from the bowels of the sea . . .

The captain wiped his mouth on his napkin. "Aye, sir, I confess a fondness for all sweets. Until now, if you had asked me to choose a favorite, I would have said nothing is as satisfying to the stomach as a slice of warm gingerbread. Having spent most of my life at sea, I've long endured meals of sour beef and the bitter taste of weevils in a ship's biscuit. So when I have the good fortune to enjoy home-cooked fare and delicacies like this, I can hardly remember my manners and restrain myself from gluttony. My apologies, sir"—he motioned to the second helping of chocolate Mrs. Culliford placed before him—"for now that I have tasted these, I fear all hope on that score is lost."

Papa chuckled heartily. "I'll have you know, Captain, my daughter made those custards you seem to be enjoying so well."

"You don't say? Well, sir, I am impressed." The captain

turned to regard Lorena. "My compliments to you, Miss Huntley. They are delicious."

"Lorena is known throughout Duxborotown for her exceptional cakes and sweets," offered Mrs. Culliford, "and gingerbread happens to be one of her specialties."

Papa gave her a wink, saying, "Perhaps, Captain, we can convince her to bake you a cake of gingerbread before you leave Duxboro."

"But I could hardly expect such a kindness," the captain replied. "No, not after Miss Huntley has already been so generous with her hospitality."

The captain's eyes turned a stormy blue. They shifted over her and sized her up, reminding Lorena of a shark about to close in and take a bite out of her composure. He fixed her with a steady gaze while one hand reached behind his head to rub the spot where Drew's stone had struck.

She understood the warning—Captain Talvis was not going to let her forget their unfortunate parting this morning.

She swallowed, and the spoon slipped from her fingers, clanging to the floor with a racket that had every eye in the room turning to gape.

"Don't trouble yourself, Lorena. I shall pick it up."

As Temperance hurried to retrieve the utensil from under the table, Lorena felt heat rising to her cheeks. With everyone's attention on her clumsiness, she assumed Captain Talvis's intimidating antic had escaped notice.

She was mistaken.

Drew pulled back on his spoon and, with the same marksmanship he had exhibited with his sling, struck the man square in the eye with a dollop of custard.

"Aaauuggh." The captain wiped his muddied eye. After

examining the sticky mess the chocolate had made of his fingers, he searched for the origin of his attack.

Lorena held her breath, for Drew was glaring at the man, boldly proclaiming his guilt when only that morning he had promised to behave.

Her father threw down his napkin. "Drew, what have you done? I don't understand your uncivil conduct and neither shall I tolerate it." Picking up the napkin once again, he mopped his forehead, inhaling deeply as though trying to draw patience out of the air. "Captain, please accept my heartfelt apologies. I am dreadfully sorry. Rest assured, the boy shall be punished. Too many people wanting to do for him, you see. Too many well-meaning folks willing to indulge him. And I am as guilty as any. I tell my carpenters no more toys, and every day I find another carved horse here, a painted solider there. Temperance runs around the house picking them up off the floor, and Drew is right behind her scattering others." He heaved a sigh that ended his rambling and added, "Lorena, perhaps you should take him up to bed now."

"Yes, Papa."

"No. Mr. Huntley, please. That isn't necessary." Captain Talvis rose, his cheek still bearing traces of chocolate. "I'm sure the lad meant no harm. I recall many a time taking out my youthful aggression on others for no good reason other than the mischief inside me." He shrugged, chuckling as though it were all a joke. "Such is the way with little boys. There's no need to banish him from the table."

Jabez Smith rolled his eyes and dropped his forehead in his hand.

But Papa, Lorena noticed, seemed genuinely impressed

with the captain's tolerance and not the least surprised at his defense of Drew, as Lorena herself was.

"Thank you for your understanding, Captain," he said. "However, we do abide by certain rules in this house."

Lorena stood, eager to put an end to an exhausting, event-filled day. Drew scooted off his chair and took refuge in her skirts, burying his face in their satin folds. He was expecting her to come to his defense, and because she felt guilty for not listening to instinct and putting him to bed sooner, she laid a protective hand on his pale curls. "I'm sure Drew regrets his actions. Don't you, sweetheart? Apologize to Captain Talvis."

A long moment of silence ensued before he mumbled, "Ah-um sss-orry," without lifting his head.

"I accept your apology, Drew," the captain said, his dejected tone leaving Lorena to wonder whether Drew's punishment of being sent to bed didn't pain him more than it did the child.

She quickly herded the boy toward the door. "I pray you don't think us ungracious for leaving, but it truly is past time Drew retired."

"Allow me to see you to the stairs, Lorena," her father said, rising himself. "I wish to speak with you a moment."

Jabez Smith stood. "A good evening to ye, Miss Huntley, and thank ye for the lovely meal."

Lorena acknowledged the compliment and wished everyone a pleasant evening, but something in Captain Talvis's manner alerted her that he was none too pleased with this turn of events. He gave her a smile, which she suspected was forced. "Good evening, Miss Huntley. I hope to be seeing you on the morrow."

Lorena started. She thought she might at least be granted a reprieve from the man on the Sabbath. "I think not, Captain. Tomorrow is Sunday."

"Sunday, aye. Which reminds me, Mr. Huntley, would you allow me to accompany your family to the Duxboro meetinghouse in the morning? I wish to attend worship services."

Her father radiated delight. Lorena had the distinct impression he was growing quite fond of Captain Talvis.

"Certainly, Captain. You are more than welcome to join us, and that invitation extends to you also, Mr. Smith. There is room enough for all in the family pew."

"A generous offer, sir," Mr. Smith acknowledged. Grinning, he gestured with a nod at the captain. "Though, for all our sakes, I do hope the meetinghouse walls don't come crashing down when the cap'n walks in."

"Very amusing, Mr. Smith," Captain Talvis returned. "It is a pity Moses did not know of your wit. He could have used it to plague Egypt."

Papa chuckled at their banter, his good humor restored. "Whatever your wishes, gentlemen, just know you are both welcome. Now excuse me while I say good-night to my children. We shall enjoy some cheese and fruit upon my return."

Brogan reseated himself as Huntley departed with his family. He dipped a corner of his napkin in a tumbler of water and wiped the remaining traces of custard from his face, then began to brush a spot off his lapel. "So, Jabez, what do you think of my son?"

"Looks like an angel, but a wee rascal lurks inside. I agree with Huntley. The lad is spoiled."

"He needs his father."

"So he does, Cap'n, but ye hardly seem to be getting off to a healthy start with the youth. Ye heard what the shipbuilder said this morning. Ye have two weeks before the *Yankee Heart* is ready to sail. Not much time to win a boy's love. Harder still to win it from such a lovely rival."

Brogan stared into the flame of a bayberry taper until his pupils lost their focus. He saw a marsh meadowland, where a willowy young beauty sat dozing on a boulder, her plentiful coils of hair bound in a kerchief and a stained muslin apron tied about her waist.

"Miss Huntley is an obstacle I hadn't anticipated. She has adopted the role of mother. Calling the boy by a name of her choosing, when in truth he is my Benjamin. What game do they play, these Huntleys? What do they hide?"

"Perhaps nothing, Cap'n. Perhaps they're just good, kind folk who have opened their hearts and home to a child."

Brogan continued as though Jabez hadn't spoken. "And she is too inquisitive by far. I noticed her taking my measure more than once this evening. I've not been in Duxboro one day and Miss Huntley has managed to intrude upon my most private moments, starting with this morning, when all I wanted was to bask in the accomplishment of becoming master of my own ship."

Frowning, Jabez Smith lifted a mug of cider to his lips and took a deep swallow. He set the mug down upon the linen-covered table and wiped his mouth with the back of his hand. "This morning? Surely, ye haven't met the girl before tonight?"

Brogan turned to meet his mate's gaze and, with the lift of a brow, said, "Surely I have."

Realization struck. Jabez asked, "Do ye mean Miss Huntley is the skinny scullery maid who knocked ye senseless?"

At Brogan's nod, Jabez lifted his eyes heavenward. "O Lord,

I pray, bestow a blessing of intelligence upon my poor, witless cap'n.'"

"You are a fine one to talk, Mr. Smith."

"I told ye to be careful," Jabez snapped, his look disapproving. "Ye are deceived. Miss Huntley is a good girl and cares only for the welfare of the child. Ye must gain her confidence if ye ever hope to get close to yer son. Be nice to her. The lad will have no regard for ye until ye do."

Brogan's nostrils flared with his annoyance. He'd been waiting three years and had no patience to waste on a mere slip of a girl, tempting distraction that she was. "Nice? And what, pray, do you mean by *nice*?"

Jabez leaned closer, his expression as serious as Brogan had ever seen it. "Be sweet to the lady. Romantic."

Brogan blinked, then gaped, lost for words. When he recovered from the shock, he broke into laughter. His sides split and he doubled over, fearing he might expire from the strain.

Slowly, his breathing returned to normal, and he turned to address his chief mate between lingering chuckles. "And what do you know of romance, Mr. Smith?"

Brogan never got his answer. Nathaniel Huntley stepped into the room just as he was wiping the tears from his eyes.

4

Brogan studied his reflection as he groomed for church. Eyes of a bright greenish blue reflected sharply back at him as he slipped a white silk cravat behind his neck, wrapped it twice around, then secured it under his chin in a tidy bow.

Something about his gaze burned just intense enough to draw attention, whether for good or bad. Aboard ship, his command was law, and it was rumored he could contain an entire crew with one menacing glare. On the other hand, and with considerably more ease, he had, on occasion, caught the attention of a lady who'd tease that his eyes resembled those of a melancholy boy. Why then, no matter how kindly he looked upon his son, did he see distrust in the lad's eyes? Had he lost the ability to convey compassion, or perhaps he'd spent too much time at sea schooling his features to intimidate so that gentlefolk could no longer see past his outer appearance?

This was not the case with Miss Huntley, however. When

Miss Huntley met his gaze, Brogan sensed she looked deeper, searching beyond the obvious to the man inside.

Such a pretty name, Lorena. But then the girl was pretty. Nay, beautiful, considering her excess of spice-colored ringlets, which, if loosed from their pins, would surely overwhelm her small face and willowy frame.

Her beauty and grace disarmed him, and were he foolish enough to indulge this preoccupation, he might easily develop a guilty conscience about his intention to abduct Drew from her home.

Her bond with his child was the relationship Brogan longed for. They made a charming pair, even going so far as to hold hands upon greeting guests for dinner. He'd seen their loving displays. And he had sensed Lorena's watchful eye, her protective manner. She was the one person who could truly obstruct his plans. How was he to compete with Miss Huntley and her motherly influence? He could not. He was a stranger to the boy.

Though he'd laughed at the suggestion, Jabez's advice was sound indeed. If Brogan wanted Drew to think highly of him, he needed to gain Lorena's approval, for only with her acceptance could he hope to win Drew's affection.

Brogan shrugged into his rust cutaway coat and donned his beaver top hat.

Lorena was unsuspecting. When he looked into those velvety brown eyes, he did not see the calculating iceberg of a soul that had been Abigail's. Nay, he saw the "good girl" Jabez heralded Lorena to be.

And here stood the "bad," unwanted and misbegotten orphan of a Boston asylum on his way to Sunday services to woo her.

"My father would not conduct business with the man were he not respectable," Lorena argued, and yet hadn't she questioned the captain's respectability herself only yesterday morning?

"It is not my intention to insult your father. However, I have proof Captain Talvis is acclaimed to be quite the privateersman." George Louder glanced down the lane to the bare bushes, which in the spring had bloomed with lilacs. They were driving to meeting in her father's one-horse chaise, Drew sandwiched between them. "I'm merely passing a warning as to the sort of character he is. Join me and Edward Hicks's family at the back of the church this morning, Lorena. I should be remiss should the captain offend you in any way."

Lorena refused to let George know he already had. Presently, however, it was George, and not Captain Talvis, who irked her. He spoke in a tone that implied possession rather than with the concern of a friend.

In no respect would she ever belong to George Louder. She turned to regard his stern profile. An aquiline nose projected sharply from his angular, clean-shaven face. "You speak harshly of Captain Talvis. I've heard it said he's a man who esteems justice and honor and loyalty. Papa approves of him. He's told me he finds the captain quite agreeable and hopes to convince him to join him in the establishment of a shipping enterprise."

"Partnering with a privateer captain." George tsked in disapproval. "Regardless of what acts our government sanctions, Lorena, attacking British merchants, thieving, and burning their ships still make a privateer nothing more than an elaborate title for a pirate."

Drew had tugged loose his cravat. "Yes," the child intoned. "Captain Talvis is a dangerous pirate."

"A remarkably clever child, Lorena. I have always said so."

"Don't encourage him, George." She retied the cravat, attempting to make Drew presentable for the third time that morning. "I know you've been calling Papa's client a pirate in front of him and I don't approve."

"I make it a point to research vessels of any notoriety," George went on without acknowledgment of her protest, "and the Rhode Island schooner *Black Eagle* gained a considerable amount of recognition during the war. Under Captain Talvis's command, she brought home some twenty-nine prizes for her owners. I was curious as to whether the schooner's success in outwitting British warships was owing perhaps to her skillful design or rigging." His left hand held the reins, while with his right he reached into his waistcoat pocket to produce a sheet of newsprint. "The *Providence Gazette and County Journal* recorded the exploits of the *Black Eagle* with some frequency. Here, read for yourself."

Drew reached for the newspaper clipping, but Lorena was quicker. She felt compelled by more than curiosity to learn as much as possible about the daring seafarer who'd invaded her life yesterday morning and had been monopolizing her energies since.

As the two-wheeled vehicle rumbled over the country road, her gaze sought the passage and she read aloud, "'That three and sixty tons of trifling fishing schooner should successfully capture and carry to its home port of Bristol, Rhode Island, three vessels of sail amounting to over one hundred and twenty thousand dollars in prizes would seem impossible were it not already documented fact. All this the privateer *Black Eagle* accomplished in but one cruise of fourteen days' duration under the command of its master marauder, Captain Brogan Talvis. Surely England takes note and proceeds across the seas with caution for his presence.'"

"There, Lorena, can you not agree that a man who has earned himself the reputation of a 'master marauder' knows how to use his resources to get what he wants?" George turned and bore his gaze into hers.

Lorena felt a stab of pride at the captain's courage and daring. Perhaps it was George's disloyalty to his country that rendered Captain Talvis appealing in contrast. "I can't disagree with you, George. He's resourceful. What, pray, do you believe he's after?"

"You, Lorena. You!" He spoke as though in grave warning.

"Me?" She laughed aloud. "What would the man want with me?"

"Dear girl, you are quite naive. I beg you to reconsider coming to England with me."

"As I've told you numerous times, George, I have no intention of leaving Duxboro."

"Well, I have no intention of staying."

Brogan arrived at Nathaniel Huntley's estate only to discover Lorena had ridden ahead in a friend's carriage.

The girl had outmaneuvered him. She'd taken Drew with her.

He'd hoped to speak with them during the drive to meetinghouse. To that end, Jabez had remained behind so that Brogan could have them all to himself. Instead, here he sat in Huntley's carriage, alone with the shipbuilder, silently stewing and vaguely aware of the man beside him.

Huntley's sights were directed on his team of bays. "You're unusually quiet, Captain. Is it in reverence to the day, or do you ponder our lively discussion of last evening? I myself have been earnestly considering your recommendation of basing a shipping enterprise and shipyard in Boston."

Brogan turned to regard him. Engaging this fellow in conversation about anything other than business proved a tiresome feat. After supper, Mr. Huntley had taken both Jabez and himself into the study for tea. Try as he might, Brogan had been unable to steer their discussion away from the shipping trade. So he resigned himself to the man. What else could he do? As with Lorena, he needed to gain Mr. Huntley's goodwill.

"I believe it to be a sound endeavor, sir. Your shipyard could easily supply the necessary fleet and your farms provision them. As for a new shipyard—well, the larger vessels of the future will require a deeper harbor than Duxboro Bay, as you admitted yourself with my own merchantman."

"Exactly, Captain. In addition to which, Duxboro has yet to prove to be a successful trading port. I think perhaps East Boston might be an ideal location. As a matter of fact, I shall shortly have some business in Boston to attend to and wonder if you'd care to accompany me for a day or two while you wait for your ship to be rigged. To be quite frank, although I may excel in shipbuilding, I have a limited background in trade. Were I to embark on such an enterprise, it should not be a sole venture but a partnership. I would require a partner with practiced knowledge of market conditions in various ports. Someone familiar with merchant routes. Do you perhaps know of anyone interested in such an undertaking?"

Amused by the discreet invitation, Brogan took a moment to consider the possibility of a partnership with Nathaniel Huntley. Could this present a resolution to his future with Drew? And would such an alternative require he share his son with Huntley?

Nay, Brogan would not share; the boy was his. "I might be interested myself if I hadn't waited a lifetime to own a ship as grand as the *Yankee Heart*. Now that I possess her, I find my ambitions directed toward a more independent way of life. I do not envision myself tied to the responsibilities of a shipping business."

"I understand exactly how you feel," Huntley acknowledged. "You are overwhelmed at the prospect. However, allow me to pass on the wisdom of my own years and experience."

A church bell rang loudly as the carriage rolled past the burying ground. Children were making a game of jumping from one stone to the next without stepping on the grass.

Brogan watched as Huntley scanned the churchyard, no doubt looking for his own children. When the chime quieted, the shipbuilder continued. "I have enjoyed a very successful career and address you in all honesty. There is an independence accompanying wealth which is unequaled, even surpassing that of being master of your own ship."

"Ah, but there is more to life than financial riches, sir."

Huntley gave a jolly chuckle, the lines at the corners of his eyes crinkling with amusement. He slowed the carriage to a halt, set the brake, and then carefully secured the reins around its handle. "Wisely stated, Captain. Most young fellows do not embrace such a sentimental view. And how can

I argue? I shall not say another word then, but my offer still stands for a day in Boston. I would welcome your company."

"Thank you, sir. I should enjoy the trip."

Brogan alighted from the carriage and glanced about. From all quarters, men, women, and children arrived, either on foot or horseback, some by carriage. Neighbors shook hands and engaged in friendly conversation. Some leaned against the fence where the horses were hitched, while others rested on benches or under the shade of a nearby tree. Children chased each other across the grounds and rolled in the grass, but Drew was not among them, and Brogan was growing impatient to see his son again.

The church bell pealed.

The windows of the Congregational meetinghouse had been opened wide to allow for the heat of the day. A stray chicken perched on one sill. Brogan entered alongside Nathaniel Huntley, and as he proceeded down the aisle, his bootheels dug into the carpet with the heaviness of each stride.

Faces turned to inspect the newcomer whose bronzed complexion announced him a man of the sea. A group of ladies giggled amongst themselves, and Brogan understood the reason. Seamen such as himself visited a parish only on occasion, when in port.

Another toll rang in his ears. He glanced toward the front of the meetinghouse and found them—Lorena and Drew.

Drew stood on the upholstered seat of the family pew, dressed handsomely in a pumpkin suit with a white blouse and ruffled collar. His jacket hung askew over a sling protruding out the back pocket of his pantaloons. Buttery curls framed his cherub face and trickled down his nape.

Both he and Lorena conversed with a comely youth suited

in gentlemen's black with knee breeches and white silk stockings. As Brogan approached, he watched with particular interest. The fellow whispered in Lorena's ear. She shook her head in response. He reached for her hand. She snatched it away before he could touch her. He grew annoyed. She looked embarrassed. Neither spoke. They stood glaring at each other, oblivious to the assembly around them, and in their obstinate expressions, Brogan detected a silent battle of wills.

"Captain, you remember George, don't you?" Huntley asked.

Brogan observed the young man's lanky build, his chestnut locks and beak of a nose, and recognition came. "It's not likely I'd forget the shipwright responsible for the *Yankee Heart*'s design. We met yesterday in the carpentry shop. How fare you, Mr. Louder?"

George Louder lifted his dark brown eyes to regard Brogan with ill-concealed disdain. His narrowed gaze met Brogan's unwavering stare, issuing a warning. Brogan failed to comprehend the reason. He found the shipwright's cockiness startling, but then it vanished to be replaced by a cold smile. Louder assumed an air of politeness, muttered a hasty greeting and excused himself, moving away as though to take a seat elsewhere in the church.

Huntley stepped into the architect's path. "Not joining us today, George? We might be entertaining a guest, but you are always welcome to sit in the family pew."

Louder stole a sidelong glance at Lorena, his look one of frustrated love. In that unguarded moment he appeared to Brogan to be immobilized by her elegance and beauty. Then he straightened and nodded courteously to his employer, saying, "Thank you, sir, but I promised Edward Hicks and his wife I would join them."

"Very well then, George. Enjoy the services and a good day to you."

"Good day, sir."

Looking thoughtful, Huntley watched as Louder departed, then turned to kiss his daughter's smooth cheek. "Is something troubling George, dear?" He lowered his voice and added, "He cares deeply for you, you know."

To Brogan's dismay, Miss Huntley responded with a becoming blush. "Papa . . . please."

Ah, he thought. A rival for the lady's affections. But where Louder's romantic attentions had been spurned this morning, Brogan was determined his would not be. The smile he bestowed on Lorena left no doubt to anyone watching 'twas meant for her and her alone.

She regarded him warily from beneath a bonnet of bright yellow satin, its brim so wide it created a funnel around her face. A puffy bow dangled from one side of her chin.

Louder had obviously said something to upset her, but what? And why had Brogan gotten the impression there was a more personal slight behind Louder's haughty stare than any annoyance he might have felt over Lorena's rejection?

Questions for another time perhaps.

"A pleasant morning to you, Miss Huntley," he greeted.

Her cautious expression faded, replaced by a welcoming smile. "And to you, Captain."

"George drove us here in the chaise!" Drew popped his head out from under the pew, eliciting a laugh from both of them, and in that spontaneous and unguarded moment, their eyes met once again. They smiled at each other, faces aglow as their innocent gaze deepened to a lingering stare, a stare so arresting Brogan found himself noticing each fleck of gold in Lorena's warm brown eyes.

Excitement shivered through his person, and then he caught himself and thought, *What am I doing mooning over this girl's eyes when my son is claiming my attention?* Self-consciousness overcame him, and it must have showed, for Lorena dipped her poke bonnet to shade her eyes with its oversized brim.

Brogan feigned indifference and turned to Drew, thinking the lad was either jealous to see Lorena's attention elsewhere engaged or simply wanted to be included in their conversation.

"The chaise, you say, Drew? That's fine. I hope it was an enjoyable ride for you."

The boy nodded enthusiastically. "Uh-huh."

This made Brogan wonder whether Louder had won the boy's affections. Then a thought jogged his memory. *George.* Could this be the same George who had called him a pirate to the boy?

Lorena removed the sling from Drew's back pocket and smoothed down his pumpkin jacket. She drew him into the pew behind her, and Brogan followed, anxious that he should sit beside his son.

Huntley joined the group, flanking Brogan's other side. "Drew, why aren't you in Sunday school?"

Lorena leaned forward and whispered across the pew, "I've excused him today, Papa." Lavender fragrance wafted up from her hair as Brogan contemplated the delicateness of the hand resting on the boy's knee. "I felt it would be beneficial for him to sit through a sermon. As I've explained to

Drew—if he wishes to be like David, he must learn David's wisdom."

Huntley's grin delivered an instant twinkle to his eye. "If he can sit patiently through a sermon, he'll be well on his way. Patience is the first step towards wisdom."

"Last week we learned again of David and Goliath," Drew said. "Do you know the story?"

"I am familiar with the story, aye," Brogan replied, perplexed by the boy's challenging glare. The strings of the bass viol began to play as the musician prepared to accompany the choir. The choirmaster walked onto the platform, and silence fell over the congregation in anticipation of the services about to begin.

"My apologies, Captain," Miss Huntley whispered, embarrassed. "Seems he's in a mood to talk this morning. Quiet," she warned the boy.

Drew crossed his arms, turning his back on Brogan. "But he's sitting in my seat!"

Nathaniel Huntley chuckled as he faced the pulpit, making himself comfortable on the cushioned seat.

Brogan felt uneasy seated between the man and his daughter in a house of worship. Neither of them suspected his relationship to Drew or the real reason he had come to Duxboro. They had no way of knowing the child they escorted to meetinghouse every Sunday morning would soon vanish from their lives.

How could he tear Drew away from the family he obviously loved? But what if Huntley intended to exploit the child once he grew old enough to be of service? The man had conspired with Abigail to steal another's son. He was no innocent, surely. But if these were indeed the good, kind folk Jabez claimed, then how could Brogan remove Drew from the only home he remembered, and yet how could he conceive of walking away from him?

Had he tied his cravat too tight or had a wave of conscience arisen to strangle him? Brogan pulled at the neckerchief, longing for a vast blue ocean and its briny spray, his only concern that of which direction the wind was blowing. Because of Abigail, he was forced into this situation. Even dead, the woman continued to make his life miserable.

Brogan rehearsed Jabez's advice in his mind and wondered where he should go from there. He longed for Drew to know him, and Lorena was his only means of accomplishing that. But what could be more awkward than trying to capture a woman's fancy while seated in the hushed stillness of a religious sanctuary, her father at his elbow?

Brogan did not care for the confinement of these holy walls. They induced a strange emotionalism that stunted the reckless cunning he knew himself capable of.

Then, out of the corner of his eye, he caught Lorena's reflective gaze. Encouraged, he returned her appraisal. She started and lowered her lashes. He had frightened her.

This was getting him absolutely nowhere.

How ill at ease she looked, fidgeting with the boy's sling on her lap. Brogan longed to reclaim her attention, to still her hands with one of his own, but he had already insulted her with his forwardness in the shipyard. He did not wish to do so again. Why was it one moment he found her such an annoyance and the next a sweet innocent he felt inclined to protect?

Nay, he was there for one purpose and one purpose only. Miss Huntley did not need his protection. He must not allow himself to think of her as anything more than a means to restoring his relationship with his son.

Glancing at the lad, Brogan recalled his own childhood. The orphan asylum. Whippings for something as trivial as sharing food with a starving alley cat. Punishment for wasting provisions, when the scraps had been sacrificed from the meagerness of his own bowl of gruel. And then there were occasions when he had done nothing wrong at all, nothing except direct the anger and bitterness in his stare at the wrong person.

One day a new orphan arrived. She wept, but no one came to comfort her. Brogan held her in his arms as she cried, and instead of receiving his usual beating, his hair was cropped viciously until nothing remained but ragged stubble. *"Boys must never touch little girls,"* he was scolded. And when his hair reached a comfortable length, it was cut again.

Again and again he was reminded of how worthless he was, until, at six years of age, he'd run away. And to this day, Brogan wore his hair unfashionably long because he could not bear to have a pair of shears taken to it without breaking into a cold, trembling sweat.

The sound of whispering lifted him from his memories, and Brogan turned to Lorena Huntley as though waking from a dream.

She was frowning at Drew. "We'll read later."

They were engaged in a small tug-of-war with the Holy Bible, which Brogan found odd.

"Not read from the Bible at meeting? What is it you wish to hear, Drew?" Brogan asked the boy.

Drew angled his head and looked up, eyes bright. "The story of David and Goliath. It is my favorite."

Lorena noticed how Captain Talvis responded most eagerly to the least attention Drew paid him. His curious behavior had not altered since last evening.

"David, aye. Now I see," he said to the child. "David and Goliath, the story of a young shepherd boy who slew a giant with a . . ." The captain trailed off to a thoughtful pause, his intelligent brow knit in concentration as he slowly lifted his gaze to hers and pinned her with a sharp stare.

Dread raced up her spine at his enlightened expression. He spared a glance at the sling on her lap before posing a question with his eyes, while with a jerk of his head and a wry twist of his lips he gestured toward Drew.

He had deduced the truth. *How could I have allowed Drew to bring his sling to meeting knowing Captain Talvis would be in attendance?* Her hand tightened around the sling, and her cheeks flamed with embarrassment.

If only she had waited for the captain's arrival this morning instead of accepting the ride George offered. She had hoped to use the opportunity to convince George to change his mind, but George's mind was set, and to make matters worse he mistook her concern for affectionate feelings.

She sighed in resignation. As for the captain, what could she do but confess? She was in God's house, after all. She nodded over Drew's small, flaxen head and shrugged by way of apology.

"God bless him," Captain Talvis praised, in a voice louder than what could be considered polite given their surroundings. Several people turned to stare.

Lorena expected he'd be angry to discover a mere child

had struck him down, or at the very least displeased, but here was Captain Talvis conferring blessings.

The strings of the church bass began to fill the meeting-house with music.

Her father leaned forward and whispered, "What is it, Captain?"

"God bless him," Captain Talvis shouted again. He shook his head, his expression full of amazement. "Only five years old, are you, Drew? That is a wonder."

"Captain . . . Lorena, please . . . the service," her father hissed.

Members of the congregation glared to let their annoyance be known. Much quieter this time, the captain whispered to Lorena, "I must speak with you privately. I feel I owe you an apology."

Apologize? To her? Here she thought she owed him the apology. Still, Lorena debated risking a clandestine meeting with this man after what had occurred the first time they'd been alone. She distrusted what she still did not know of the captain, and yet she was beginning to regard him in a more generous light, as not quite the threat he first seemed.

He was waiting for an answer.

She couldn't help but have reservations.

"Tomorrow at the launching, then," she agreed, and strangely enough found herself looking forward to the meet-ing. What had she done?

He nodded, pleased. And when he smiled, the hard edges and broad planes of his masculine face came aglow with boyish charm.

Her father huffed in exasperation. "What is so important about the launching, it needs to be discussed during meeting?"

Eyes still on Lorena, the captain inclined his head to her poor, confused papa and said, "Tomorrow, in honor of the occasion, your daughter has promised to bake me a gingerbread."

At that moment the congregation stood to face the choir loft. Rising to her feet, Lorena repressed a giggle. For all his size and arrogance, Captain Brogan Talvis was full of surprises and the mischief of a boy.

In some respects, he reminded her of Drew.

5

Lorena thought this was possibly one of the loveliest days her father had ever chosen to launch a vessel. By eleven a.m. at high tide, a few scattered clouds had woven a feathery pattern of white against an otherwise azure sky. She watched from the top of a gently sloping hillside as Papa stationed himself beside the *Yankee Heart*'s keel along the marshy shore. He prepared to deliver his speech to the waiting crowd.

Nearly everyone in town was in attendance. Children had been released from school, and hundreds of citizens ventured out—her father's workers and all those tradesmen whose skills had contributed to the *Yankee Heart*'s construction, their families and friends, in addition to neighbors and towns-folk—each one curious to see how the town's most ambitious craftsmanship to date would maneuver into Duxboro Bay.

They'd seen launchings before. Many times over. But this one was special, because the *Yankee Heart* held the record for being the largest vessel ever built in a Duxboro shipyard, the largest merchantman to originate from New England waters.

Admirers down along the river's south bank gazed up at the fullness of her towering hull. Some had rowed out in small skiffs on the river. Others stood scattered throughout the shipyard, some as far as the fitting wharf by the forge and blacksmith shops, partaking of the free lemonade and punch.

"I find no gingerbread among the refreshments, Miss Huntley."

A breath stirred the wisp of curls at her nape, and Lorena whirled about to be greeted by a pair of the most hauntingly beautiful, melancholy eyes ever to grace a man's face. Eyes of intense ocean blue surrounded by thick lashes.

"Oh, good day, Captain. I did not hear you approach."

He assessed her with a narrow stare. "Then it would seem you have great powers of concentration, Miss Huntley, for I have never been one to step lightly. Now, about that gingerbread . . ."

"There was hardly time."

He feigned a frown. "A likely excuse."

Like some gypsy pirate, his shaggy hair dusted his shoulders, but today was tied back in a queue. With a gold earring he might complete the look. But then looks were deceiving. By his own admission, Captain Talvis was no pirate, but a true Yankee patriot.

He grinned playfully, and as they continued to exchange glances, a silence fell between them. At length, he chuckled.

"I fear the sun may be obscuring your vision, Miss Huntley, else you look as if seeing me for the first time."

She realized she'd been staring without saying a word. "Not at all, Captain. Forgive me, I could not help but notice your coat. I find it oddly familiar, though at the moment I cannot place where I might have seen one before."

He looked down at his military blue cutaway coat, its wide cuffs, red facings, and brass buttons. He explained, "My privateer captain's uniform."

It appeared somewhat worn, a well-used garment, but clean and obviously cared for, marred only by the right shoulder area, where a series of jagged tears had been repaired with an overcast stitch as though something had torn through the fabric.

"Allow me to state my reason for seeking you out," he said. "I was wondering if you would do me the honor of sponsoring my ship."

Lorena was caught off guard, convinced she had not heard correctly. "I beg your pardon, Captain, but are you asking *me* to christen the *Yankee Heart*?"

He nodded. "What say you? Will you stand on her bowsprit to dash the bottle before these spectators and shout out a blessing for all to hear? I realize it's a lot to ask, and there's a bit of an unstable foothold standing on that spar while the stern plunges into the river, but those nearby will steady you, and I should be honored to have you accept."

Usually the privilege of dashing the bottle went to one of the master craftsmen responsible for that vessel's construction. But the captain wasn't asking George or master carpenter Edward Hicks to christen his ship; he was asking *her*.

In a small seaside town like Duxboro, young boys grew into men who dreamed of one day being chosen for the occasion, and here Captain Talvis wanted *her*.

Why would he make such an unlikely choice? What lurked in the heart of this rugged seafarer, a man of passionate emotion and concealed melancholy, who'd been hailed as a "master marauder," that he should desire to befriend a small orphan and flatter a humble girl?

Not long ago his presence had been disturbing and unwanted. Today, a bit of unexpected attention from the man and her insides were all aflutter.

He grinned, encouraging her to accept the challenge.

"I have no fear of balancing on the bowsprit, sir."

"Then your answer is . . . *yes*, Miss Huntley? I need you to decide quickly, please. Your father has nearly finished his speech. See there. I believe he searches for my whereabouts among the spectators."

To refuse would be to insult both the captain and her father. "Yes, Captain. My answer is yes. I will gladly sponsor your ship."

She could see her answer pleased him. His eyes shone with merriment.

"Thank you, Miss Huntley." He turned and glanced about, anxious that he should join her father. "I'll signal you when the moment arrives. And I've not forgotten I owe you an apology. I'd prefer we speak privately, however."

Again, Lorena thought of how she'd intended to apologize to him for Drew's attack, yet it was the captain who felt the need to beg her pardon. She commended him for it and nodded quietly in agreement. If they must speak on the matter, she'd rather it be in private also. "I hope you understand, Drew is not a bad child. He was merely doing what he believed necessary to protect me."

"Well, I can hardly fault him for that, can I? He is a brave lad, and I should like nothing more than the chance to get better acquainted. I say, let us forgive the past and start fresh. Perhaps we might all grow to become . . . *friends*." His eyes held hers only a moment longer before he backed away and turned, hastening through the crowd.

Lorena had to chase after him so that he might hear her. "After the ceremony, meet me in the carpentry shop."

"I shall be there, Miss Huntley."

Lorena craned her neck, following him with her gaze as Captain Talvis threaded his way through the multitude to proudly take his place at the *Yankee Heart*'s keel.

A warm feeling settled in her stomach, contentment that Captain Talvis was sincere in his efforts to make amends. Or could he have another reason?

"Good morning, Lorena."

Recognizing the voice, she turned. "George, you surprise me. Your place belongs beside Papa and Captain Talvis, not here with me."

Lorena gestured to the *Yankee Heart*, where the captain had begun to address the multitude, telling everyone how it had been his dream as a child to own a ship as grand as the one before them. An impossible dream, he'd thought . . . until today. She mourned every word she would miss at George's interruption, but there was no help for it other than rudeness and so she gave the shipwright her attention. "Need I remind you, that ship you designed is the largest of New England's merchant fleet?"

George's fair-complexioned cheeks glowed with pride. "No, my dear girl. No need. Her dimensions still ring in my head. One hundred thirteen feet and one inch on her keel, thirty-eight-foot beam, thirteen-foot depth. But I bring you news, Lorena. News I cannot wait to share. Arrangements have been made. I shall be leaving soon."

"Soon?" Lorena's spirit grew troubled, just as it had when

she first learned of George's plans. Now that the war was over, the young, gifted shipwright had secured employment in Whitby of North Yorkshire, along the banks of the River Esk, working for Turnbull's shipyard. Turnbull's was an old, established yard, where the *Discovery*, one of the ships on Captain Cook's last voyage, had been built in 1774. Whitby ships were heralded throughout England, and for a generous salary George had agreed to share with British shipbuilders the secrets of excellence in American-made sailing vessels.

He nodded. "I have found a merchantman bound for England, the *Lady Julia* harbored in Plymouth. She shall sail just as quickly as her hold can be filled with cargo. I will need to check with her master daily to know exactly when that date shall be. I've informed your father, and he's told me again he is sorry to see me go. He says I have a fine future in store and asked me to reconsider and make that future here."

Lorena agreed. "You'd be wise to listen to Papa. No one knows more about shipbuilding than he. He's done you a great service in handing down his trade secrets and skills to you. He's treated you kindly as a man would his own son."

His face reddened. "Am I to be chastised for ambition and a desire to procure a better life for myself than what can be had in this simple New England town? I have given my best to your father."

"True. And yet, George, 'Every way of a man is right in his own eyes, but the Lord pondereth the hearts.' No matter how hard we might try, sometimes the right path eludes us. But if our hearts are turned toward God, He will make that way clear. I know you desire to seek your fortune, but I promise you, God can deliver your riches to Duxboro as well as to England."

"I am sorry, Lorena, my mind is set. But it is not too late to change yours." Taking hold of both her hands, George lifted one to kiss her knuckles. "You are of an age when it is expected you should leave the nest to start a family of your own. But you allow your attachment to Duxboro and the responsibility you feel toward your father and another's child to keep you from me and the life we could share together. You know what I'm capable of. You know I settle for nothing less than the highest achievement in everything I put my mind to. There is nothing I could not give you. I would lay the world at your feet. If only you'd open your heart to me. Tell me you've reconsidered and will sail to North Yorkshire as my wife?"

Lorena's breath caught. George frightened her with his insistence on a marriage between them. She took insult at his ridiculous arrogance that he could continue to press his suit after she'd explained the deep emotion that accompanies marriage she had not to give him.

But George could not accept defeat. He'd learned early to make his own way. He'd grown so self-reliant, he trusted only in himself and his abilities, not in God . . . or love . . . or friendship. Lorena felt sorry for him. He had not always been that way.

His parents, being too poor to bear the burden of another mouth to feed, had indentured him as an apprentice to learn the craft of shipbuilding. Lorena had welcomed him as an equal, careful to show no notice of his thin and tattered appearance. She encouraged him, as George trained hard at her father's craft, from hauling buckets of oakum and learning how to wield an adze, to understanding the four key aspects comprising a ship's plan and then practicing them for hours in his sketches. When it was discovered he had an uncommon genius for ship design and mathematics, George worked diligently to achieve the title of master shipwright he held today.

Today he was honored and revered, impeccable in his image and manner. A perfectionist. Cold.

If she had to repeat it a thousand times, she would remain compassionate, but she must be truthful. Lorena knew she must be fair.

"You shall always have my friendship, George, but my feelings do not rise above that. You've never hidden the fact you resent my devotion to Papa and Drew, but you fully expect that I should abandon them and transfer this same devotion to you. I forgive you your jealousy, because I know you did not have the good fortune to be born into such a loving home."

George pierced her with an indignant glare and promptly dropped her hands. "You forgive me?" he squawked. "Forgive me for offering you marriage!"

Lorena stared him full in the face and narrowed her gaze at the obstinate set of his chin. "You can't understand, can you, George? My world is here in Duxboro. And each day that passes I grow wearier in the hope you'll realize that loyalty to those who call you friend is more precious than any amount of financial gain."

Neither her father nor any of his workmen or even George's closest friend, Edward, knew the truth behind George's accepting employment in North Yorkshire. What havoc might be caused if they did. They believed he desired to join a brother of his in England, which was, in a measure, correct. George had confessed all to Lorena in confidence, hoping to impress her with his ambitious plan.

"The truth is, I view your scheme as ingratitude to my father and traitorous to your country. Yet as strongly as I disapprove, I shall not break my promise to remain silent in the matter. The confession is yours to make. There is nothing to gain by hurting Papa and upsetting his shipwrights, but in your greed for money, you can be certain you have sacrificed my affection forever."

Lorena thought that if not for the throng of people gathered to witness his most highly praised achievement to date, George might have exploded back at her.

"Pray, how is it you scorn me yet smile favor on some fellow you don't even know?" His dark eyes flashed angrily in anticipation of an answer.

Lorena drew back, disturbed. "On whom do you presume I smile favor?"

George closed the distance between them. "You know full well I speak of Captain Talvis. First dinner in your home, then yesterday he joined you in the family pew. Privateering may be declared legal, but robbery on the high seas is piracy no matter what the title given to it. God only knows the crimes that fellow has committed, for who can be certain what atrocities take place on a forsaken sea? I am asking for the opportunity to bestow you love—everything in my power to give—but be warned, Lorena. Brogan Talvis is naught but a glorified pirate who won't hesitate to help himself to whatsoever he desires."

The fierceness of George's conviction gave Lorena pause, reminding her of that startling assertion the captain had made to Drew not two nights past.

"Taking back what rightfully belongs to you is not stealing."

The captain's eyes blazed angrily at her for challenging

him, and now Lorena wondered whether he'd been referring to something closer to the heart than privateering. What then? What did he so passionately believe he was entitled to?

She was struck with the thought—not a *what* but a *who*. Who, indeed?

Suddenly she found herself actually considering George's warning.

From a distance, Temperance could be heard calling their names.

"Keep a goodly distance from Captain Talvis," George insisted, "and allow him not the least familiarity." His face puffed with anger, he departed without a farewell.

Lorena recoiled. Despite her hopes for a better outcome, she couldn't help but breathe a sigh of relief he'd soon be gone.

Temperance arrived with her good friend Mercy Larkin just as the Reverend Potter prepared to convey a blessing over the *Yankee Heart*.

"Bow your heads, ladies," Lorena advised, grateful for a chance to hide the disquiet that followed every encounter with George. She felt shaken. Disappointment burned inside her to have missed Captain Talvis's speech, but with Temperance watching, she forced her attention on the reverend's booming voice.

". . . and so we commend the *Yankee Heart* unto the hand of God. May He always send her a prosperous voyage and a safe return."

"Amen," the three women chorused aloud.

Lorena raised her head while across the assembly Captain Talvis smiled, then waved, beckoning her to join him. And there stood Drew at her father's side. His face beamed with excitement.

"Look there," Temperance bid, pointing. "Why, I believe it is you the captain calls for, Lorena. He wants you."

The *Yankee Heart* towered over the surrounding buildings and sheds of the shipyard. A launching cradle held her upright, its slipway greased with tallow and soft soap to ease her descent into the water. Beneath the shadow of her hull, the spectators grew restless. Excitement filled the air.

With a steadying breath, Lorena took her first step down the grassy slope, hurrying to the front of the crowd to join the captain.

Brogan was now master of 880 register tons of the finest merchantman ever crafted. Decks outfitted with yellow pine, imported off the coast of Georgia. Frames of live oak, copper fastened throughout. Gun ports painted on her sides to deceive potential attackers. Even her stern was sheathed in specially imported red copper from the Boston-based Paul Revere silver and copper works.

Full of wonder, he asked himself what prize befitted such a fine lady merchantman. Did a cargo exist rich enough to fill her hold? Would she transport fine silks and brocades from the Orient? Gold dust and ivory from the West African coast? Bales of cotton and hogsheads of tobacco from the port of New Orleans?

Nay, he mused wistfully, nothing so elaborate as those. Nothing but a spirited towheaded lad, a treasure more precious than all the tea in China.

The *Yankee Heart* had yet to be fitted with her three masts or rigged with square sail. Still, she was magnificent in every respect, a wooden manifestation of his hopes and dreams, but no more so a vision than the one strolling toward him now.

There was a bold statement. Likening a woman to his precious ship. Ah, what matter? Any less praise would be an injustice, for here she came now in a silver gown of Empire fashion, dotted with tiny lavender flowers. The dropped shoulders and short puffy sleeves exposed her white throat and slender arms, of which his eyes could not drink their fill.

As she reached his side, Brogan harnessed his energies into playing the role of a gentleman shipmaster. He greeted Lorena with a formal bow, then directed her attention aloft to the *Yankee Heart*'s bow and the ladder she must scale in order to reach the main deck. Drew waited up there for her, looking down over the rails alongside several other very excited Duxboro boys and several of Huntley's workers preparing for the launch.

He removed the bottle tucked under his arm and presented it to her. The champagne had been awarded him from a prize cargo. Brogan had saved it in the hopeful anticipation that one day this moment would arrive.

"You know what to do then, I presume?" He did not pause for her answer, but continued, "Tie the stem of the bottle to that short piece of halyard on the bow, and once the ropes have been cut and the ship takes to water, you let go of the bottle and say—"

"I know what to say, Captain. Far better than you, I daresay. You were not raised in a shipyard."

He blinked at her impudence, then saw the twinkle in her eye and burst into a grin. Could it be? Was Miss Huntley flirting?

Brogan wished he did not feel the blood so warmly beneath

his skin as he leaned forward to whisper, "I shall meet you as soon as I can get away. Good luck."

He guided her to the ladder, holding it steady behind her as she made the climb up the *Yankee Heart*'s side, where Huntley's men received her and helped her aboard. The bottle was tied, and Brogan watched as she stepped gingerly out onto the large spar extending out from the stem of his ship. Drew stood beside her, encouraging her on.

When Lorena was ready, she looked down at him and nodded.

The thrill of the moment rushed through him. Brogan gave the signal. The axes were swung, severing the ropes that held the weights and kept the props in place and the cradle from sliding. His stomach knotted in anticipation.

At first there was nothing but his racing heart. He kept his eye on Lorena and she on him, and even though people thronged about them, Brogan felt as though he were sharing this moment with her alone.

A great creaking arose from the *Yankee Heart*. Brogan sensed Lorena holding her breath along with him.

As the ship began to pull away, Lorena gripped the bottle's stem and shouted, "I christen thee *Yankee Heart*!" She dropped the bottle and it went flying and then swung back against the bow with a spray of shattering glass and a shower of champagne. "Success to all who sail her!" Lorena cried out.

"Success to this ship!" the crowd shouted back.

The *Heart* gathered speed on her way down the incline into the Bluefish River. She hit the water with a mighty splash and the spectators erupted. They cheered. They tossed their hats in the air. People thronged about, congratulating him. Brogan searched, but Lorena had disappeared from off the bowsprit.

"Have you ever been to Russia, Captain?" Nathaniel Huntley asked once the numbers had begun to disband.

"Russia, sir?"

"Precisely, Captain. Russia. That is one of the places I'm considering sending my new fleet. Ladoga, Russia, to bring back Manila hemp and iron for the purpose of making our own ropes, tools, anchors, fittings, and the like. We shall discuss it in detail at a later time, once you've finished celebrating," he promised, clapping Brogan soundly on the back.

Did Huntley think of nothing besides economics? And what was there to discuss? Brogan had already explained he had no interest in a partnership. Nay, something else entirely occupied his thoughts. Someone, rather. And as he scanned the faces before him, Brogan realized it would be several moments more before he could steal away to meet her.

A flash of white-gold curls caught his eye, and Brogan glanced down to find his beautiful young son had returned. The boy stared curiously at his privateersman's coat. Having spent so much time searching above the crowd, he'd failed to appreciate what awaited beneath his nose. Brogan squatted before the boy and offered him his hand.

"Truce?" he asked. He longed to hold the lad as he remembered, to fill his arms with his precious child and give thanks for the breath that filled his tiny body. But three years had stolen all recognition, and if Brogan could not embrace his son, he would settle for a handshake.

At Drew's worried frown, he explained, "You've proven yourself as skilled as David with a sling. I'd do well to call you friend and not enemy. So what do you say, Drew? Will you make peace with the giant?"

Drew narrowed his eyes in a scrutinizing stare, as if debating whether to trust Brogan or not. He crossed his arms. "I don't shake hands with pirates."

The words cut into Brogan's heart. How he ached to call the lad Benjamin and pretend these three years had not been lost between them. But they had passed.

Drew bore not even a glimmer of recognition for the papa he'd once loved.

Brogan withdrew his hand. "Well then, I guess I am going to have to prove to you I am no pirate."

"Aha, and what is the nature of this meeting?" Nathaniel Huntley arrived, smiling down on them. "A secret, hmm?"

Jabez Smith joined the group. "I believe, Mr. Huntley, the cap'n might be trying to recruit the little mite into joining his crew aboard the *Yankee Heart*. And what do ye say to that, sir? Do ye believe the boy hearty enough?"

"I should say so," Huntley responded. "In fact, it is almost a pity the war is over. I am sure Drew would have given the enemy good and proper recompense."

Brogan rose. "I was about to ask him if he'd like a tour of my ship and perhaps a short cruise once she is rigged. Would you like that, Drew?"

"May Lorena come with us?"

Brogan inwardly cringed. He knew all along this would not be easy. But this was not the time to wean the lad away from his mother figure, not when their own relationship was so very fragile. And yet their future together depended on his doing just that.

6

From the opened doorway of the deserted carpentry shop, cawing gulls could be heard as they swooped in graceful circles over the bay. Lorena had told no one where she was going, so if Captain Talvis did not arrive soon, she would be forced to leave before her family began to wonder as to her whereabouts.

She turned to pace the depths of the interior. The afternoon sun streaked through the westward-facing windows with a lazy warmth that filled the shop, raising the smell of dust, wood shavings, and drying paint from a nearby corner where Drew's toy ark sat under construction. In their spare moments, several of the carpenters, under the direction of the dockyard foreman, Edward Hicks, had been constructing a two-foot replica of Noah's ark to go along with the carved animal pairs they had given the boy on his recent birthday.

She bent to admire it, but her thoughts would not be diverted.

How long had she been waiting? Twenty, thirty minutes? Plenty of time to reconsider the wisdom of a clandestine meeting with a man who, two short days ago, she'd regarded as an arrogant and unwelcome stranger.

And yet it had been her suggestion to meet here. And what had been the need when they could have just as effectively spoken on the outskirts of the launching crowd, in plain sight yet out of hearing?

Whatever possessed her to be so daring?

Lorena made a dash for the exit, only to be brought to an abrupt halt as Captain Talvis came striding into the shop.

"Captain, oh, I was beginning to think you might not manage to get away."

"Were you about to leave? My apologies, Miss Huntley. I came as quickly as I could, which is the reason, I fear, for my hurried and ungainly entrance. I hope I haven't startled you . . . again."

"Certainly not." With a shake of her head, Lorena dismissed his apology as unnecessary, but the captain's steady gaze told her he'd heard the breathlessness in her voice.

"No?" There was mischief in his eyes, and a smile played at one corner of his mouth. "Dare I hope I've redeemed myself and now have your trust? Or are you simply playing the brave girl? This time we are most certainly alone, Miss Huntley, for when last I saw Drew, he was listening to one of Mr. Smith's yarns. And I can assure you, Mr. Smith does not release a captive audience in quick time."

He advanced with long strides, with the heavy clunk of his bootheels, his laughter echoing throughout the room, until all that separated them was mere inches, a thin passage of soundless summer air and a few floating dust motes.

Lorena found herself once again at eye level with his strong jaw.

She glanced up to meet his gaze. It got her hot with exasperation how he endeavored to best her in their encounters, always with a confidence to overshadow hers. Make no mistake, she wasn't foolish enough to believe she was a match for the likes of a privateering war hero. No, what got her dander up was the little boy inside who enjoyed watching her fluster. Well, not this time. Lorena had plenty of experience with little boys, and she saw through their games.

"If you've lured me here simply to bait me again, I shall leave," she announced.

He chuckled, eyes bright, and removed his hat. The heat and sunshine had dampened his brow, and his sandy hair clung to his forehead where the brim had been resting. She found his shaggy hairstyle to be more roguish than fashionable, and yet it seemed to complement him.

"Not at all," he said. "I realize the inconvenience of meeting me privately, so I thank you for coming. The truth is, I have no excuse for my behavior in the shipyard except to blame my high spirits and an eagerness to make your acquaintance. As a lady, you were undeserving of my forwardness. For that, I beg your pardon. Also for any ill manners I may have shown the evening I dined in your home. Your identity took me by surprise, to say the least."

He regarded her humbly. In his eyes shone a sweetness of expression.

"I accept your apology, Captain." Lorena felt warmth in her cheeks. "As for myself, I am ashamed of the way I ran off. I was frightened. I thought—"

"You made the wise decision. I did not offer my name, and you had no idea what sort of man you were dealing with. I take full responsibility and pray Drew does not bear me any ill will. Perhaps you could help me in that respect. He is such a fine lad. It would please me greatly if we three could become friends."

Lorena contemplated him a moment, surprised by his request. "How is it, Captain, that a famous privateersman, a man both feared and respected, displays such amazing tenderness towards a child? Most men do not concern themselves with little ones, finding them more nuisance than not. But not you, sir. Why, your face fairly glows whenever Drew is near. One minute I find you an arrogant fellow and the next quite surprisingly . . . sentimental."

She watched him absorb this information, his expression grave, then thought better of herself and said, "Forgive me. I speak too personal."

"Nay, I respect your honesty. May you always feel this free to share your opinion. Which makes me wonder myself how a refined young lady finds the courage to be outspoken. It seems we are like most people whose characters are more complicated than what first appears on the surface. It takes time to get to know the heart of the person within. And is that not what we are doing here? Getting to know one another? In which case, it would please me greatly if you'd call me Brogan."

This pleased Lorena also. "Very well . . . Brogan."

He brightened. "Then we can be . . . friends?"

"Indeed. The three of us." There was gaiety in her voice and a lightness in her spirit. "You shall enjoy getting to know Drew. He's a delightful child. A good boy . . . most of the time."

The captain chuckled. "I'm sure I shall, and I look forward to a closer acquaintance with you, as well. Speaking of which, something has been puzzling me since our first meeting." At her quizzical look, he asked, "For what reason does a beautiful young lady sit dozing in a shipyard before the dawn?"

Lorena had not been dozing so much as waiting upon the Lord. But how to explain her unease, as though she was being warned, when she did not understand the danger herself?

Instead, she told Brogan the tale of her cranberry tarts. How, as soon as she had finished baking them, she'd headed for the marsh and its cool breezes. She told him of the tarts' disappearance, of how Drew, her father, and Temperance had gobbled them up for breakfast before the pastries had even had a chance to cool. And how, when only four remained, it had been necessary to make a new dessert.

"All that for me? Now I truly do feel the scoundrel."

Reaching up, he surprised Lorena by skimming his knuckles down her cheek in a caress soft as a whisper, gentle and affectionate, with a look that thanked her for her troubles. He gazed into her eyes, holding her spellbound and causing their surroundings to fade, until there was nothing but the earnestness of his handsome expression and a sudden flutter of her heart.

His stare lingered. Perhaps propriety demanded she turn away, yet she could not. She stood transfixed, and it wasn't until Brogan dropped his hand and stepped back, as though remembering himself, that Lorena was able to recover her voice.

She felt a necessity to lighten the mood with a smile. "I daresay, if it weren't for my family's gluttony, you may have had the opportunity to sample my cranberry tarts."

"In fairness to your family, Miss Huntley, if you recall, I devoured your chocolate custards with equal piggishness."

She laughed at his frankness. "I do. And, Brogan, please do call me Lorena."

"Lorena," he whispered flatteringly, while behind him another male voice called to her in a slightly whiny yet sharper pitched tone.

"Lorena!"

The interruption took them both unawares, and Brogan spun toward the intruder, placing himself before her as if to shield her with his body, though there was hardly need. Lorena knew George's voice and stepped out from behind the captain.

"What is it, George? What's the matter?"

She had her answer the instant she saw his face. His jealousy was evident. He made no reply, but eyed Brogan disapprovingly, absorbed in his own misplaced possessiveness.

Brogan stared stonily back. At length, he gave the shipwright a slight nod of greeting. "Mr. Louder."

"Captain," George returned. "I've come to escort Miss Huntley back to the house. Mrs. Culliford has a meal prepared and the family is gathering."

How did he know to find her here? Lorena wondered, doubtful George spoke the truth. Oh, Mrs. Culliford was indeed preparing a celebratory meal, but Lorena did not expect it would be served this early. It unnerved her to think she had been followed, that George was spying on her.

"That won't be necessary, George," she said. "You may inform Mrs. Culliford I shall be along directly."

"Aye, Mr. Louder, I am quite capable of escorting Miss Huntley myself," Brogan said.

George stood resolute, disdain etched plainly on his thin, angular face and in the sharp glare of his dark eyes. "I am sure you are capable of a great number of things, sir, and given your reputation, a man used to taking what he wants. It is your familiarity with Miss Huntley which raises concern."

"George!" Lorena rebuked.

"You distrust my character?" Brogan asked George coolly.

Lorena burned with embarrassment and silently willed the shipwright not to provoke Brogan further, but George dismissed the question with a sneer and in a manner more insulting than any answer he could have given. He turned his focus on her.

"I had always thought you a smart girl, Lorena," George chided. "I gave you warning, and then no sooner do I find you here in a shocking dalliance with this flirtatious fellow."

"Clearly, you do not approve of me, Mr. Louder." Refusing to be ignored, Brogan advanced on the slighter man with an authority that caused George to retreat several paces. "However, if you have some grievance, I expect you should address it to me and not Miss Huntley."

George retreated another step, then steadied himself and straightened his lace cravat. "I have come merely for the lady. I have nothing more to say to you."

"And yet you have plenty to say behind my back, I hear."

She should intervene. She should step between them and demand an end to this ridiculous quarrel, but curiosity held her tongue, and Lorena found herself listening with piqued interest. It seemed the direction of Brogan's upset had turned to something other than George's rude intrusion.

"Privateering is an unscrupulous business," the shipwright announced, his guilt confirmed. "And a letter of marque does not make you any less a freebooter."

Brogan placed himself in George's face and snarled, "Then

it was you who likened me to a pirate to Drew? Did you not tell him I was no more than a thief? Who are you to speak critically of me to others and especially to an impressionable young boy?"

George snickered, unaffected. "You don't fool me, Captain Talvis. Here I find you trying to beguile an innocent girl, and you pretend to be angered over my comments to a child. Why such concern for Drew? You may be able to charm Lorena, but you cannot deceive me any sooner than you can catch a weasel asleep. In my opinion, you are no better than a pirate!"

Brogan's jaw clenched. The cords in his neck bulged. "I don't give a wooden cent for your opinion, Mr. Louder. Besides, you'd be surprised at how well I can catch a weasel."

"The devil take you first," George spat back.

For all George's priggish ways, it took pluck to fling insults into the face of such a large and formidable foe. Pluck or ignorance, Lorena thought sadly, then started anxiously as, like a thread pulled taut, Brogan's control snapped and he exploded with a fist to George's angular jaw that sent the shipwright crashing into the wall.

Lorena shrieked in horror, and as Brogan advanced again, she stepped in between them. "Don't you dare! Only yesterday you greeted each other in a house of God. Captain, I allow you are a passionate man whose emotions dwell close to the surface, but I do not condone fighting any more than I care for George's contempt."

Brogan glanced past her to sneer at the master shipwright as though he were something quite foul.

George stepped forward rubbing his jaw. He had provoked the argument with his harsh words, and Lorena turned her disapproval on him with a glare. "Whatever your personal views, George, privateering is an accepted practice in times of war. You judge Captain Talvis unfairly, and not as a matter of morality but because you are jealous of his association with me."

"Do you not see, Lorena? He doesn't care about Drew. He's merely pretending in order to have the advantage with you."

"Shut your foul trap," Brogan growled. "You know nothing of what I feel."

Lorena found her growing appreciation for Brogan blurred by confusion. To her, the severity of his emotion seemed irrational. Rage brewed beneath his rigid exterior when annoyance would have sufficed. What consequence was George's prejudice and poorly concealed envy to a man who'd been hailed in the papers as a hero? To a man who had won the approval of Duxboro's citizens and had just lately received their cheers and congratulations? And yet Brogan was vehement.

"What exactly are you feeling, Captain?" she challenged. It was as though being called a pirate to Drew had ignited such a rage within him, Brogan lost all control. "Am I correct in assuming there is more going on here than the fact that George happened upon us alone?"

Moving to the open doorway, she turned to flash the shipwright a cold stare. "Come, George. For your own sake and on behalf of my father, I feel a responsibility to see you removed before you insult his client further. In which case I do not know that I can trust Captain Talvis not to retaliate again."

George made to hurry her out the door. "And so I've been trying to tell you, Lorena."

"Wait." Brogan eyed her, incredulous. "You defended me and yet . . . you are leaving . . . with *him*? None of what he says is true, Lorena. Don't let this fool's chatter sway you.

We've done nothing here to be ashamed of." He held out his hand to her. "Please, let me be the one to escort you."

Lorena stared at his strong, extended hand.

"I am puzzled, Captain. I believe your desire for Drew's good opinion to be genuine. Your regard for children bespeaks wisdom and compassion, yet you discredit such sensitivity by assaulting George when he never raised a fist to you. What inspired such anger?"

"My reaction was in defense of you."

"Really? To my ears, it sounded like you were defending yourself. But as you say, there is more to you than what can first be perceived on the surface."

Lorena waited. When no further response was forthcoming, when Captain Talvis held his expression in check and did not protest as she stepped with George into the open air, it was all she could do to hold back the tears.

She grew suspicious, clever girl.

Brogan remained in the deserted carpentry shop for near an hour, staring out the empty doorway, considering her.

What was it about Lorena Huntley that drew him?

Her loveliness and grace, obviously. That refreshing combination of innocence and intelligence? The lively spirit beneath her modest exterior? Perhaps her love for his son.

He only knew he was fast developing new respect for the girl, which if he wasn't careful could grow into something more.

He could not help but feel she had taken the advantage, not the other way around, as Louder had claimed. She evoked sentiment in him that Brogan did not care to feel, making what he'd thought such a seamless plan increasingly more difficult to carry out.

But was attraction to Lorena Huntley more powerful than his duty to his son? Of course not! Then what was he to do? He'd have to make amends. Again. He'd have to exercise gentlemanly restraint at all times if he was to gain Lorena's goodwill and trust. Without them, he could not hope to get close enough to restore his relationship with his son.

He'd been wrong to let anger get the better of him, but Louder had no right calling him a thief to Drew, no right to increase the distance between father and son with slander.

Brogan massaged his pounding temples. He was quickly running out of time. He had not come to Duxboro to make nice with Miss Huntley or defend himself to a weasel. He had come to claim his child.

He must push these feelings aside for the attainment of a much higher prize—his son—and stop allowing himself to be distracted by that graceful young dove.

He must not entertain thoughts of Lorena. No matter her beauty or how great her charm, he must keep his wits about him.

Somehow, this gentle, soft-spoken slip of a girl had proven a more formidable opponent than any he had yet faced.

7

August temperatures rose high enough without suffering the added heat of the baking ovens. To spare the household unnecessary discomfort, the summer kitchen had been built—a one-room structure located to the rear and separate from the main house. Outside its cottage door, Lorena's flower, herb, and vegetable garden grew.

Scarlet poppies, cucumber and muskmelon vines, lettuce and cabbage heads sprouted alongside pink sweet Williams and the more savory parsley, thyme, and sage. Leafy greens like parsnips, beets, and radishes crowded around the leaden sundial until not one patch of naked soil remained.

Each time she passed, Lorena was reminded of the abundance God had provided her family. They had much to be thankful for, and yet, as she bent to the harvest—noting the imprints of Drew's plump bare feet running in and among the green beans and the holes he'd left digging for worms—she felt an alarm go off in her conscience.

It was that same queer nervousness, an impression not in her head but in her heart, an uneasiness that warned she was headed into an area of potential harm.

Uncertainty of the future weighed heavily on her shoulders, yet what reason could she have for worry? By nature, she was careful in thought and deed. The household ran smoothly. Each of them was in good health. Her father's business prospered.

Her thoughts wandered, so too her gaze, along the ground where movement by the old crab apple tree caught her eye. Among its gnarly roots she spied a pair of black buckled shoes with thick heels and lean calves covered in white silk stockings.

Lorena jerked upright with a start. "George, how long have you been hiding there?"

They hadn't spoken since exiting the carpentry shop yesterday. Lorena had returned to the house while George joined her father and a group of other shipwrights in conversation on the fitting wharf.

"Not hiding. I've been waiting for you." He cleared his throat and removed his topper hat, stepping out from beneath the low-hanging branches to be plainly seen. "I cannot bear to leave Duxboro with ill feelings between us."

Lorena felt for his bruised face, though she could not help but remain leery of George's intent. "I would not wish that, either."

"You have been a dear friend. I hoped for more, but if I cannot win your love, Lorena, then I would preserve our friendship," he said, joining her in the garden. "I promise there will be no more talk of coming to England with me, and no matter what you may tell another yourself, I shall never speak of what I saw in the carpentry shop, to your father . . . or anyone."

"George, you saw only two people in conversation."

"Meeting in secret. Because of which I am now forced to walk about with a battered jaw and blame it on my own clumsiness."

Her spine stiffened when Lorena realized she had no defense. George's point was well made. She had been meeting the captain in secret. She'd sent him to the carpentry shop, where she knew they'd be alone. Alone, for a moment, when Brogan had caressed her cheek. He had gazed into her eyes with abandon and she into his.

"Lorena?"

She snapped her attention back to George with a blink of her eyes. She tried to see the situation from his perspective. Perhaps in his own misguided way, like Drew, George had been looking out for her. Perhaps she could give him the benefit of the doubt.

"George, let us not speak of this again. Let us accept that there are certain things on which we shall never agree. You choose ambition and fortune, while I hold fast to home and family. Each of us to our own path. I am sorry I accused you of being disloyal. I strive to be Christian in my views, but I am as human as any. You are of course free to go wherever your heart leads. You have much talent and much skill to offer any shipyard, and so I wish you success wherever you travel. May your vessels be heralded throughout the world, for in the end I do believe our lives work out according to God's will."

His intensity eased with a sigh of relief. "Lorena, you have no idea how much your blessing means to me. In that respect I beg a favor, if I may. I ask that you and Drew accompany me to the docks to see me off when I set sail."

She had never seen his expression so humble, so hopeful.

There was no question she would accompany George. She could not in good conscience allow someone she'd known since childhood to embark on such a journey without a proper farewell and a party on the dock to wave him off.

"Of course . . . of course we'll come," she said.

George beamed with pleasure. As Lorena watched his departure, she wondered why she did not feel the relief she'd expected. Soon George would be out of her life. No more offers of marriage, no further contention with the captain. They had agreed to part amicably. His doings need no longer concern her, so why this nagging foreboding?

Greater than ever, she felt the need to shake it off through her outlet of baking. Lorena entered the kitchen and mixed ingredients for a cake batter. Only a fool would choose to work with the ovens on what promised to be another sunny day. A fool or someone in search of solitude to toil away the demons that plagued her.

She worked at the breadboard table, blissfully lost in the task and her busy hands.

"I've heard it said that no one prepares sweets to rival those of Lorena Huntley. For just as like creates after its kind, so does the sweetest woman in all of Duxborotown bake the most toothsome desserts."

Surprised to find she had a visitor, Lorena lifted her gaze to where Brogan leaned against the doorjamb in buff trousers, a striped waistcoat, and rolled shirtsleeves. He wore no hat. Sunshine gilded his sandy hair, and with his smile, his sharp masculine features softened.

Perspiration trickled down the back of her neck.

He studied her with a sprig of mint between his teeth, probably expecting her to blush and titter at the compliment, which could not even be credited as his own, for the captain had just quoted her father.

Wiping her brow with the back of a hand, Lorena stepped away from her large earthenware bowl of batter to blow at a stray tendril. "Come for an early check on your ship, Captain?"

"Captain? I see I'm going to have to earn my way back into your good graces before you'll address me by my given name." His heels beat the floorboards as he strode inside, tossed the sprig into the hearth, and then joined her at the breadboard table. "As it happens, that is precisely my reason for coming, Lorena, so let's get to it, shall we?"

He braced his hands on the back of a yellow-painted Windsor chair. "I confess. Perhaps I was trying to win your favor with my attentions to Drew. But please, don't fault me for that. It does not diminish my affection for the boy."

Lorena gave him a stern eye. "After your roughness yesterday, I find you a bad influence. I have a mind not to let you anywhere near that child."

"You've been listening to Louder."

"I'm not one to be influenced by anything George or anyone else has to say. I form my own opinions."

"Good, then there's hope for me yet." His eyes pleaded for understanding, and as Lorena gazed back at his rugged face bordered by long side whiskers, she found him impressively handsome.

Her thick hair was bound inside a kerchief. Its heavy coil threatened to unfurl. She felt sticky and wilted and likely had at least one smudge of flour on her face, but if she felt self-conscious about her appearance, she preferred not to show it. She glanced down, testing the firmness of her batter with a finger.

He followed her movements with his eyes, stared at the contents of the earthenware bowl, then leaned over it to take in its aroma. "Is that molasses I smell?" His tone was expectant.

Before she could reply, he reached for her wrist and raised her hand to his mouth to taste the gooey batter on her finger. His eyes glittered with delight. Lorena knew at once he recognized the flavor.

"Gingerbread. And here I thought you were angry with me. I've been pacing the wharf, reluctant to confront you for the reception I'd get."

Lorena snatched back her hand. "Insufferable man. You actually believe I am baking for *you*?"

"Aren't you?" he asked.

She wiped her finger on her apron, unable to remove the feel of his lips from her skin. He overwhelmed her senses, awakened her to feelings she'd do well to turn away from.

"Very well, Captain, you have extracted a smile out of me, as was your intent the moment you entered my kitchen. I have experience with little boys and I see through their games. That does not forgive your savage behavior yesterday."

"Aye, my actions were impulsive. I was wrong to strike George Louder. Still, I do not care for his accusations. That fellow uses his tongue as rashly as I raised my fists. The thing is, I've learned to react when threatened. Sometimes I forget I am no longer at war. And Louder poses no threat. At least I have no reason to believe he does, but something about him warns me he's not to be trusted. Why is that, Lorena? Is there something more I should know about him?"

"Why would you ask such a question? What do you know of George?"

He regarded her with an assessing stare. "Nothing. It is you who know something, I believe."

"I know that very soon he shall be leaving my father's employ to make a fresh start in England."

"England?" He took the news with great surprise and some measure of suspicion. "Lorena, may I ask the nature of your relationship with him?"

She found Brogan's question presumptuous, but refusing to say anything could very well give him the wrong impression. And strangely, Lorena did not wish that.

There might have been a time she felt romance blooming between a young George Louder and herself. Having grown up in the same environment, they had things in common, confidences to share. But with maturity had come ambition, and George's pursuits had turned exclusively to his studies. No longer the eager, playful friend of her childhood, George's passion had become shipbuilding and his drafting. This pleased her father, certainly, as George had grown into one of Duxboro's most skilled shipwrights.

Lorena, however, felt an estrangement from her friend and focused her affections on the motherless boy who had joined her household. With her days filled, she forgot any romantic interest in George. But George, who didn't require emotion, who seemed to understand nothing of romantic love, believed career success alone would win her hand. Marriage to him was to be just one more triumph on his list of achievements. Perhaps for many women, a man's ability to provide financial security was reason enough to consider him, but it wasn't enough for Lorena. Not nearly enough.

"I have known George from girlhood," she said. "Ours is a friendship based on long acquaintance. Nothing more."

"Nothing more you say, and yet you traveled to meeting with him on Sunday. I've seen the possessive glances he casts your way. Nothing more and yet you jump to Louder's defense at a bit of justly deserved bullying, but leave me rotting in the wet marsh grass while I lay unconscious."

She'd grown increasingly flustered by his speech, but *rotting*? His word choice affronted her. "And for that you have no one to blame but yourself!"

"True." He nodded with a wry, crooked grin. "I take responsibility for getting knocked on the head. But, Lorena, yesterday you spoke of being confused. What about that which lies beneath your exterior, eh? What secrets do you keep, I wonder. Could it be you don't know or trust me well enough to share them? And yet you demand to know my innermost thoughts. Which leaves us exactly where we were before Mr. Louder so rudely interrupted. With a desire to get to know one another. Do you still have that desire, Lorena?"

She pondered her answer, then at length said, "Captain . . . pardon me, Brogan, promise me there will be no more fighting between you and George. I will not have Drew looking to you for example, only to have him believe fighting and war bring excitement to a young man's life. I do not condone violence."

"Neither do I. I give you my word. I'll not raise my fists again no matter what insults are flung my way."

"Well, in that case, you are invited back to the house this afternoon for a slice of freshly baked gingerbread and a tumbler of Mrs. Culliford's cool raspberry water. Perhaps you might apologize to George, and I could convince him to return the gesture."

His brows knitted together. His smile disappeared and so did he.

But Brogan returned later in the day, and then the following morning he called again. He spoke with her father, who sent them off with his blessing, a picnic lunch prepared by Mrs. Culliford, and the loan of his chaise for a drive into Duxborotown. They took Drew for a drive along the two-mile main street, watching the bay and counting the masts that lined the shore. Lorena could tell Duxboro pleased Brogan. It was, after all, a town given almost entirely to the sea and its related industry.

At the town square they turned the corner of Harmony Street onto Washington. Here stood the squarish white Federal houses of Duxboro's shipping magnates, in addition to boardinghouses for the single young men who worked the shipping trades. All along the lane, to the east, was a clear view of the bay as most of the town's trees had been hewn in the building of ships and homes.

On foot they climbed the heights of Captain's Hill. Brogan spread the picnic blanket, and Lorena unpacked their lunch. She removed biscuits, cooked sausages, and a covered dish of thick ham slices, and then pointed across a panoramic view in the southerly direction of Plymouth.

"See there, Brogan, the southern end of that peninsula?" she said as he stretched his long legs, reclining back on his elbows. "That is the area we here in Duxboro refer to as the Nook. There lies the garden plot, where tradition has it that Elder Brewster brought the first lilacs to the New World when the Pilgrims came to America two centuries ago. Today lilacs bloom throughout Duxborotown every spring."

He chuckled. "And I take it you favor lilacs, eh, Lorena?"

"I pick them for her," Drew piped up, "don't I, Lorena?"

"Yes, sweetheart. You are a very thoughtful boy, but please don't pull off your shoes."

"I must. I remove my socks so I can feel the worms in the grass with my toes, or how else will I find them?"

"You won't need worms today. We have a beautiful lunch here, which we are about to eat. You're not going anywhere, young man."

From the corner of her eye, Lorena saw Brogan's smile as she removed a jar of pickles from the basket. She lifted another of boiled eggs, only to spot something unexpected behind a pot of raspberry jam.

"Oh, Drew, look. Look who clever and thoughtful Mrs. Culliford packed for you," she said, plucking Captain Briggs up by the collar of his blue jacket to hold him aloft. "I'm surprised you didn't think to bring him for yourself."

As Drew glanced up from picking his toes, Brogan sprang forth to snatch the doll from her grasp.

"Captain Briggs," he whispered in a voice thick with emotion and hoarse with wonderment. He took close inspection, turning the doll over in his hands.

Drew jumped to his old friend's rescue, stretching forth his hands in a silent plea for his return, but Brogan held fast to the doll. "I would have thought him long gone, but I see you've managed to hold on to him all these years."

Drew's eyes rounded at Brogan, as Brogan stared intently back at him. His gaze rolled over the boy with, if Lorena's eyes did not deceive, a look of intense love and pride.

"Drew carries him everywhere," Lorena said, attempting to include herself in whatever was happening, but Brogan had eyes only for the child. He placed Captain Briggs reverently into Drew's chubby little hands. Lorena turned her attention from Brogan to the doll, thoroughly confused, trying to look at Captain Briggs with the same fascination.

"Brogan, how is it you are familiar with Captain Briggs? I do not recall mentioning him. Drew, have you been showing the captain your doll?"

The boy shook his head no.

Brogan seemed to gather himself before speaking. "Forgive me, I merely meant to comment on the doll's age. He looks quite worn. He must be well loved and a very special doll if you carry him everywhere, Drew. How long have you and Captain Briggs been together?"

"All my life," the child said, positioning Captain Briggs in a seat against the jam pot, whereupon he immediately burst into a sermon on the virtues of the raggedy captain. As master of his own home, Drew insisted Captain Briggs would one day occupy a place of honor at his dinner table. Anyone who disapproved would not be welcome.

Lorena had begun to notice Drew no longer referred to Brogan as "the giant." He was more at ease, more outspoken in Brogan's presence, as was his nature. And she understood perfectly what was going through the child's mind. Although he might be allowing a new friend into his life, a friendship with a new and different captain, Drew needed to affirm— not only to Brogan but to himself as well—that his loyalties remained with his old friend Captain Briggs.

She and Drew were obviously both experiencing the same inner tug-of-war. They each felt a bit of reserve, some timidity, but at the same time excitement to be welcoming this unlikely stranger into their lives. What a surprise to find themselves opening their hearts to a man they once mistakenly viewed as a threat.

A new captain and yet . . . something about him so familiar . . .

"Oh, your coat," she cried, as it suddenly occurred to her. "That is why your coat intrigued me at the launching. It is the same coat Captain Briggs wears, isn't it?"

Brogan nodded. His expression had sobered. "A blue military coat with pleated tails, red facings, and brass buttons. It is the uniform of an American privateer captain."

"Not just a sea captain, but a privateer captain," she mused. "That still does not explain how it is you know of Captain Briggs."

"Captain Briggs was my commanding officer on the privateer *Wild Pilgrim*, and it was he who made the recommendation I be given command of the *Black Eagle*. The *Wild Pilgrim* employed a sailmaker, a Mr. Thomas Pinney, who being skilled with a needle made costumed dolls in his spare hours. He was commissioned to craft a doll in the likeness of a privateer captain, and we on board christened it Captain Briggs. This is that doll. I would recognize it anywhere. I have never seen another like it and have at times wondered what became of it."

Lorena got a chill at the mention of a seaman commissioning Drew's doll. She'd known of his existence of course, but never his name.

With all the colorful and dangerous experiences one would expect filled a privateer captain's career, why would the crafting of a child's toy stand out in Brogan's memory?

Drew listened, intent on every word, though Lorena doubted he understood their full meaning. She was certain, however, he sensed their import. They spoke of a papa he'd been too young to remember, yet still he mourned.

"Who gave you this doll?" Brogan inquired of the boy.

Drew's soft cupid's mouth rounded. He glanced from

Captain Briggs to Brogan and stared as though seeing him with fresh eyes.

"My papa gave him to me," he said.

"He means Papa Huntley." It was not the truth, but then it was the story given to all who asked, so to Lorena it hardly felt like a lie. "My father gave him that doll."

Brogan turned to her, disbelief in his eyes. What reason would he have to doubt her? This could not possibly be the doll he spoke of. There could be no connection between Brogan Talvis and Drew's toy. Only she and her father knew that Captain Briggs had been taken from a Boston townhouse that had long ago burned to the ground. Those associated with that place lay silent in their graves.

"Obviously this sailmaker stitched more than one doll," she said.

With his melancholy blue eyes, Brogan Talvis drew her into the scrutiny of his gaze. He probed her conscience, until Lorena felt her heart pound against her rib cage. Her cheeks burned.

The enigma surrounding the captain deepened. Now Lorena had something new to disrupt her thoughts, something not so comforting and deeply puzzling.

8

*L*orena enjoyed Brogan's attentions in the days that
followed.

Together they'd stroll with Drew along the beach, at
times venturing far enough to admire the view from Harmony
Bridge over the Bluefish River. Sometimes they'd cross Squire
Huntley Road to stand on the wharf. Drew would sit upon
Brogan's shoulders as they watched the *Yankee Heart*'s trim
and spars being fitted out.

Huntley shipwrights oversaw the erection of each of the
three masts, and once completed, the riggers set to task.
Working high in the masts, others on deck, they wove an
elaborate network of hemp rope, which was then trimmed
with square sail, all new canvas, crisp and bright, until the
running rigging had been completed from jib to royals.

Lorena found something so natural about Brogan's interac-
tions with Drew, as though he had been with the boy countless times before. In moments like those, it was not the ship
Yankee Heart that captured her attention, but its captain.

He'd once called the boy Ben. And then it seemed Brogan

had been acquainted with the sailmaker who'd crafted Captain Briggs. Was it just coincidence or did he know more than he let on? Should she be alarmed? Did she have reason to suspect him? Suspect him of what? Lorena sensed no ulterior motive in Brogan, merely a genuine regard for all members of her family. More, she saw something decent and good in him, an innate strength of character she had grown to trust.

No, the warning nagging her spirit these many weeks was not to do with Captain Brogan Talvis.

Now, weeks into the fitting out of the *Yankee Heart*, Brogan had embarked on a business excursion with her father. Papa was off to Boston to meet with his cordage supplier— John Gray & Son, the famous rope makers.

But Brogan and her papa were not the only ones departing on a journey this day. Jabez Smith had left for Rhode Island to assemble the *Yankee Heart*'s crew, and very shortly the brig *Lady Julia* would weigh anchor on a course set for England, George Louder aboard her.

Lorena waited with Temperance on the cobblestone street of a busy Plymouth seaport, preparing to say farewell.

Crates, hogsheads, and barrels lined the wharf while the waterfront buzzed with activity and an assortment of inharmonious sounds that nearly deafened her. Sailors shouted from the docks, some in foreign languages. Great drays loaded with merchandise rumbled over the cobbles. Shoppers milled about the sidewalks of the hardwares and groceries. Blacksmiths, carpenters, and coopers hammered at their trades, and the air reeked of tar and oil from the refineries, candle factories, and ship chandlers across the street.

Amid the chaos, Lorena grew sentimental. More than waving good-bye to an old acquaintance, she was, in a respect, bidding farewell to the past and starting anew. This morning Brogan promised to return from Boston with gifts. When he had asked what she would like, Lorena assured him she did not need anything for herself, thank you. But he insisted, so she confessed that she had misplaced her thimble.

The pleasant thought vanished the moment Lorena noticed George returning.

He came alone.

She hastened to meet him. "George, where is Drew? You promised you would keep careful watch over him." The boy had asked permission to accompany George during the loading of his trunk.

George dismissed her alarm with an indulgent smile. "He's with Edward. They've gone to fetch the bag of tools I left in the carriage."

Edward Hicks could be trusted, and Lorena turned her focus to George. Now that the moment had arrived and he would leave their lives forever, she did not quite know how to say good-bye.

Not so Temperance, who was never at a loss for words. "Godspeed, George. We shall miss you. Will you miss us?"

George stuffed his hands into his trousers' pockets and bowed his head. He kicked a stone across the cobbles. "I shall. I suspect England shall seem quite tame without Temperance Culliford in residence."

Temperance giggled. "Oh, George."

Slowly lifting his gaze, he stepped forward while withdrawing something from his pocket—a folded note, Lorena saw—which he immediately pressed into Temperance's palm. "For you. But, please, promise me you shall not read it until after I've gone."

Temperance nodded, flustered and slightly embarrassed, though not half as surprised as Lorena, who wondered why *she* did not get a note.

George turned to her then, drawing Lorena into his stare until she grew uncomfortable. She handed him the still-warm packages in her hands.

"These are for you, George. The remainder of the cider cakes we had with tea, and your favorite—a couple of mince pies. I baked them for you . . . for your trip." She pecked him quickly on the cheek and stepped back, unable to look him in the eye.

Her gaze strayed behind him, where she caught sight of Edward Hicks strolling toward them, a carpenter's tool bag tucked under one arm. She grew alarmed.

"Edward, where is Drew?" she asked in an accusing voice.

The shipwright's brows creased, and a look of concern washed over his face. "Why should he be with me? When last I saw him, he was with George."

"What are you saying, Edward?" George's voice rose excitedly. "You must have seen him. He followed you. I swear to it."

Edward scowled. "Of a fact, I left him with you, George. If he had followed me, I would have kept my eye well on him."

"Meaning to say that I did not?"

"Two grown men to look after him, and neither of you knows where he's gone?" Lorena bounced her annoyance from George to Edward, infuriated with them both for not minding Drew, infuriated with herself for entrusting the child to them.

"How could this have happened? Edward, no one is more responsible than you. And, George, Drew would never disobey you by running off." She darted a glance across the

124

wharf. Lorena tried to remain calm, to hold the panic at bay, but already queasiness was forming in the pit of her stomach. "A busy waterfront is no place for a small boy to wander alone."

A small hand slipped over hers and squeezed Lorena's fingers. "We shall find him," Temperance assured. "Drew's a clever boy. He knows better than to stray far."

George nodded. "Edward, do you suppose he could still be aboard the *Lady Julia*? Let us go check." He tugged at his friend's sleeve and started toward the brig.

Edward made to follow, but Lorena stopped him. "No, let me go."

George regarded her a moment, then tucked his bundles under one arm and offered her his hand. He turned to the others with renewed enthusiasm. "Edward, while we're gone, would you be so kind as to go back to the carriage for another look? Temperance, you had better wait here in case Drew returns on his own."

He led Lorena away, hastening toward the *Lady Julia*. He swept her into a bustling scene of activity and at a pace more expedient than Lorena could have managed on her own.

She'd heard seedy tales of the waterfront, even horrors involving children. They'd no time to waste, and suddenly Lorena found herself putting her trust in George and in the quick manner he had taken control.

With her free hand she held on to the rope alongside the gangplank as they boarded. She was feeling somewhat light-headed as she stepped onto the deck and grabbed the rail for support. Already the wind was snapping the white cotton sails. Between the noise and commotion of the passengers, those working the brig and others still trying to load last-minute baggage and supplies, it was unlikely Drew would hear his name being called.

"I'll search forward," George shouted, releasing her hand, his voice echoing strangely in her ears. Suddenly she wasn't feeling so well. "You check the stern."

Lorena knew her way around a vessel, as did Drew. When he was not to be found on the main deck, she wended her way to the waist of the brig, where the last crate of chickens and wooden casks of grog waited to be stowed. Pausing at the fore hatchway, she made one last sweeping appraisal of the area before descending the ladder below.

The boy could be anywhere if he were playing an imaginary game of captain, as he'd played only recently with Brogan when they inspected the *Yankee Heart*. Or had something happened to Drew already? Was this the manifestation of her uneasy feelings these many weeks?

She hoped she was overreacting, but it did not help her fearful disposition, this sickening dizziness that had come upon her. And in this state Lorena could not tell whether it had been brought on by physical or emotional distress.

She followed a small, dark companionway that reeked of the whale oil burning in the lamps. They creaked on their chains. The fumes irritated her eyes as she made her way down into the cargo hold. At the bottom she found very little air or light. She covered her mouth to hold back the bile rising in her throat, then steadied herself with a breath before calling out Drew's name.

It returned unanswered in a cavernous echo.

Above decks a shrill whistle blew, and then Lorena heard the cry, "All visitors to shore!"

Her head swam dizzily. This time she could not shake it

off. She needed to make haste, to return above for a breath of air, but found herself unable to move swiftly as she grew increasingly unsteady on her feet. For caution's sake, she tread deeper into the hold, calling for Drew, until she was forced to stoop for lack of headroom. Other than a scuffling of tiny rodent feet among the barrels, her cries were met with silence.

Lorena began to pick her way back toward the companion-way, convinced Drew had not ventured this far below, when a shadowy figure descended the ladder. Hopefully George had come to tell her the boy had been found.

"Hello," she called. "George? Are you there?"

The brig rolled heavily. She straightened, grappling for balance, only to hit her head with a shattering crash on a crossbeam. Lorena cried out, the pain nearly blinding her, blazing through her skull. She staggered forward. The vessel pitched suddenly and she was hurled flat onto her face. A wave of nausea overtook her and she heaved onto the deck.

Was someone there?

As she waited for aid, her stomach settled, but relief vanished the instant she tried to raise herself from the puddle of her own mess. Nausea returned afresh, immobilizing her. Lorena could scarcely raise a brow without the movement making her so ill she felt she would die. *What is happening to me?*

She retched again.

Footfalls sounded nearby and then a pair of black buckled shoes with thick heels stepped into her line of vision.

Lifting her face, she drew a shaky breath, but the stench of vomit and lamp fumes combined with bilge water and waste odors sickened her. She reeled dizzily, her skull throbbing from the blow, while blackness seeped in from behind her eyes.

"George," she croaked on barely a whisper. Why wasn't he answering? "Help me."

She grew fainter, having lost any sense of balance. Was the vessel in motion or was the swaying inside her head?

Panic started her heart racing. With her last moments of consciousness, Lorena lamented she had failed Drew. Then all went black.

Lorena awoke with a flutter of her lids, and through the blur and grogginess a face fell into focus.

The face of a handsome, well-groomed woman of thirty-plus years. A cluster of tight reddish-gold curls gathered at her temples like two rosy bouquets. She gazed down on Lorena with concern, pressing a damp towel to Lorena's brow and then again to the side of her neck.

The woman's expression offered comfort, and in response Lorena managed a smile.

"You are awake." The woman balled the damp linen in both hands, her eyes widening before she returned the smile. "Won't Mr. Louder be pleased. He's been terribly anxious."

Memory of recent events returned and Lorena jerked upright. "Drew!"

Her chest constricted in panic. She attempted to rise, but the sudden movement brought a wave of nausea so fierce, she'd time only to roll on her side before heaving. Thankfully a commode had been set beside her berth.

Lorena swooned, but the red-haired woman slipped a hand behind her neck, supporting and guiding her upright. "Rest easy, Miss Huntley, please. Don't fret. Mr. Louder is just outside the door." She brought a small cup to Lorena's lips and, at Lorena's hesitation, explained, "It's salt water. Drink it. It will help settle your stomach."

Lorena nearly gagged on the stale, salty water yet managed a swallow. Her head ached, though she began to orient herself.

Perched on the edge of the bunk and stripped down to her chemise, she surveyed the narrow, windowless compartment and tried to think. A second bunk stood against the opposite wall along with a bench chest, one large traveling trunk, and a lantern swinging by the closed slotted door. She recognized the rolling motion of the ship, quiet and still but for the occasional squeak from the jaws of its boom. A lonely, eerie sound.

"How long have we been at sea?"

"Thirty, forty minutes," the woman explained. "You've been quite ill, soiling your clothing, in and out of consciousness. Brought on by the bump to your head, I believe, in addition to a bout of seasickness."

No, that could not be right. Lorena was feeling ill before she'd hit her head. And now she was shipbound on the *Lady Julia*. What she should have done was gone directly to the brig's captain, she realized too late. But what of George? He'd stood there in the hold, silent and unmoved, while she lay ill. Why hadn't he stayed the ship?

And what had happened to Drew?

The red-haired woman frowned at the confusion on Lorena's face. "I am Jane Ellery, traveling with my husband and his brother to North Yorkshire. We are to be cabin companions, Miss Huntley. When you're feeling better, perhaps you'll eat some crackers. I believe it will help."

"Thank you, Mrs. Ellery," Lorena croaked, her throat raw and strained, though already her stomach was feeling a trifle more settled. "Tell me. Have you seen a young fair-haired boy anywhere on this boat?"

"Jane. Please. And no. You must be mistaken, Miss Huntley. There are no children—"

A sharp knock silenced her, followed by George's voice projecting through the slotted door, "Mrs. Ellery, I hear voices. How is she?"

Opening the door, he popped his head in without waiting for permission. "Why, Lorena, you're pale as a ghost."

Lorena did not trust the sincerity of his anxious expression. She eyed him warily, unwilling to believe the worst . . . that he could have had a hand in her being stuck on this brig. Worse, that he'd allow anything to happen to Drew. George had his faults, but he wasn't evil.

"Mr. Louder, please. Miss Huntley is still indisposed." Jane Ellery stepped before him, blocking his view. "However, when she is feeling up to it, I would suggest you take her above for a walk on deck. I have some experience with seasickness, and it does relieve the nausea. In a measure, at least."

"No, Jane, wait," Lorena called before George could be dismissed. "I must speak with him on an urgent matter."

Jane hesitated, but seemed to reconsider the necessity for propriety given the circumstances. "Very well, let me cover you." She dug through her trunk and produced a paisley Kashmir shawl, which she wound around Lorena.

Lorena spilled a tear at the kindness. Jane offered an encouraging smile, then bent down to collect the commode from the deck. She scooped Lorena's white day dress, bonnet, and cranberry floral spencer off the opposite bunk and into the crook of her free arm. "I shall see about getting these cleaned for you. In the meantime, Mr. Louder, see if she won't take some more salt water."

"You have been too kind, Mrs. Ellery, bless you." Stepping aside to let her pass, George glanced briefly into the commode, likely drawn by morbid curiosity against his will. He gave a flinch of disgust and slipped inside the spartan quarters.

Mrs. Ellery quit the stateroom, closing the door softly behind her.

At the woman's retreating footsteps, George attempted to touch her arm, but Lorena shrugged him off.

"What's happening, George? Please tell me that Drew is safe. Where is he?"

He studied her intently. "You have my word. Drew is safe. It is you who worry me. You have been grievously ill, in addition to striking your head, and even now I can see you are still weak and pale. Pray, don't excite yourself unnecessarily. You'll grow unwell all over again."

Lorena wanted to breathe easier at his words, but her pulse quickened in suspense of what news he was holding back. "What is it you're not telling me? How do you know Drew is safe?"

"When last I saw him, Temperance had him firmly by the hand as they stood on the wharf. While we were searching here, he was across the street, patronizing the waterfront candy shop with the dime I'd paid him for helping load my bags."

Lorena was finding George's manner more and more disturbing. "You gave him money for candy and didn't tell me? You knew he was at the shops? Explain to me why I am here then, sick in the cabin of some outbound vessel, when I should be standing on the dock with Drew and Temperance. The nausea came on me suddenly and for no apparent reason. I stumbled and, in trying to regain my balance, struck my head. But you were there. You saw. You could have helped me get off this brig before it sailed."

George swallowed as though readying to speak, but no explanation was forthcoming. He simply stared back, shamefaced.

"Answer me, George!" Frustration rose in her so great, a sob welled up within her.

His brow furrowed the longer he continued to study her. "You shall see, Lorena, once you're faring better and have time to dwell on matters, that the situation is not so unfortunate after all." His voice was a malevolent whisper.

Lorena thought him absurd. He was truly beginning to frighten her. "There is no time for reflection, George. We must act quickly before the *Lady Julia* moves farther out to sea. You must go to the captain. Perhaps he can drop his longboat to row me back."

"There will be no going back," he announced with finality. "Even if the captain were agreeable to sacrificing his long-boat and several of his crew, which is entirely unlikely, we have been too long under sail. But I have seen to everything. I've secured your passage and arranged your lodging in this stateroom with Mrs. Ellery. She's a lovely woman, don't you agree? Look how attentive she has been already. I hope you don't mind, but I think I shall make her a gift of one of your mince pies. It's the least we can offer for her trouble. Don't fear, my little girl. I shall provide and care for you. You understand now, don't you, Lorena, how far I'm willing to go to prove my devotion? You'll see, we'll be very happy together."

Lorena felt sick to her stomach in a way that had nothing to do with her earlier nausea. "You've tricked me! And what of my family? They are sure to be sick with worry, wondering what has become of me."

George's grin sent a foreboding down Lorena's spine. "I have taken care of that, as well. The note I passed to Temperance on the wharf? It tells a romantic tale of how you reconsidered my proposal and at the last minute decided to accompany me on my voyage. We are to be married in North Yorkshire. It explains how, in fearing they would try to discourage you from leaving, you chose to say nothing directly, but left me to write this parting note on behalf of us both."

The insensitivity of George's cool, frank tone rang in her ears, numbing Lorena with shock, even as she tried to absorb the horror of what he was admitting to. "You planned this? Planned that I should be shipbound on the *Lady Julia* . . . helpless?"

"Bound for England with no money, no belongings, no contacts, dependent on me for your very survival, you shall experience firsthand, Lorena, how very well I can provide and see to your needs. You need me, Lorena. You've always needed me. Now circumstances will give you the opportunity to see just how true that is."

"And did you have a hand, then, in my taking ill?" A twitch in his left eye confirmed it. "George, what have you done?"

"Forgive me, that. I never meant you should have become so very sick. I must have slipped too much vomit powder into your tea while you were removing the mince pies from the oven."

"Vomit powder?" Lorena felt faint, reeling from the depth of George's betrayal.

"Just enough to prevent you from disembarking. Truly, what alternative did I have? You would not agree to accompany me otherwise." Righteous anger fired from George's dark eyes. "I pleaded that you become my wife. I offered you everything. But you refused me and proceeded to keep company with that, that, ugh . . . pirate!"

"You have never been more wrong. Captain Talvis is not the pirate. He is not the one who's stolen me from my home!"

Lorena could see her words stung. George stumbled backward for a seat on the opposite bunk. He slipped his folded hands between his knees and hung his head, shoulders slumped in exasperation. He raked a hand through his chestnut waves as, slowly, he raised his face to hers. "Oh, Lorena, can you not find room in that Christian heart of yours for forgiveness? Make the best of this journey. Away from the demands and responsibilities of your family, I know we shall find great happiness together. Will you not at least try?"

Lorena thought him mad.

Her soul cried out in sadness. Who would read the psalms to Drew at night? Who would pour Papa's evening tea and take it to his study as he sat at his desk, chest-deep in ship designs? Who would lecture Temperance against spying on the shipwrights who had removed their shirts while toiling under a hot sun?

Her gaze narrowed angrily over George's conservative features—the wide forehead, the aquiline nose and angular jaw. And in the midst of her helplessness, Lorena remembered her faith. She would not accept this dire fate.

"Understand this, George Louder. I have no intention of sailing to England. Even less of ever marrying you." She attempted to stand, but between the lightness of her head and the deck rolling beneath her feet, she could not find purchase.

George reached out to steady her.

Lorena recoiled at his touch, swatting away his hand. "I suppose you have told Mrs. Ellery I am your betrothed?"

He nodded.

"That is a lie, and well you know it!"

George's impatience revealed itself in an unforgiving scowl. "Then what should I have told her? That I am your *friend*, I suppose?"

"You are no friend of mine, George Louder."

"You try my patience with these criticisms. I suggest you learn to treat me with more respect."

His coldness chilled her. Lorena had found aspects of George's behavior both suspect and disturbing for weeks now, though she'd chosen to ignore those misgivings so that she might preserve their long friendship. Now, too late, she realized how naive she'd been. The warning in her spirit had not been for Drew's sake or for the sake of her family.

The warning had been for her.

By the following morning, Brogan was looking forward to his return to Duxboro and the moment he'd present Drew with the driving hoop he had bought the lad. Hoops were the most popular child's amusement of the day. Yesterday, Brogan had watched young boys parade up and down the Common, driving their hoops in companies of fifteen or more, sometimes single file, sometimes two by two. Other times, they marched all lined up together in a row.

They looked to be having grand fun, and he'd immediately thought of his son.

For himself, he'd purchased a few supplies—some fishing lines and hooks, a knife, and a couple of shirts. And one thing more, quite unlike his other purchases for its sentimentality—an elaborate silver thimble, gaily wrapped in paper and presently tucked inside his waistcoat pocket.

After securing his other packages to his saddle, Brogan set off on horseback, traveling south with Nathaniel Huntley down the Bay Path, the principal inland road and stage route that ran from Boston to Plymouth. Later in the afternoon, they rested in the coastal farming community of Hingham, for it was Huntley's desire that they should patronize the Old Ordinary.

"I think you'll enjoy the fare," said the shipbuilder. "This local gathering place and stagecoach stop has been serving warm drink and wholesome meals since well into the previous century."

Outside, it featured weathered clapboards and a beautiful colonial garden. Inside, Brogan found wide-plank flooring and a central chimney. Public notices, printed circulars, and hand-scrawled advertisements papered the front wall. They sat in the dining room beneath the yellow glow of the oil lamps hanging overhead from hand-hewn beams. As Huntley spoke grace over the meal, Brogan couldn't resist contemplating the crockery bowl set before him. It appeared to contain some sort of hash, browned and crispy around the edges and releasing a tantalizing vapor of sage and onion.

The prayer concluded, he reached for his silverware and forked into its moist center, sampling the fare. Chicken hash. It was hot and satisfying to his taste, with a pleasing sour edge of cranberry.

"Lorena would enjoy this dish," Huntley said with a thoughtful smile. "My daughter loves a good home-style Yankee casserole. She shares that in common with her mother. There are many ways, in fact, that she reminds me of dear Clara."

Beside them, a group of travelers bowed their heads in a lively discussion of politics, but to Brogan the voices were nothing more than a collective hum amid the pipe smoke and cigar rings as he sat listening to Huntley reminisce about his late wife.

A shame it was too, to hear of the grief this good fellow bore for a spouse several years deceased. He reminisced of her delicate beauty, her gentle spirit, her unending compassion for others.

"Qualities she passed on to her daughter," praised Huntley.

Brogan nodded. Aye, Lorena Huntley lived her devotion and commitment to family with the same passion that Brogan yearned to be a part of one.

He felt for the shipbuilder, who was still fairly young to have lost such a wife—the kind of devoted and faithful life companion Brogan could only imagine. Huntley's was nothing like the relationship Brogan had known with Abigail. Extreme sadness and guilt rose within him that he did not mourn his own wife so.

"I am deeply sorry for your loss, sir. Not only of your wife, but I believe you also lost a brother a few years back." Brogan tread carefully and in a tone inviting further discussion.

Huntley winced before gazing thoughtfully in the direction of the hearth. To Brogan, the man's eyes appeared misty, but whether as a result of the smoke-filled room or his memories, it was impossible to tell.

"Died of pneumonia," the shipbuilder confirmed.

"I read of the tragedy in the Boston papers."

Huntley gave a grim nod. "God have mercy on his soul. Stephen was richly blessed. If only he'd taken more responsibility with those blessings."

Brogan stared into his cup of mulled cider, confused as to the shipbuilder's meaning. "His death was rumored to have been linked with a mysterious house fire in which a Boston woman perished. Were you acquainted with her?"

How well did you know my wife? The question burned

on the tip of his tongue. *How did you manage to take possession of my son?* With bated breath, Brogan anticipated Huntley's answer.

"I hear she was a social woman, acquainted with a great many people."

The man's evasiveness gnawed at Brogan. He'd been at sea, captaining the privateer *Black Eagle*, when Abigail perished. Upon his return he learned only what the newspapers had revealed and what little else he'd been able to garner through his own inquiries.

Abigail had succumbed in a fire that began quite late in the evening, burning their home—the brick waterfront she'd inherited from the estate of her first husband, wealthy Boston lawyer and merchant, Hezekiah Russell—beyond repair. The papers portrayed her as beautiful and haughty, referring to her as the "widow Russell," as she had been more widely recognized throughout Boston society due to her first husband's prominence . . . and as opposed to her second husband's commonness. She was hailed as a woman of means who had made a surprising marriage to a younger man, a lowly seaman to whom she had borne a son.

It was an insult to Brogan that his name was not mentioned, nor Benjamin's. No infant's body was found at the scene, and yet the child was reported to have died in the blaze. No one cared enough to investigate further, and no mention was made of the babe again. Reportedly, no mourners attended his mother's funeral. Abigail had no other family.

Brogan visited her resting place often once he returned, as though she could speak through the grave and tell him the whereabouts of their son.

He continued to search, knocking on neighborhood doors,

though he was not always well received. When necessary, he waited on street corners in order to question certain folk as they were leaving or returning from their homes. He interviewed the seafront community, from merchants, sea captains, and sailors to the seedier characters of Boston Harbor and its taverns. He visited orphanages and churches throughout the area into outlying towns. He chased any lead, any possibility of a clue, yet found nothing that might lead him to Ben's whereabouts.

Then he uncovered the hint of a rumor which had circulated at the time.

A witness was reported to have seen Boston merchant Stephen Huntley, Nathaniel's younger brother, fleeing the scene of the fire. The story was discounted and the witness viewed as unreliable, not only because of him being a ship's master, well known for having business disagreements with Stephen Huntley, but because, at about this same time, Stephen—a graduate of Harvard College, a respected member of Boston society, a devoted husband and father—had been struck grievously ill and was bedridden. He died shortly thereafter.

His passing was received as a great tragedy, and all of Boston lamented his loss. Family, friends, and business associates rallied to protect his good name from slander, and the rumor was promptly hushed.

Only through his tireless research did Brogan stumble upon news of it. But with nowhere left to turn, he'd made haste to Duxboro to call on Stephen's shipbuilder brother. As it happened, Brogan was in the market for a merchantman, and Nathaniel Huntley came highly recommended. Though three years had passed since he'd set eyes on his son, one glimpse past the open draperies of Nathaniel Huntley's study window to the ruggedly built, towheaded child playing in the garden, and Brogan knew he had at last found his precious child.

Relief washed through him, victory sweeter than any prize he'd taken during the war, for Brogan could see his son was in health and had been cared for.

He wavered between a smile that split his face to a shout of joy and a tearful outpouring. Yet Brogan revealed nothing of the whirlwind of emotion inside him and instead channeled his excitement into laying out what he required in the design of his merchantman, then placed an order for the *Yankee Heart*. Once the documents had been signed, it took every bit of strength and resolve to leave Huntley's estate. Brogan had no choice but to bide his time until the *Yankee Heart* was built, counting the months until he could execute his plan and reclaim his son.

Which caused Brogan to often wonder . . . if the rumor had been so unfounded, as everyone believed, then how had it managed to be the only bit of information to successfully lead him to Duxboro and his son?

Obviously there was a connection between the Huntley brothers and Abigail. But what was the connection? One a Boston merchant, the other a Duxboro shipbuilder—how was it they'd both been acquainted with her? And what had been the nature of that involvement? It would seem even more likely that it was not Stephen at all who'd been spotted the night of the fire, but Nathaniel. Did the two brothers bear a strong resemblance?

In the weeks Brogan had spent in Nathaniel Huntley's company, in careful observation of the shipbuilder . . . and in knowing Abigail as well as he had . . . Brogan could not imagine these two conflicting personality types having had any sort of close association.

And yet they most definitely had.

As far as Brogan could tell, the only thing they had in common was the child Benjamin.

Why his son?

Only the fellow seated across from him knew the answer.

Brogan leaned forward, eager to turn the conversation to his advantage and gain the information he sought, but he must proceed with caution, for beneath Huntley's humble and affable exterior lay a shrewd, accomplished fellow, careful in all respects and keen to keep his wits about him.

Brogan grew weary of hiding his identity. Should he confess all to Huntley right now and be done with it? Unburden his secret and trust in the shipbuilder's goodwill to help him resolve the fate of his relationship with his son? Here they sat, man to man; it was the perfect opportunity. And yet how could he, not knowing what reaction his news would bring? Brogan couldn't risk alienating Huntley before he'd had a chance to restore his relationship with Drew.

Nathaniel Huntley, what dark secret do you hide? The man had intentionally avoided his inquiries about Abigail. What influence could she have exercised over him that would have caused Huntley to act so extensively on Benjamin's behalf? Kindness?

Brogan had a difficult time believing such goodwill existed.

He might never learn the truth of what happened three years ago, never know why Abigail had rid herself of their son on the day before the *Black Eagle* was scheduled to sail into war. But unwittingly she had saved Benjamin's life. If she had not given the boy to Huntley, Ben would have been in their townhouse when the fire broke out. He would have perished alongside her.

Abigail had been gone nearly three years, and in the passing of that time, Brogan's bitterness and resentment had turned to pity.

He realized he was only half listening to Nathaniel Huntley, who had moved on to the topic of his merchant venture and was debating what goods he should invest in to trade.

"Cod," Brogan heard himself blurt.

"Cod?" repeated Huntley, inviting an explanation.

"Indeed, sir." Nodding, Brogan laid down his fork. "There's a wealth of Atlantic cod to be caught in the shallow waters of the Grand Banks of Newfoundland. My recommendation is that you start your enterprise by constructing a fishing fleet. Schooners you could easily outfit through your farms. Crew them with fishermen and launch them on expeditions off the east coast of Canada. The catches could be sold to Boston merchants or ferried back home to Duxboro, where you could have the cod salted first."

"There is indeed a fine profit to be made in the fishing industry," Huntley agreed, thoughtful. Brogan could fairly see the man's wheels turning. "Especially with markets in Nova Scotia and the French Indies."

"Aye. But in trading as near as Boston you could oversee the operation of your fleet yet remain close to your family." But in offering this suggestion, Brogan wondered, was he referring to Huntley or himself?

Huntley continued to discuss the prospect as they resumed their journey along the Bay Path. They rode a sun-dappled turnpike, bordered on either side by a dense stand of trees, but as the afternoon wore on and daylight began to fade, shadows obscured ruts in the gravel road. They progressed carefully on the last leg of their journey, both travelers and horses growing weary as they reached Duxborotown, when suddenly Brogan spied a man on horseback galloping toward them. The fellow called out and waved for their attention.

Huntley turned to Brogan with alarm. "I believe that is Edward Hicks, my dockyard foreman."

The approaching figure was a young fellow of medium build, dark hair, and the hale appearance of one employed at working with his hands. Brogan nodded in greeting as Hicks reined his horse alongside theirs, but he could read in the foreman's expression he had not come to bring good tidings.

"Mr. Huntley," Hicks greeted, somewhat breathless, "I and several others have been searching for you, even riding as far as Boston. We had expected your return earlier."

Huntley's brow creased in concern. "We dallied a bit at the shops this morning. What is it, Edward? Has something happened?"

"I am sorry to say I have unfortunate news, sir. Your daughter is gone. Gone on the ship that carries George Louder to England. She departed with him yesterday."

"Departed with George? But . . . how is that possible?" Huntley sat frozen with woe, his face white. "Edward, are you certain? With no word to anyone?"

"A note was left with young Miss Temperance Culliford."

Huntley squeezed his eyes shut in painful reflection. "About a month ago, George requested my permission to propose marriage to Lorena. I assumed she had refused the shipwright, for she never mentioned any such offer to me, not even when I hinted at the subject one evening after supper."

Brogan saw the shipbuilder's anguish, and his jaw clenched with the effort to contain his own stinging pride. Had he mistaken Lorena's affection? Had he imagined fondness in those soft chocolate eyes? He was shocked to realize the severity of his disappointment. His gut burned.

Anger and jealousy flashed hot within him. He had been played the fool. Lorena had accepted Louder's proposal without consulting her father. It seemed inconceivable and yet another horrible possibility occurred to him. "And what of Drew? Tell me she did not take the lad," he demanded.

His outburst took Hicks aback. The foreman quickly assured them that the boy was safe at home, then further explained how Lorena had boarded the vessel in search of Drew, whom they all believed had gone missing.

Nathaniel Huntley turned to Brogan in appeal. "We must make haste to home."

Urging his horse onward, Brogan tore after Huntley and his foreman down the coastal road leading to the shipbuilder's estate. He insisted on tending to the horses and offered his further assistance. With an expression of devastation, Huntley beseeched him to join the family inside.

Upon leaving the stables, Brogan marched around to the front of the house and knocked on the large black door. When no answer came after his third knock, he attempted to peer through the sidelights, then let himself in and followed the sound of conversation to the west parlor. He recognized the voice of Edward Hicks.

". . . and I tried to find a boat to dispatch immediately after her, but no master would agree, no matter how much I offered as payment. So we hastened home to tell you, hoping you'd make a timely return and would know what to do. As the evening wore on and you still had not arrived, several of us set out to search but had no luck in finding you until today."

Brogan paused in the entry, scanning the faces of those gathered in the parlor. Such sadness. On the sofa, Temperance sobbed in her mother's arms, while Drew sat by the corner windows in a mahogany lolling chair, staring out at the bay while he clutched Captain Briggs.

"There is no vessel available, or ready to sail after her, sir, save the one now at our fitting wharf." Edward Hicks addressed Huntley and then redirected his focus to Brogan.

Whereupon every other eye in the room sought him with the same pitiful stare. Nay, it could not be. Were they thinking to send *him* after Lorena?

Huntley rose and approached slowly, his expression full of hopeful anticipation. "And no man more capable of seeing Lorena safely home, I'd say, than the one now before us. Will you do it, Captain?"

Brogan held the man's gaze expressionless, then inclined his head toward the shipbuilder. "I beg your pardon, sir," he said, one brow raised and lips twisted in a wry smile at the irony of the situation, "but you think to launch the *Yankee Heart*, an 880-ton merchantman, in pursuit of an impulsive girl who has chosen to run off with her sweetheart?"

Temperance pulled away from her mother to sit erect. "No, that is not the way of it. Lorena did not accept George. She told me so herself. She said, 'I seek a better life for myself than marriage to a man I do not love.' She assured me she would not leave us." The girl swiped at her runny nose. "It is all quite unlike her. It must have been an accident, you see."

A man she did not love. Louder. Something inside Brogan found satisfaction in the knowledge, but he quickly tempered any emotion rather than explore it. Instead, he stayed his course of skepticism. "An accident? How could such an accident occur? Lorena need only have disembarked if that were her wish. Besides, she left a note. With you, I'm told, Miss Temperance. Perhaps Lorena changed her mind."

Nathaniel Huntley moved closer. "Even if Lorena did perchance change her mind—which if you knew her as we do, you would agree it inconceivable—she took no clothing or baggage with her. This was no accident. Something must have happened we are unaware of. I do not know what that something is, and that worries me. I fear she did not depart of her own accord. The letter was not written in her own hand, but by George Louder. I beseech you, Captain. Will you sail after my daughter and return her home to us?"

Brogan considered the roomful of tear-stained faces and pleading stares, but his attention was drawn to the small, forlorn Drew.

When their eyes met, Drew bounded off his seat to rush forward. He came to a skidding halt before Brogan, craning his neck to peer upward. "May I come also, Captain?" he asked, excited and hopeful, fully trusting in Brogan's assent to the voyage.

It was the opportunity Brogan had been waiting for.

10

The thrill of success overwhelmed him. Brogan squatted before his son, thinking that at last he felt whole. A piece of his heart once torn from him was now restored—his son, his own flesh and blood. The love that welled up inside him was stronger than any emotion Brogan had ever experienced.

He'd regained the little lad's trust and affection, and now with the *Yankee Heart*, he could give the boy a home. He had only to sail away with Drew and their future together would be secured. All he'd desired lay within his grasp.

He smiled tenderly. "I dare not leave without you, Drew. But we must first ask your papa Huntley."

Brogan looked to the shipbuilder, throwing it all back to him. Huntley had requested something dear of Brogan. Now Brogan requested something dear in return.

Huntley paled.

Brogan explained that, as he had promised Drew a cruise, he should very much like permission to take the boy along.

He hastened to add that Lorena, when rescued, would be comforted by the child's presence.

The shipbuilder was hardly in any position to argue. He assured Brogan that as he trusted him with his daughter, likewise he trusted him with Drew. Just that easily, Brogan found the opportunity he'd been waiting for. The *Yankee Heart* could sail away with her prize.

But at what cost?

The uncertainty of Lorena's fate vexed him. Brogan could not get her out of his thoughts.

Preparations for provisioning the ship began that evening. Jabez gathered the crew and returned to Duxboro the following day, but more had needed to be recruited. Huntley volunteered two of his own men for the duration of the voyage—Edward Hicks, ship's carpenter, who had petitioned earnestly for the job as he felt, in part, responsible for Lorena's misfortune, and Frederick Mott, cook, whose culinary skills came along with everything necessary to prepare not only palatable but delicious meals as opposed to dull, standard ship's fare.

If Lorena had freely chosen to travel with George Louder to England, then his conscience needn't be troubled. Just his pride.

She'd made her loyalties clear the day of the launching when she'd walked out of the carpentry shop with that weasel, leaving Brogan with naught but troublesome thoughts. Had she indeed run off, leaving her family to agonize over her welfare? It would not be Brogan's first experience with a woman's coldness.

But suppose the family was correct in their belief and something had happened to prevent her from disembarking? What if she'd been harmed?

Under less desperate circumstances, Brogan would have enjoyed a rescue mission. Drew thought it an adventure. What would he think of a father who refused to come to the aid of his mother figure? How could Brogan ever explain such unchivalrous behavior to his son? The boy would never forgive him.

Back and forth he weighed his decision. In saving Lorena, he would be a hero in his son's eyes. The price, of course, would be to forfeit the opportunity to reclaim his child.

A painful choice. If only there were not so much at stake.

Indecision tormented him well into the evening, which Brogan spent for the first time in the quarters of his new ship. With all he'd accomplished to date, he should have been enjoying the most restful night of his life, but sleep would not come. His internal debate continued, and with nowhere left to turn, Brogan humbled himself to reach for his old ship's Bible.

He hadn't opened it in years, but as he untied the laces that held it closed, then pressed his palm upon its cracked leather binding, it came to him, not as a thought in his head but in words transmitted directly to his heart:

"A good man out of the good treasure of the heart bringeth forth good things: and an evil man out of the evil treasure bringeth forth evil things."

Matthew, chapter twelve, verse thirty-five. Though he'd tucked it away and turned from its teachings, once read, the Bible continued to live inside him.

Brogan gritted his teeth, and the tension in his jaw traveled to his temple, where he experienced a painful throb. Like a child begging for attention, something within this "bad" misbegotten orphan desired acceptance from a God who demanded obedience yet bestowed indifference.

He quit his sleeping cabin and strode the length of the day parlor to a smaller sleeping cabin beyond. With his permission the Huntley clan had transformed the room into a cozy nest for their precious girl. They had dressed the bed with quality bed linens, laid an Oriental rug, and hung a silk brocade drapery over the porthole.

They'd brought her possessions aboard—a trunk of clothing, books, and needlework to keep her occupied. Gifts and notes of endearment from each member of the household had been left with messages that conveyed their love and contained prayers for her swift and safe return.

It was all rather touching, and as Brogan inspected their work, he could not help but realize his defeat. He had deceived himself in believing he ever had a choice in the matter, in believing it could still all go according to his plan. That he, Drew, and Jabez could sail away and happily live out their lives. Oh, the plan was still in place. Nothing had changed, and yet everything was different. Brogan had changed. Changed, here in this quiet Duxborotown.

Brogan added his own gift to the others—a tiny wrapped package.

And now the *Yankee Heart* awaited, ready to embark on her maiden voyage, a good three days behind the *Lady Julia*.

Brogan stood with Jabez at the end of the fitting wharf, waiting for the Huntley household to say their good-byes. Word had spread throughout Duxborotown, and a curious crowd had gathered on shore.

Full of smiles, Drew lugged a ditty bag nearly as big as himself.

"What have ye brought there, young lad?" Jabez asked.

Drew attempted to heave the bag over his shoulder. "I have brought my sling. In case of danger I shall be ready to fight. And Captain Briggs must come with me. Captain Briggs knows everything about sailing ships."

"Aye, a fine sailor," Brogan agreed. "Briggs is welcome aboard, but you must both understand, there is only one captain aboard the *Yankee Heart*. What say you, Master Huntley and Seaman Briggs, are you prepared to obey my command?"

The child stuck his finger in his mouth and nodded.

Brogan inclined an ear. "Eh? What is that? I did not hear a proper answer."

Drew glared, then straightened, removing his finger to say, "Yes, sir."

Nathaniel Huntley pushed his way forward to stand before him. The shipbuilder eyed Brogan closely. "Are you certain, Captain, that Drew shall not prove a distraction for you? He has the tendency to get underfoot and is prone to asking many questions."

At Brogan's side came Drew's quick intake of breath, followed by a pitiful moan of "nooooo." He felt the lad's pudgy hand press against his thigh, Drew's fingers clawing at his tight-fitting trouser leg as though clinging to Brogan for dear life. Nothing could have pleased him more.

"I assure you, Mr. Huntley. Drew is no burden. No harm shall come to him under my watch. You can depend upon me to protect him with my life. On that I give you my word."

The uncertainty in Huntley's expression washed away, though not replaced by his usually jolly grin. "I believe you, Captain. In truth, I'd be lost without your assistance. My daughter is worth my very life, and all that I have means nothing without her. I promised her mother before she died that I would protect her and see to her happiness." The man's voice began to falter, and he paused for composure.

Brogan knew well enough what pain and turmoil came with loving a child.

"Sailing with the prevailing winds and currents, it shall take the *Lady Julia* approximately four weeks to cross the North Atlantic," he explained to the shipbuilder. "From our inquiries in Plymouth, we know from the boat's agent that she travels eastbound at the latitude of New England, following the main sailing route and taking advantage of the Gulf Stream. As long as weather and wind hold, my confidence remains with the *Yankee Heart* in being quite swift to overtake her, not only because of her superior design but because she has the cleanest of hulls, this being her maiden voyage. And with her copper bottom I expect she'll exceed a speed of thirteen knots. Rest assured. Luck is with the hunter, Mr. Huntley."

"Oh no, Captain, more than luck, I should say. God's blessing is upon your ship. Lorena was the one to christen her. May the Almighty send you a successful voyage and a safe return," Huntley said, offering his hand. "I trust you'll bring my children safely back to me."

Brogan took firm grasp of the man's hand and shook it. "That I shall, sir."

"Then Godspeed, Captain." Nathaniel Huntley released Brogan's hand and turned his attention to Drew. He held out his arms. "Give me a hug, then, and you can be off on your adventure."

Brogan left man and boy to exchange a private farewell while Mrs. Culliford and her daughter Temperance bestowed proper and polite kisses to both Jabez and himself. His chief mate's face flamed to the roots of his bristly red hair over a minor peck on the cheek from the diminutive Wealthea Culliford.

He chuckled. Jabez's admiring glances at the housekeeper had not gone unnoticed by Brogan. And who could blame the mate for his attraction? Mrs. Culliford was a comely woman, and with the exception of Temperance's plumper figure, she'd produced a near replica of herself in her daughter.

A nod of farewell accompanied by a parting smile and then Brogan shouted loud enough for the sake of the crowd, "Prepare to board, Mr. Smith. We are off to rescue one of Duxboro's own!"

He scooped up Drew's ditty bag, amazed at its weight, then glanced down at his son with renewed respect. "How is it you've managed to drag this dunnage? What have you in here, lad? Rocks?"

"How else shall I use my sling? There are no rocks to be found on the sea."

"Rocks indeed, Mr. Smith." Brogan cocked a brow at the reproof, then looked to his chief mate.

Jabez tapped his temple. "He thinks like a privateer."

They exchanged a grin and boarded the *Yankee Heart*. On deck, Brogan handed Drew's rock-filled bag off to his thirteen-year-old steward, who winced at the unexpected weight.

Brogan had confidence the slightly built Warrick Farragut would fill out with time given the strenuous demands of working aboard ship. When Brogan first met the lad, he and his older brother William had been little more than children, fending for themselves and barely getting by after their destitute parents had released them to their own fates. They sought to sign with his privateer.

Brogan had expressed strong reservations. Then he considered his own humble beginnings as a seafarer, thanks to the charity of Jabez, and found he could not turn them away. He appointed the younger Warrick his steward, where he could keep him the safest, and now it would be Warrick's duty to watch over Drew whenever duty called Brogan from his son.

They continued aft from the waist and ascended the ladder onto the *Heart*'s quarterdeck. Brogan called his chief mate aside while Drew and Warrick waved to the cheering crowd.

Already the sea called, stirring his senses with a blend of oakum, paint, pine, and sailcloth, fresh scents from the new vessel that awaited his command.

"Set all plain sail, Mr. Smith. Pilot us out of the bay, and then I'll have the topsails and jib sheets on a course southeast by east."

"Man the capstan there!" Jabez shouted to the crew.

Brogan ran a discerning eye over his merchantman, inspecting her lines, from her three towering masts to the crew that worked the rigging and the square sail that unfurled at their labors. Proud at what he saw, his focus turned to the direction of the wind, to the currents and tide, then finally to Nathaniel Huntley's folk gathered on the wharf.

"You realize another opportunity like this shall never come along for us again," Brogan confessed to Jabez. "The westward journey home takes longer, naturally, because of having to sail into the wind. Huntley knows this. We would have had plenty of time to disappear. My plan could not have been executed more smoothly."

Jabez returned a sympathetic nod. "I'm proud of ye,

sacrificing yer own desires to save Miss Huntley. It cannot have been an easy decision, and yet I always knew that when the time came, ye would choose the honorable thing."

Perhaps he'd come to regret this course, but a part of Brogan was actually looking forward to time spent with Lorena Huntley.

Until then, for a few days, a week at most, he'd have his son all to himself, Brogan and young Benjamin Talvis sailing the seas on their own merchantman, just as he'd dreamed.

And one thing more.

Before this voyage was over, Benjamin would know the truth.

His father lived.

All hands were called to breakfast at seven bells, and within the hour their tramping feet could be heard overhead as they began to swab the deck, followed shortly thereafter by the steady clank of the pumps siphoning out the brig's daily bilge.

Lorena knew these sounds well. She lay awake nights listening to them, from creaking planks and whistling winds to the working rudder. During the day she tried to keep occupied and not let her imagination wander to the uncertainty that awaited her in North Yorkshire, while George bore the passage with his usual smug confidence.

"Three more weeks would you say, Thomas, until we reach England?" He tucked into his breakfast of broiled meat followed with a bite of bread.

Jane's husband inspected the oyster on the edge of his fork. "Mmm, likely that, yes."

Lorena had little appetite, yet forced herself to gnaw on a ship's biscuit, washing down the dry crumbs with a sip of lukewarm tea.

Muted light from an overcast morning shone through the skylight onto the long table of *Lady Julia*'s main cabin, where passengers gathered for meals and passed their days reading, socializing, or employed in needlework.

Jane sat beside her with needle and thread, altering one of her own dresses for Lorena, a turkey-red calico trimmed in narrow white lace. Only Jane's kindness kept Lorena from falling into total despair of missing her loved ones. Jane traveled with her British husband and brother-in-law and had assured Lorena she'd be welcome in her home for as long as necessary.

"Lorena, perhaps you'd care to join me in a game of draughts after breakfast?" The inducement in George's voice drew curious glances from the table. Jane looked up from her sewing.

George had manipulated to win the favor of all aboard. First, endearing himself by sharing the mince pies and cider cakes Lorena had baked, while she sat with a commode in her cabin fighting back nausea. Then he set himself in good standing with the brig's company and captain by correcting the fitting of the bowsprit so rainwater no longer leaked into the men's living quarters.

It enraged her, the gall with which he continued to press his suit. Quite unlike her usual self, there were moments Lorena longed to slap his face. This was one of them. "Find yourself another to play, George. Myself, I feel the need for some air. Perhaps a promenade on deck." Turning to the woman she could truly call friend, she asked, "Would you be so kind as to accompany me, Jane?"

"Allow me a few moments more to finish these last stitches and you can change into your new dress before our walk."

George would not be dismissed, however. Glancing from one to the other of them, he said, "Very good, ladies. Allow me to offer my services, for you shall require the protection of an escort."

Eighty feet above from a mainmast yard, a lookout gave the cry, "Sail to windward!"

Brogan pulled his glass from inside his jacket pocket. Extending the lens, he raised the telescope to his eye. As the horizon fell into focus he saw a vessel hull down at three points over the starboard bows. Only her topgallants and double masts were visible.

All hands on deck rushed to the larboard rail for a look. Drew moved closer to his side. Beneath the shadow of an overcast sky, the sea had turned a dark olive gray.

"Mr. Smith, reef out all tops'ls. And I'll have the jib sheeted, if you please."

"Aye-aye, sir." From his position at the waist, Jabez relayed the order and several of the crew went clambering up the ratlines.

"Mr. Fletcher," Brogan shouted to his helmsman, "weather us a course northeast by north and fetch me those sails."

"Northeast by north, sir!"

"Carry her as close to the wind as she'll bear, Mr. Fletcher. Full and by." Brogan was interrupted by a tapping on his lower thigh and glanced down.

Drew stretched forth his arms, fingers wriggling, begging for the glass. Brogan gloried in the bond of blood between them and felt it to the marrow of his bones. This small, precious child was the only living soul he could rightfully call family, which might easily have him cowing to the lad's wishes like Nathaniel Huntley was wont to do, except that Brogan was impressed with a responsibility to instill discipline in his son. He snapped the glass closed and returned it to his jacket pocket.

"Is that a proper manner to address your captain, do you suppose?" Brogan spoke next to the doll hanging by Drew's side. "What say you, Captain Briggs? Does the lad deserve a look in my glass?"

The boy stomped his foot impatiently. "Captain Briggs wants to see."

"Does he?" Brogan eyed the lad with correction in his gaze. "You forget I am long acquainted with Captain Briggs. Captain Briggs has experience with authority. He follows proper etiquette aboard ship, and he would not make grabbing motions at his commanding officer. He would ask permission in a proper, respectful manner."

Drew worried his bottom lip, unused to the reproof, confused perhaps, likely even contemplating resistance. Yet when he spoke, it was without his earlier whining tone. "May I have a look in the glass?"

"Did you not hear me use the word *respectful*?"

"Please, sir. Please, may I have a look? I want to see Lorena."

"Aye, me too." Brogan rested his hand affectionately on the crown of Drew's straw hat. "Soon we'll draw close enough to that speck of sail out there to know whether she is the one we seek. If Lorena is aboard, then we shall see her before the day is out. If not, then I promise we shall keep searching until she is found. Will you wait here with me, Drew?"

In response, the boy slipped his stubby fingers into Brogan's much larger hand.

Topmen in the rigging edged to the far end of the yards to loosen sail. The square canvas sheets unfurled with a great rustle. Then came a loud report as they filled with wind. Jabez kept careful watch over the hands, making certain all yards were trimmed to his satisfaction, while Drew absorbed it all with interest.

Brogan took delight in his son's wonderment. There was nothing he wouldn't do for this lad. He'd sail the seas to fetch back the woman Drew loved as a mother. He'd honor a Father God who had not shown the same compassion to Brogan as a child. But in saving Lorena, was he sacrificing his precious son?

The *Yankee Heart* gathered way with all good speed, and half an hour later Brogan withdrew his glass once more. This time what appeared in the lens was a two-masted square rigger with a gaff spanker on her mainmast identifying her as a brig.

He helped Drew position the telescope for a look. "Do you see her?"

Drew gasped in delight. "A ship, yes!"

"A brig. With a figurehead. Can you make out what it is?"

"Yes, sir. It is a painted lady."

"Not just any lady, Drew," Brogan whispered in his son's ear. "I do believe that is the *Lady Julia*."

"Perhaps not the prettiest day for a walk," Jane Ellery observed as Lorena strolled with her, arm in arm, "yet I would daresay it is ideal. The sun is not so bright as to blind our eyes or burn our noses, and we have the added entertainment of sighting our first vessel since leaving Plymouth."

The appearance of another vessel—a reminder to all aboard

the *Lady Julia* that they did not sail the Atlantic alone, along with the break from monotony on their lonely travels—had passengers and crew alike hugging the rails with interest.

Whether due to the pleasant companionship of her friend or because Lorena wore a fresh change of clothing for the first time in a week, she felt herself being swept into the excitement. Just a simple cotton dress, yet it had been tailored to her frame by loving hands, and in it she dared step a little lighter.

Jane's husband, Thomas, Thomas's younger brother Matthew, and George escorted them on their walk, keeping several paces behind. Both Thomas and Matthew shared the opinion of the crew—that the approaching vessel carrying the American flag was a fellow merchantman eager to offer a passing hello.

It appeared to be gaining on them with all good speed, and the closer it drew to the *Lady Julia*, the more agitated George became. At their third turn around the deck he excused himself and hastened up the companionway ladder to the quarterdeck. Lorena watched him engage Captain Winsor in a passionate exchange, whereupon the captain handed George his spyglass.

Lorena turned her attention off the starboard quarter in the same direction George held the glass and gave the ship careful and particular examination for the first time since its sighting.

She was of new construction to Lorena's trained eye, and there was a certain familiarity in her architecture and the craftsmanship of her carvings. Lorena watched her copper-bottomed bow cleave the harsh waves, and something within her reacted with a spontaneous burst of joy. Suddenly she understood what George was looking at.

"Jane," she said with a gasp, curling her fingers around the woman's forearm and drawing them both to an abrupt halt. Lorena glanced again at George. His back to the forward ship, he slowly lowered the spyglass. "Jane, it's possible I know this ship!"

As though he'd heard her, George turned around to catch her eye from where he stood on the quarterdeck. The look of crazed, angry panic he shot back confirmed what Lorena had dared not let herself believe.

It was true then.

She smiled as she had not since her feet stood on dry land. "No, I must take that back, Jane," she said in a clear, bright voice. "I *do* know this ship. I christened her myself in my father's shipyard less than two months ago."

Jane's mouth fell open and she turned her surprise on her husband and brother-in-law, who had just joined them. "Then it is your father, do you believe?" she asked Lorena. "He has come for you?"

Lorena's thoughts whirred. "I don't know. I don't know what to think." But Lorena was imagining not her father, but a handsome Yankee captain with sharp features, a hawkish nose, and sandy blond side whiskers framing his lean cheeks.

Brogan had come for her. Already some of the other passengers were waving a greeting, and she was reaching up to join them when her wrist was seized from behind.

"Silly girl, you're making a terrible mistake." George's words spewed forth in a hiss.

"Here, here," called Thomas Ellery, stepping forward. "I'll not tolerate roughness to a lady." He glared a warning at George, then turned his stare upon the hand that held Lorena.

"Forgive me, Thomas." As George released her, Lorena snatched back her hand, glowering.

"I believe the apology you owe is to Lorena," Thomas corrected.

George assessed her with his dark stare, and even now with help so close at hand, she couldn't help but feel uneasy.

"I believe you are correct, Thomas. I owe her much by way of apologies." George beseeched those surrounding her in hopes of privacy.

Lorena reached for Jane's hand. Her eye remained warily on George, sending him an unspoken message. *You may speak to me in front of my friends or not at all.*

He straightened, studying her with a penetrating stare until his expression softened. "I have loved you since we were children," he declared, his voice a controlled whisper. "My means of showing it of late may have seemed desperate and extreme, I confess, and yet if not for that desperate act, you would have been lost to me forever. Lorena, you cannot leave with Captain Talvis. The good people of this ship will not allow you—a kind, respectable Christian girl—to be taken off by this ruffian. I cannot allow it! It is not too late for us. We will be happy in England." He stepped closer. "I assure you."

Disgust and pity rose in her throat like bile. Lorena stood erect, facing George with resolve. "Matters have gone far beyond reviving any further tolerance of you. I believe if you examine your heart, you'll realize it is not me you love at all but personal achievement. You set your mind long ago that I was to be part of that success. Marriage to the daughter of the man you were once indentured to. What a testimony to how far you've come up in the world. And because you have never failed to accomplish anything you've put your mind to, it is inconceivable for you to accept defeat in this one thing. For if you loved me, George . . . if you even understood the meaning of the word, you would have respected my wishes. You would have considered my happiness. Not just your own. You would not have deceived me in order to get me to come with you. Accept it, George. I could never be persuaded to marry you! I'll be leaving with Captain Talvis, and this time no amount of trickery or vomit powder can stop me."

George's expression turned to stone.

"You admit it?" Jane's tone rang of shock as she draped an arm protectively about Lorena's waist. "You poisoned her, Mr. Louder? Not that we did not believe you, Lorena, but he does have a manner of presenting himself to be everything amiable and helpful."

George's color rose along with his defenses. He shot Jane an indignant glare. "Vomit powder is not a poison, Mrs. Ellery. By all accounts, it is most often considered a remedy."

"A remedy?" Jane scoffed. "No remedy for unreturned love, Mr. Louder, surely!"

Heads turned on the *Lady Julia* as the *Yankee Heart* forged up alongside the brig. Brogan signaled Jabez from the quarterdeck to issue the command to ready the longboat. Warrick had shined his boots and assisted him into his cutaway coat. As Brogan shrugged it onto his shoulders, the young steward presented him his leather baldric and sword.

"I don't recall asking for my sword."

"He insisted, sir." With a jerk of his head, Warrick indicated Drew watching earnestly at his side.

The boy stepped forward. "How shall you defend Lorena with no weapon? Shall I come and bring my sling? I'm quite an excellent shot. I protect what is mine."

Brogan held his grin in check. "I'm well aware of how excellent a shot you are, but we've discussed this and my orders are that you remain out of sight with Warrick. I believe I'm capable of handling this myself, thank you."

The boy pushed the encased sword in Warrick's hands toward him. "If I were captain, I would do it myself, but you, sir . . . you must do it."

"Here now, mind your tongue, lad, when addressing your captain," Brogan said, but found he could not disappoint his son's sense of adventure and so slung the baldric across his shoulder, allowing the sword to rest at his hip.

Drew's little shoulders relaxed. He handed Brogan his speaking trumpet, which Brogan took up to shout, "Brig ahoy! What brig is that?"

"The *Lady Julia*, seven days out of Plymouth," her captain returned.

"*Lady Julia*," Brogan announced to his crew, whereupon their voices rose together in three shouts of "hurrah."

He cast his gaze over the *Lady Julia*'s deck, searching through the crowd. "The ship *Yankee Heart*, four days from Duxboro," he hailed back through the trumpet. "I request an audience. I am sending a boat."

His crew rowed him to the brig, where Brogan scaled the *Lady Julia*'s side ladder. He swung himself over the rails, planting his Hessians firmly on deck. Doffing his hat to a sea of curious faces, he gave them no more than a quick glance, as a stout fellow of middle years with dark red muttonchops stepped forward.

"Captain Josiah Winsor." He extended a hand, which Brogan eagerly accepted.

"Captain Brogan Talvis of the ship *Yankee Heart*." As he bowed he heard William arrive behind him. "Allow me to introduce my second mate, William Farragut."

The two officers nodded to each other, upon which Brogan continued, "I have a grave matter to present before you, Captain Winsor. I have information that you may have a young passenger on your brig made to board against her will. I am come to make certain of her safety and to ferry her home to her much concerned father."

Captain Winsor responded with a mixture of disbelief and confusion. "I can assure you, Captain. There's been no sign of foul play aboard this vessel. If a lady had been abducted, don't you think I'd be aware of such? This has been a peaceful voyage."

"And peaceful it shall remain once I remove the young woman in question. I am prepared to make compensation for her mistaken passage and the delay of your voyage, but you can depend upon this, Captain—we are not leaving until she's found."

"Brogan! Brogan, I am here."

With a tug of his heartstrings, Brogan harkened toward the voice and found Lorena separating herself from those gathered about. Her eyes burned into his, velvety brown and gentle, aglow with hope and all the purity of her soul.

Dressed in homespun with her hair tucked inside a white cotton bonnet, her humbled, weary appearance stirred his compassion. Yet her cheeks glowed as she smiled back at him, leaving Brogan awash with relief that she was found safe.

He was hastening to meet her as she came running to take

the hand he offered when a voice rose from the assembly behind her.

"Captain Winsor, be warned, I beseech you." George Louder shoved his way to the front of the crowd to grab Lorena gruffly by the shoulder before Brogan could reach her. She gasped in midstep as the shipwright pointed a finger accusingly. "That man is a privateer. He's guilty of engaging in acts of piracy on these very waters. You mustn't permit him to remove a woman passenger from this good brig."

Brogan stepped forward and gave Louder a shove that forced him to release Lorena and sent him staggering backward into the crowd of alarmed onlookers. "It is a pity I am not the authority here, as you, Louder, are a passenger under Captain Winsor's command. But you speak ill of the lady being in danger of me. It is *you* who are the guilty party. You who needs be exposed before these witnesses as the coward you are. For you forced Miss Huntley aboard this brig against her will, and under no circumstance will I let you mistreat her further."

The weasel straightened and shot him a glare of pure disgust.

"Young lady," said Captain Winsor, "is it your desire to remove with Captain Talvis to his ship?"

As she turned her soft gaze upon him, Brogan explained, "I don't understand how an intelligent woman like yourself came to be separated from Drew and aboard this vessel against your wishes, but your family was of the absolute opinion that was indeed the case, and so I am come to escort you home."

Her eyes spoke as loudly as her simple "Thank you." Lorena turned and nodded enthusiastically to Captain Winsor. "I wish to remove to the *Yankee Heart* very much so, yes."

"And you go of your own free will?"

"I do, Captain."

"Then so be it. I bid you depart peacefully, Captain Talvis, so as to not frighten these good people nor disrupt my voyage any longer. I'll suffer no fighting aboard my brig."

"Aye, Captain."

Brogan began to escort Lorena to the gangway, when George Louder's bitter laugh rose above the assembly. "Yes, be the hero, Captain Talvis. Rescue this damsel you believe to be in distress. Take her, I say, and with my glad tidings. Her presence aboard has been most disagreeable. She's been nothing but an annoyance, and I can't recall why I ever allowed her along. But no matter, for I have already had my pleasure and now I throw my leavings back to you."

In a swift move of unleashed fury, Brogan drew his sword and poised its lethal, polished edge beneath Louder's chin. "You filthy weasel," he spat. The insult on Lorena festered hotly within him, and Brogan burned with the injustice.

A collective gasp rose from the deck. Passengers and crew drew back. Brogan could feel the tension in their silence. He heard William's steps behind him and knew the mate stood ready to defend his captain, just as Brogan sensed his crew aboard the *Yankee Heart* go on the alert.

"Here, here, now!" Captain Winsor opened his coat in warning of reaching for the pistol he had tucked into his leather belt.

Brogan raised a hand to stay them all, though he doubted whether he could stomach the sight of the weasel a moment longer without anger getting the better of him. "I should like nothing better than to make fish bait of you, Louder, but I promised Captain Winsor there'd be no violence.

However, if I truly am the despicable character you accuse me of, it should take little to provoke me into breaking that promise. Perhaps I shall gut you right here. Then, rather than arriving in England, you be traveling straight to Davy Jones's locker."

Louder's eyes burned with hate and rage, which never wavered from Brogan's, as he stepped closer to Captain Winsor in a show of alliance . . . or perhaps, Brogan thought, he merely sought protection.

"I see you've no qualms about a public display of brute force, Captain. A chance for all to see the fruit of your life's work," Louder taunted, appealing to the crowd. "Terrorism at sea."

Brogan's anger swelled. Lorena curled her fingers around his forearm and gave it a squeeze, staying him. She lifted her face to his with calm assurance, lingering over his features in an expression of hero worship Brogan did not feel worthy of. She was beautiful to such a degree that he could not stand in her presence without awareness of that beauty stirring a reaction in him, but suddenly her loveliness took on a force that seemed to reach into his very soul.

"He hasn't yet apologized," he protested, eyeing Louder.

"What good purpose is an apology made at the point of a sword?" Lorena asked him.

She was expecting him to rise above his desire to strike the coward, and something inside him could not disappoint her. He placed some distance between them with a step backward and sheathed his sword. "I once promised Lorena I'd not strike you again, and it is only for her I step aside. But before we leave, have you anything to say to the lady, Louder?"

Brogan waited for an apology that didn't come. "No? Very

well then. Let us not delay your voyage any further, Captain Winsor."

He turned from Louder's cold stare to take Lorena's elbow, but she pulled away and slapped the shipwright soundly across the face.

Brogan stood in awe.

"Best you do well for yourself in England, George, for you are no longer welcome in Duxboro," she said. "You're a cruel, selfish man."

Turning her back on him, she addressed Brogan, saying, "Allow me to say good-bye to my friends and then we can be on our way. As you can imagine, I'm anxious to sail home on the *Yankee Heart*."

Brogan watched her proudly as Lorena stepped into the embrace of an older woman with striking red hair. Louder watched also, his complexion paling to near white. He turned toward Brogan, and as they glared at each other, the weasel began to tremble with rage. No sooner did Brogan recognize the madness in those dark eyes than Louder whipped around and grabbed the pistol from Captain Winsor's waistband.

He leveled it straight at Brogan's chest.

12

I'm thrilled to be going home, though I wish that didn't mean I must bid farewell to you, dearest Jane."

The arms embracing Lorena stiffened as Jane gave a frightened scream. Lorena glanced into her friend's face, then whirled in the direction of her horrified stare. George had a pistol trained on Brogan.

How could this be? Fear squeezed her heart until it felt she could scarcely draw a breath. George was guilty of many selfish acts, but he wasn't a murderer. Was he? Lorena just didn't know what to believe anymore.

Brogan eyed him unflinchingly. "Let me caution you to think this through, Louder. You may shoot me, but you still won't have Lorena. My crew have been trained in battle. Formerly privateersmen all . . . pirates, as you prefer to label us. Think what they'll do should you harm me. I would not be surprised if my chief mate didn't have a musket trained on you this very moment. And Captain Winsor won't protect you once you've fired that pistol."

"He's correct, Mr. Louder." Captain Winsor stretched

forth his hand. "This action is most ill-advised, sir. Return me my weapon."

"Think of your hopes and dreams." Lorena stepped closer, but Brogan warded her off with a raised hand. "Think of the prosperous future you've planned for yourself in England. Look at me, George. Do you really want to sacrifice everything you've worked your entire life for—your freedom and maybe your life—all for an impulsive moment of retaliation against Captain Talvis?"

The pistol began to tremble in George's hand. "You were wrong about me, Lorena," he said, though he kept his focus on Brogan. "I do recognize how precious you are. My love has always been true. Know that. And that I wish you happy. I-I-I'm sorry."

Lorena was taken off guard. "George, I can't believe I'm saying this, but I do believe, for the first time, you may actually be sincere."

George nodded. "I am."

"Then I accept your apology. Drop the pistol, George."

He hung his head and his arm went limp. Brogan snatched away the pistol while Captain Winsor's men seized George from behind.

Brogan returned the weapon to the *Lady Julia*'s captain. "We shall leave immediately, sir," he said.

Captain Winsor gave a grave nod. "That would be most advisable."

Jane and her family followed Lorena to the gangway. Below, the longboat bobbed and rolled on the waves splashing against the *Lady Julia*'s side. Three pairs of seamen sat at the oars.

Jane blinked back moisture from her eyes. "I will miss you, Lorena Huntley. Perhaps it is selfish of me to feel saddened to see you go, but this voyage shall seem lonely without you. Go with God's blessing. It's good to see a smile on your face."

Lorena nodded, sobered by how quickly fortune had turned around for her since only that morning. "I shall miss you too, Jane. Please take my day dress and spencer. I wish it were more of an offering, but at the very least, you will have my dress and I shall have yours . . . as a remembrance. Not that I'll need a reminder of you. I'll never forget your care of me throughout this misadventure of mine. I've been blessed to have met you kind Ellerys," she added with a smile for Thomas and Matthew, "and now to be returning home. Good-bye, Jane, Thomas, Matthew. God see you all safely to England."

"And you, Miss Huntley," Thomas returned, draping an arm across his brother's shoulders so as to include the young man in the sentiment. "Godspeed."

Matthew gave her a shy smile. "I swear I shall never taste an equal to your mince pie."

Lorena glanced behind to hide a smile and found Brogan overseeing the hauling of gifts of vintage port, coffee, teas, cheeses, and fruit up from the longboat, which he then bestowed on Captain Winsor.

He'd come to her rescue when he'd no obligation to do so. When not even the delicate affection of their budding friendship would have warranted the expense and inconvenience of taking the *Yankee Heart* on this unexpected maiden voyage.

He was a fine man, as it turned out, despite their early confrontations. Yet so much more than his charity attracted her. Lorena admired him in profile, speaking with Captain Winsor as a lock of sandy hair fell across his brow to partially cover one eye. His was a strong, masculine face. An appearance made all the more authoritative by the proud set of his shoulders and a masterful stance that reached into his black leather Hessians.

I adore him.

With that thought came a new and startling sensation that had every cell in her body stirring to life and bubbling with excitement. Embarrassment warmed her cheeks. Still, the truth remained. Lorena craved nothing more than to be sheltered in the protection of his arms.

Having concluded his business, Brogan beckoned her to join him, where he introduced her to his second mate. He swung himself onto the rope ladder, pausing to instruct her. "Follow me down once I have reached the boat. Mr. Farragut will assist you from above, and I shall be waiting below to receive you. Do you think you can do this?"

"I can assure you, Captain, my excitement to be going home prevails over any hesitation I have in navigating a rope ladder."

He looked at first surprised by her confidence, then amused. "It is a wonder, then, that such an adept young woman managed to find herself in this helpless situation. I am curious to hear the tale."

"And I will tell it, if I must. But not here."

He descended into the longboat, where he stood balanced in the rocky boat and waited with a self-satisfied smile.

Lorena stepped over the *Lady Julia*'s side after him, finding purchase for her slippers on the first rung of the rope ladder before continuing with her descent. Three quarters of the way down she felt Brogan cinch her waist from behind, holding her secure until she was close enough for him to lift into the boat.

In the tossing boat she lost her bearings and stumbled. Brogan held steady behind her, solid as a tree, righting her, then guiding her to a seat in the bow.

As he settled down beside her, awareness of his masculinity left her silent.

The oars were lowered and they shoved off, all six crewmen putting their backs into rowing across a choppy sea. It swelled like a living thing about them, rocking the boat and dampening her face with spray. Lorena found Jane amongst the faces lining the *Lady Julia*'s rails and waved a final good-bye.

In the opposite direction, the much larger *Yankee Heart* loomed closer and closer in all her lofty magnificence. Lorena picked out Mr. Smith at the gangway, waiting to receive them. He drew a small figure forward, closer to the rails. Was that . . . Drew? Happiness filled her so completely, Lorena thought she must be dreaming, and yet she'd never felt more alert. Drew was aboard and would be traveling with her.

The longboat closed alongside the massive hull, and Brogan stood, securing the boat hook to the *Yankee Heart*'s chains. One of the oarsmen caught the rope ladder, and Lorena was ushered up first.

"Welcome aboard, miss," Mr. Smith called down as she scaled the ship's great wooden side. He lent a hand to assist her on board while the crew gave a round of cheers. Having manned the yards, several returned to the deck, sliding down a single rope.

Lorena whooped along with them, and then Drew hurled himself into her arms. Dropping to her knees to receive him, she squeezed him in a hug and covered his face with kisses. He giggled and clung to her neck. "You don't know how relieved I am to see you, my little man. I should never have let you out of my sight that day."

"It's ye we are relieved to see, Miss Huntley." Jabez Smith assisted her to her feet. "And won't yer papa be happy for this day. Ye are a fortunate lady to have a family who loves ye watching over yer welfare. Ye have not been harmed?"

"I am well, Mr. Smith, thank you. And fully aware of my blessings, make no mistake. Though I think we both know I owe thanks to more than those within my own family."

She caught the eye of Brogan, who by now had joined them on deck. She was moved by the warmth in his gaze, drawn into the high spirits and excitement circulating among the crew.

"I won't easily forget this day," she said. "I have seen this ship countless times under construction, and now I feel honored to be sailing with her. I say hurrah to the *Yankee Heart*, to her captain and to all who sail aboard her."

Holding fast to Drew's hand, Lorena was pleasantly surprised at the crew's response. They raised their voices, cheering, "Huzzah to the *Yankee Heart*! Huzzah to Captain Talvis! Huzzah to us all!"

She empathized with their loyalty and shared their pride. As she glanced at the many faces gathered round, two shocked her as decidedly familiar.

"Edward! What's this? You are here, as well? And Mr. Mott! Can it be? Have you both signed articles with the *Yankee Heart*?"

Her father's men approached her with greetings. They asked after her travels, eager to know how she fared, then explained their temporary roles on board.

Poor, dear Edward expressed especial pleasure to see her. "I blame myself for not taking better care," he said. "I should have been watching out for you and Drew, but George was my friend . . . at least I believed him to be so. I had no reason to distrust him or to suspect that he would use me to trick you. Forgive me, Lorena."

Lorena touched his hand consolingly. "All is forgotten now, Edward. Do not berate yourself. Believe me when I say no one was at fault for what happened, save George Louder. I considered him a friend also, but he misused our friendship."

Brogan strode into their midst to take Lorena's elbow. "Perhaps we should allow Miss Huntley to retire to her cabin for a rest before dinner."

He appraised his deck of idle crewmen. "Mr. Smith, see everyone returns to their duties. Let us be quick about changing course and sailing our young miss home. Mr. Mott, I'll have you break out the finest of Mr. Huntley's stores, if you please, and prepare us a meal in celebration of Miss Huntley's safe return."

As the sailors dispersed to obey orders, he turned to Lorena with a twinkle in his china blue eyes. "And now, Miss Huntley, if you would care to accompany us, a surprise awaits you in your cabin. Is that not right, Drew?"

He hoisted the boy in the air, tossing him playfully while Drew squealed with joy and, through his giggles, answered, "Yeeeeeeessss!"

It was a heartwarming exchange that had Lorena recalling all over again the curious affinity for the boy Brogan had displayed from the first. Memories returned of Brogan's upset when she'd removed Drew from the supper table to put him to bed, the way Brogan had praised Drew's skill with a sling even though the weapon had been turned on him, and how subsequently Brogan made certain to include Drew in their plans anytime he came calling for her.

And now, in her absence, the pair seemed to have grown closer still.

How was it so? That an unfettered, childless, widower captain, who'd spent these past few years at sea embroiled in war, showed remarkable tenderness for a boy he barely knew?

What bond had forged between them during the course of their short voyage? It was as if they shared something to which Lorena was not privy. A connection she could not define.

"Lead the way, then, young sailor," Brogan charged as he set Drew back on his feet.

"Come, Lorena," the child urged, pulling her aft toward the quarter gallery. "Come see."

Hand in hand they walked, taking care to keep from getting underfoot of the crew. Drew smiled confidently as he led her about, drawing her attention to particular points of interest. Everywhere seamen moved about the ship. Those sailors who did not have their feet planted firmly on deck hung from a confusion of rigging and sails.

Brogan followed close behind, though at the midship bulkhead he stepped forward to open a door.

Lorena knew well the ship's plan, but allowed Drew to guide her down a corridor into the great cabin. Here was the grand seagoing parlor just as she remembered, paneled in mahogany and trimmed with the yellowish luster of satinwood. The difference now being the fully furnished compartment, seeing those articles that had been either purchased or commissioned during the weeks the *Yankee Heart* was being rigged placed in their rightful home, transforming the once cavernous cabin into a comfortable living space as fine as any house built on New England soil.

Lorena skimmed a fingertip across the large mahogany

dining table. Damask curtains of willow green dressed the stern windows with matching cushions on the window seats. Daylight reflected off the fresh white paint of the ceiling and the silver lanterns hanging from its beams. There was also a settee and matching wing chairs.

Lorena curled her toes inside her slippers, pressing them deeper into the Brussels carpet. "It's all so lovely."

"I could not have expected less." Brogan's gaze followed hers around the cabin, the corners of his lips crooked slightly upward in pride. "If you recall, it was you, Lorena, who helped me choose these fabrics and several of the furnishings."

"How satisfying a surprise to find them all looking so well together. I believe I shall enjoy this cruise very much."

"This isn't your surprise," Drew said with a giggle as though she were quite silly.

"It is not? What else could there be?" Sifting her fingers through the boy's pale curls, she glanced down at his sweet face with a raised brow. "Truthfully, sweetheart, I do not think anything could make me happier than I feel right now." In a matter of hours she had gone from despair to a contentment her heart could barely contain.

"Step this way and we'll show you," Brogan said, directing her portside to a closed cabin door.

But Lorena's curiosity was already drawing her to the opposite end of the suite, where ledgers, charts, a divider, and parallel ruler lay sprawled across a large writing table. An old desk held journals and accounts with rolled documents stored carefully inside each pigeonhole. As she moved closer, Lorena inspected a small bookcase. One well-used book in particular caught her eye on a shelf of its own. Thin leather strips wrapped around its worn nut-brown casing, holding the pages together.

"This book. Is this—?"

Brogan grabbed her wrist before she could touch it. This surprised her, for she hadn't realized he'd been standing so close behind. "Drew has been waiting patiently to show you to your cabin," he said.

Lorena saw eagerness in the boy's wide-eyed expression and offered him her hand, the book forgotten. "Of course. Show me your surprise."

Drew led her back to the closed cabin door. With a turn of the latch she opened it to reveal a modest stateroom as luxuriously built as the great cabin but decidedly feminine in décor.

Decidedly familiar also.

Lorena spun about and sat on the bed with a bounce. She ran her hands over the blue-and-white-diamond coverlet. "This is from my own bed in Duxboro." Gaily wrapped packages lay across her pillow, but her gaze did not linger, as there was much to see. The cabin held many of her own personal items, from her grandmother's framed sampler on the wall to the rug beneath her feet.

"And those draperies on the porthole there, I believe they are sewn from the very same silk brocade Mrs. Culliford helped me select with the purpose of making pillows for the settee in my room. And here is my trunk, I see." She leapt off the bed to look inside and found it filled with her clothes and slippers, the book she'd been reading before her unfortunate departure, and her needlework and embroidery basket.

"I feel so at home. But that, I suspect, was the whole intent, was it not?" It was more statement than question. Still, Lorena directed those words to Brogan, who remained standing at the threshold as though he preferred observing from a distance.

She offered him a grateful smile, then bending down scooped Drew into her arms. Brushing the curls from his face, she pressed a kiss to his temple. "As miserable a time as I had, knowing I was sailing away from home, we are now going to have the most wonderful adventure returning together."

He nodded, then wriggled from her embrace to climb on the bed. "Open your gifts!"

"They're from your family," Brogan said. Lorena sensed a sudden reserve in his tone and bearing, in stark contradiction to Drew, who quaked with excitement.

The child presented her with a small painted tin. "This is from me."

Lorena seated herself beside him as they conspired to open first the lid and next a layer of tissue paper. They peered inside together, heads touching.

She made certain to gasp with delight. "Maple sugar fudge. Thank you, sweetheart, you thoughtful boy. How long you must have been waiting for me to open it, when we both know how well you enjoy candy. Shall we celebrate with a piece before supper?"

His enthusiastic nod was answer enough. Drew reached into the tin with one hand and then the other.

Lorena then offered the tin to Brogan. "I know you won't mind, Brogan. You and Drew are two of a kind in that you both share a taste for sweets."

He surprised her by refusing with a shake of his head. Moments ago he'd endeavored to make her welcome merry, and now that she was indeed bursting with gaiety, he seemed to have gone strangely pensive.

Lorena puzzled over him, then selected a piece of fudge for herself and bit into it.

Drew handed her one package after another. There was a small painted fan from her father, a pair of white silk stockings embellished with embroidery from Mrs. Culliford, and a shell comb from Temperance. Lorena skimmed their notes, preferring to read them in private later when the day's excitement did not have her thoughts so distracted.

One very small gift remained. It bore no note.

Drew dropped it into her palm.

Lorena loosed the ribbon and peeled back the paper. A shiny silver thimble shone up at her. She held it up and saw that it was etched with tiny hearts and cupids.

She knew immediately whom it was from and scooted off the bed, before thoughts of propriety or self-consciousness dissuaded her, and stood openly before Brogan with affection shining in her eyes. "Thank you." Two simple words, but in her heart they meant so much more, words she could not express. "I will cherish it always."

As she gazed into those intense blue eyes, what shone back awakened her soul. Burning like a flame, a reflection of her own passionate feelings, a surrender, a humbleness that for a moment allowed her to peer into the heart of his being. And what she saw was a man haunted by pain and guilt.

It seemed he wished to tell her something, but whatever Brogan's thoughts, he chose to keep them hidden as she watched him withdraw into himself.

"George said some awful things about me," she said. "He spoke in anger. I want you to know they aren't true in the least."

All vulnerability in his expression disappeared. He gave her no more response than a nod. Lorena presently was feeling too weary and uncertain to push him further.

"Get some rest," he said. "I'll have you called to supper."

He spoke as though relations between them were proper and formal. Lorena suspected not. She suspected their guards had been lowered in the realization they shared more in common than either of them could have imagined. Perhaps much of it had to do with their mutual affection for Drew, but during their short time apart, feelings of friendship and attraction had grown into a deeper respect and caring.

Brogan paced his quarterdeck and stood facing the sea. His throat constricted, strangled by the emotion rising inside him. Emotion Brogan did not comprehend. He'd succeeded in his mission. Lorena was safely aboard the *Yankee Heart*. He'd been wrong to believe she'd ever willingly flee with Louder. There'd been no love for the shipwright in her eyes, nor even sympathy. Brogan never believed Louder's lie about having Lorena, not unless the weasel had forced himself on her, and Lorena's spirits were too high for a woman who had undergone such an ordeal.

No, what bothered Brogan was that within a short period of being reunited with her, Lorena had managed to touch something inside him he'd thought long dead. A frozen place in his heart was melting, leaving him vulnerable in a way he strove never to be again.

It frightened him in a respect, thinking from force of habit that he might be punished for allowing such tenderness to affect him, and yet Brogan had no idea exactly what he was feeling that made him afraid.

13

Behind the drawn draperies, lantern light cast quivering shadows throughout the great cabin.

"Who would care to give the blessing?" Lorena asked. She glanced expectantly around the supper table.

Brogan nodded to Jabez. It was the mate's habit to give thanks, because if left up to Brogan there'd be no prayer. Yet before Jabez could begin, Drew announced, "I should like to say it."

Brogan made quick note of Lorena's proud smile. No mother had looked more adoringly upon her son and certainly not Drew's natural birth mother.

"By all means," he said, experiencing a tightening in his chest as he clasped his hands with those of Lorena on his right and Drew on his left.

"Almighty Father," the lad called in his clear, sweet voice. "We come before you with grateful hearts for bringing Lorena back. I especially give my thanks. Please let her not be taken from me again. And everyone else here does feel the same. Show your favor to Captain Talvis and Mr. Smith and the ship and the crew and may they always remain under your care. Amen."

Jabez cleared his throat and Drew opened his eyes. The mate smiled approvingly, then nodded to the repast set before them.

"Oh! And thank you for this food," Drew added.

Here sat the folk who mattered most to him, Brogan reflected. The closest he'd known to a family meal, including any he'd shared with Abigail during their married life. He gripped the hands he held that much tighter before releasing them. "Amen," he said.

"That was wonderful, sweetheart," praised Lorena.

Brogan gave the lad a wink before contemplating his bowl of creamy chowder. He dipped in his spoon and brought a sample to his lips, first inhaling the scent of bacon before actually tasting the corn chowder. He let the flavor settle on his tongue before swallowing. Made from a lobster base, the corn was sweet and the potatoes hardy. It was delicious, and yet . . .

"Warrick," he called to his young steward now setting before him a serving platter of golden-brown fish cakes. Brogan gave them a queer eye. "I'm curious as to our cook's choice of dishes. I specifically told Mr. Mott to prepare a meal with the best of our provisions. We are celebrating Miss Huntley's safe return, and he sees fit to serve us the fare of a public supper?"

"I see exactly what the dear fellow has done." Lorena beheld the platter of fried fish cakes with an expression of shining delight. "As wholesome a meal as this likely appears, these dishes are among my favorites. Fred Mott has obviously prepared them in my honor."

"And there is bread pudding for dessert, miss," Warrick added.

"Bread pudding? I do love bread pudding. Did you hear that, Drew?"

The boy nodded excitedly as his mouth was full, and while he chewed, a bit of mushy potato escaped the corner of his mouth.

"I see I'm not the only one who enjoys a public supper. And what have you to say, Mr. Smith?" she asked. "You seem to be enjoying the chowder and cakes."

"Aye, miss. You'll hear no complaint from me."

Brogan's attention was drawn to her long, slender hands as Lorena lifted the teapot and began to pour Jabez's tea and then a cup for herself.

She had changed into a pretty pink calico frock with large puffed sleeves that tapered in from elbow to wrist. A wide, ruffle-edged satin ribbon cinched her high at the waist. The modest, straight neckline covered her collarbone yet disclosed the lovely curve of her long white throat as it met her shoulders. It was there that the lanterns' quivering light played on the paleness of her skin.

"And you, Brogan, as a man who admittedly prefers the simplicity of gingerbread, you can't deny Fred Mott's Yankee fare makes for a satisfying meal. And yet you scowl. Are you displeased?" She offered him a cup of tea.

As he reached to accept, his fingertips brushed hers. They both held the saucer, yet neither took full possession.

No longer could Brogan dismiss his feelings for her as mere regard for her delicate beauty. His heart betrayed him, harboring affection for a woman who had fouled up his plans. What part had she played in the taking of his son? What knowledge did she hide? He still did not know.

"I find the chowder very tasty." He accepted the teacup

and sought to hide his woolgathering by reaching for the fish cakes. As he ate, he glanced up, surprised to find Lorena observing him.

"Drew tells me you and Mr. Smith share tales of your travels at dinnertime, and that the stories are even more exciting to him than the exploits of Captain Briggs. Imagine my surprise to hear it. I did not think anyone could rise above Captain Briggs in Drew's esteem . . . in any regard."

Her tone held a challenge, her eyes mild curiosity as though she insisted upon an explanation.

Brogan swallowed, then followed her gaze to the cloth sea captain lying idle on the table beside Drew. Instead of falling into whispers with his doll, inventing his own stories, as Brogan learned was common of Drew at mealtimes, the lad now took animated interest in the dinner table conversation.

Even now, Drew followed their exchange. He set down his tumbler of milk, licking his upper lip. "Are we going to hear a story?"

"Aye, I believe it is indeed time for a story." Brogan leaned toward Lorena. "Mr. Smith and I have many stories, but this evening no one has a more interesting tale than you. So tell us, Lorena, for we've wondered, what turn of events led you to be shipbound for England with George Louder?"

She cleared her palate with a sip of tea and then swallowed uncomfortably.

She stalled and Brogan had to wonder why. "Now that you are on my ship, I feel an even greater responsibility for your welfare, a sense of duty separate and apart from my command of this vessel." What he felt was fierce protectiveness, similar to his feelings for Drew and far stronger even than any emotion he'd felt for his late wife. "You claim you were not injured, and to my eyes you do not seem to have been. Still, I understand you have been through a trial, and I don't mean to be insensitive, but you sit here in good spirits. Therefore, I believe we deserve an explanation. So, tell us. What happened to prevent you from disembarking the *Lady Julia*?"

"Be warned. You are not going to like what I have to say," she mumbled into her teacup before carefully returning it to its saucer. She stole a warning glance at Drew before meeting Brogan's gaze.

"Let me start by explaining that George and I became friends when we were both children. But as we grew older, his priorities changed to follow wealth and success, whereas mine remained with home and family. When he made his decision to depart to England in search of his fortune, he asked me to marry him. I refused as gently as I could. He grew most insistent, and recently I thought he had at last accepted that I did not have the love of a wife to give him. We agreed to part as the friends we had always been. To that end I baked his favorite mince pies for the trip and invited him to tea in the summer kitchen before seeing him off to Plymouth. Little did I know, he never had any intention of taking no for an answer. He somehow slipped a vomit powder into my tea."

"Vomit powder?" Outrage on her behalf boiled inside Brogan. He felt it hot and urgent, the way he'd felt the injustice of England's tyranny or Abigail's deceit. "Louder poisoned—"

"I accused him of the exact same, yes," Lorena commented with a finality that warned Brogan against further interruption and pointedly put a halt to his rising anger. She continued in a composed voice. "As the powder was beginning to take effect, George deceived me into believing Drew had boarded the *Lady Julia*. We took off in search of him. While looking in the hold,

I became violently ill and hit my head. I could not distinguish my own dizziness from the movement of the brig, and in either case I was too sick to move. By the time I was found, taken to a stateroom, and revived, we were well out to sea."

Brogan gaped, letting his horror be known. His brows knit as he pinned Lorena beneath the displeasure of his stare. "So this is why you've waited till now to tell me? To the last, you protect that weasel."

"I was protecting *you*," she shot back.

"Me?"

"From yourself. She gave him a pointed stare and to such degree that Brogan quieted and let her continue. "You did the right and wise thing in not acting on your anger. Especially when it would have served no good purpose but to distress Captain Winsor and his passengers, not to mention the wrong example it would have set to a certain *impressionable* young passenger of your own." With a sharp jerk of her head, she indicated Drew. "Thank you for choosing the most appropriate course and behaving like a gentleman."

"George was bad," Drew growled. He slammed a fist down on the tabletop.

"George did a bad thing," she said to Drew, "but then you and Captain Talvis arrived as an answer to prayer. And now George is gone from our lives."

Lorena sighed. She fidgeted with her fork, twirling it between her fingers. "You were right all along, Brogan. George was not to be trusted. I didn't want to believe evil of a childhood friend. I failed to accept the man he had become." Her voice grew thick. "Bless you and Mr. Smith and dearest Drew for coming to my rescue. I should not be having such an enjoyable evening otherwise."

Jabez slipped her a look of awe. "Well spoken, miss."

Brogan raised his teacup. "To your voyage aboard the *Yankee Heart*. May it reside in your memory as fondly as corn chowder, fish cakes, and bread pudding."

Her laughter pleased him, and dinner proceeded with everyone's energies directed toward Fred Mott's good Yankee fare. It was a satisfying meal in all respects, so much so that after dessert was consumed, they lingered over another cup of tea.

As he sipped, Brogan noticed Lorena's eyes wander the length of the cabin to his bookshelves.

"Earlier I noticed what I suspect is the Holy Book on one of your shelves there," she said. "Is it your personal Bible, Brogan?"

He answered cautiously. "Aye."

She offered him a sweet smile. "It looks to be well read."

"It is old."

"I've had a look through my trunk and it seems my family neglected to pack my own Bible. Would you mind—"

"You are welcome to it," Brogan heard himself reply a little too quickly. "I have little use for it myself, other than to keep it on hand for the ship."

The soft expression in her velvety brown eyes grew saddened at his words. "Oh? I had thought otherwise. You seem to know Scripture. And in getting to know you, one would think the Good Word had left its impression and that you carried it in your heart. Your Bible sits by your desk in a place of honor. Do you not turn to it for prayer and guidance?"

Jabez cleared his throat and grinned into his cup of tea.

Brogan grew uncomfortable with this conversation. "I've trained myself to rely on hard work and bravery, on study and careful thought to carry me through life and battle." He'd learned not to trust his hopes to a God who would close His ears to the prayers of the baseborn.

He rose from his seat and strode to the far end of the cabin, where he retrieved the Bible off the bookcase. As he held the worn leather-bound pages in his hands, Brogan felt his unworthiness like a darkness surrounding his heart. "Yet there was a time I read it faithfully," he said in reflection.

A time of shining youth when Brogan was grateful to be at sea. No matter how hard he must work, he was learning a trade. He was free of the orphan asylum. He was traveling far from those whose cruel misjudgment viewed the circumstances of his ill birth as a crime instead of a misfortune. It was a time when some measure of virtue and innocence still lived in him and Jabez's teachings could stir his faith. Enough to inspire Brogan to believe that God would show mercy to an honest, upright heart, even if that heart belonged to the lowly and baseborn. Enough to make Brogan believe there was more to life than survival.

Then along came Jefferson with his embargo against all shipping to and from foreign ports, leaving hundreds of seamen unemployed, their families left to starve. Soon just trying to survive became all there was.

But life changed after Benjamin's birth. Brogan had a son. Someone in the world he was connected to by blood. Someone he was responsible for. Suddenly he understood what it felt like to truly love. He grew fiercely ambitious, determined to make a future for his family.

He found not only employment but purpose, for himself and Jabez among the American private sector, businessmen both eager and equipped to participate in the naval war with

England. They would be doing more than earning a living. They would fight for the rights and freedoms of their country.

As Brogan sailed the open seas, his wife grew distant. Soon Benjamin became the only link to the love they once shared. He worried about his son during those absences, knowing Abigail resented his time away and grew impatient with the confinement and caretaking of an infant. There were times he even suspected her of being with other men.

Brogan's last wavering flame of hope for his family had been snuffed out the day Abigail told him Benjamin was gone. It was as though the Almighty had noted his unworthiness and turned His face.

Or perhaps His face had been turned all along.

Sometimes Brogan thought the only thing keeping him alive during the war was his desire to find the boy.

The cabin had fallen deathly silent, all eyes upon him. Embarrassed, Brogan shook off his dark thoughts and returned to the table to offer his Bible to Lorena. "Here. I hope it will comfort you. It has done little for me."

She observed him with a sweetly curious expression, then turned to Jabez seated beside her. "Do you know why he is angry at God, Mr. Smith? He hasn't stopped scowling since this conversation began."

Jabez nodded knowingly. "Unfortunately, miss, the cap'n believes the Almighty does not smile favorably upon him, keeping those things he desires most out of reach."

She straightened, taken aback. "But how can that be, Mr. Smith? Captain Talvis is a successful and acclaimed war hero. He is possessed of wealth and master of his own ship. What more, pray, does he desire?"

"Avast talking about me as though I were not standing

here." Brogan forced the scowl from his face. "Here, Lorena. You wanted the Book. Take it."

She pressed it back into his holding. "I was hoping you would do the reading."

His irritation returned. "Me? Surely Mr. Smith would be better suited. Aboard ship he conducts Sunday services. That is his collection of hymnbooks on my bookshelf. He's been active in the religious revival to improve the moral condition of seamen and promote temperance."

"That is very good of you, Mr. Smith," Lorena acknowledged. "But allow me to explain my predicament. Before recent events, I'd been reading to Drew from Psalms. I thought, considering the bond it seems you've forged with him, that you, Brogan, might wish to read in my stead. It has been a long day and my eyes are tired. If not, I'm sure Mr. Smith would agree."

Brogan's throat went dry. His gaze jumped to Drew, who stared back in earnest. This opportunity would allow for one more way in which he could be a father to his son. "I would enjoy that very much. And you, Drew? Would you like me to read to you?"

The lad's eyes widened excitedly. He reached for his cloth doll. "Oh, yes. Captain Briggs likes to hear, too."

Brogan resumed his seat and opened the weathered Bible to the book of Psalms.

"Clever girl," he heard Jabez whisper to Lorena. "I've not known man or woman to have such good influence on the cap'n as ye. In getting him to open his Bible again, ye have accomplished in one evening what I have been trying to do for years."

Brogan lifted his gaze from the page to eye his chief mate

with annoyance. And yet not so annoyed as he might have expected.

"The dust flying from that Good Book is fairly choking me." Jabez coughed and hacked, making a show of waving a hand before his face. "Quickly, Miss Huntley, cover yer mouth."

Lorena laughed at the jibe, then sat back, hands folded, and gave Brogan her attention. "What have you chosen?"

"Nothing until I have quiet."

Drew shot her a glare from across the table, pressing a finger to his soft pink lips.

Lorena repressed a smile, but not the gaiety in her eyes.

Brogan gave his son's curls a tousle, then turned his focus to the page. Dismissing all else from his thoughts, he began to read, "'They that go down to the sea in ships, that do business in great waters . . .'"

He projected authority in his voice for his son's enjoyment, but as the moments wore on and he reached the passage "'Then they cry unto the Lord in their trouble, and he bringeth them out of their distresses,'" Brogan began to feel a conviction from the words he recited aloud. It had been so long since he'd dared have faith, and even then what good had come of it?

"'He maketh the storm a calm, so that the waves thereof are still.'" His voice grew hoarse and thick at the promise. Dare he trust it? "'Then are they glad because they be quiet; so he bringeth them unto their desired haven.'"

What was his desired haven? His son, of course. A family of his own, bound in blood and loyalty and love. Folk to whom he truly belonged and who belonged to him.

He finished the last remaining lines of the psalm as though

offering them up in prayer. *Whatever the outcome upon reaching Duxboro . . . please don't let my son be taken from me again.*

A light touch on his forearm burned through Brogan's shirt and flesh to his marrow. He looked down into the sweet face of his young son, gazing up at him with an expression that could be . . . love?

"I had a papa once," he said. "He sailed into war on a ship with cannons and guns, but he never came back. He gave me Captain Briggs, but I was too small to remember. I think he was like you."

Brogan felt the breath flee his lungs. *I am your father, Ben.* The truth festered inside him, and now Brogan could feel the ties of kinship revive between them. He took Drew's chin in his hand, tilting his face so he might smile more deeply into those sincere eyes. The lad smiled back. Drew may not yet know who he was, but some part of Benjamin remembered.

The only course left to him was to find the proper moment and reveal himself. Then hope for acceptance, not only from Drew but Lorena, as well. Would they forgive him for believing, not unlike George Louder, that he could take what he'd felt was his by right, when all along he'd needed to earn their love?

Whatever had transpired between Abigail and the Huntleys, he was grateful to Nathaniel Huntley and Lorena for opening their home and hearts to the boy, for giving Drew the love he never would have received from Abigail. Together, they had raised him into a fine, brave lad.

The mystery behind it all, however, continued to eat away at him.

Lorena thanked him again for the day's events and tonight's

reading, then rose to herd Drew off to bed. "Will you read to us again tomorrow, Captain?" she asked.

Brogan nodded, still thoughtful. "Aye, I shall. Sleep well now, both of you."

"And you, Brogan," she bid. "A very good night."

14

Deep within the abyss of slumber that evening, Brogan was having a hard night. Dreams had dragged him back to the last time he saw his wife alive.

"The child is gone, Brogan. Do you hear me? Gone. How many more times will you have me repeat the words before their meaning sinks into that infernal thickness between your ears? Benjamin is gone . . . forever!"

Reeling from disbelief, he searched for a sign to the contrary, all the while fearing the worst. He scanned the parlor, furnished in Abigail's ostentatious preference for dark floral chintz décor, heavy Empire furniture, and lacquered screens. Not a trace of motherhood remained. Abigail had rid herself of their two-year-old son.

Brogan steadied himself, straining against the rage coursing through him. He envisioned his son frightened and crying among unfamiliar surroundings, and his ire rose to where steam fairly blew out his ears. He clenched his right hand into a tight fist, then slowly unclenched it, his patience waning.

"Tell me where he is." The words spewed forth as a plea,

although that was not his intent. The last thing Brogan wanted was to sound desperate.

Abigail tossed back her head of silky golden curls and postured herself on the edge of the settee in a well-practiced manner that drew attention to her petite frame and the generosity of her endowments. Her dressing gown draped loosely off one shoulder, her skin a perfect alabaster. Six years his senior, she could pass for much younger than her actual twenty-nine years.

Suddenly her beauty disgusted him.

She raised her face to him in defiance, and even the dim lighting could not disguise the exceptional brilliance of her exotic blue eyes. "It is done. He shall be provided for far better than you or I ever could. I no longer have the means to care for an infant, and you, Brogan, most certainly do not. An occasional visit when in port does not make for a doting parent, as you may seem to think."

Brogan winced at her harshness. By "means" she meant she no longer had any desire to care for Ben. She'd shown little love for the boy, and not for one moment did he believe her attempt at reassurance. Nay, he was not so naive as to trust the motives of anyone who'd condone a mother abandoning her son, anyone who'd agree to spirit away their child. "You believe Benjamin will benefit from the sponsor of strangers, more so than with a father who loves him? To grow up never knowing his origins, his own people?" It was a terrible fate. Brogan knew from experience—a loneliness that tore at the fabric of his being.

She glared back. "You needn't worry. He'll be well taken care of, I assure you. Very well."

Ah, was this her true purpose revealed at last? She was a

sly one, this woman. "I see then. It's money, is it? You sold Benjamin for money?"

His mind grappled for something to persuade her to reveal the boy's whereabouts. "You know you've no need of that money, Abigail. You are more than comfortable, and besides, I've been advanced to captain. It's a captain's wages I shall be sending you from now on. I've been sought in the service of a vessel under my own command. I promise, I shall return whenever and as often as I am able, but what else can I do? I must work; I must provide for my family and aid in the defense of our country."

"Ah, yes." She rolled her eyes, a twist of disdain on her lips. "You are to captain a privateer."

Brogan nodded, hoping he had finally caught her ear. "The schooner Black Eagle, with a crew of forty-two and guns of two six-pounders and three twelves, all waiting to sail. One half of the net proceeds from her prizes goes to the vessel's owner. The other half belongs to the crew. Of that, I shall receive twenty-two shares. That's very generous. This venture could prove quite prosperous. For all of us."

Her bitter laugh slashed through his pain with the sting of a whiplash. "Don't be a fool, Brogan. We are 'us' no longer. You shall not see the boy again. And don't mistake me for ignorant, because I assure you—I am not. Your missions grow more dangerous each time you sail. In truth, there is no prosperity in your future. I hold little hope of my husband returning with his life. Besides, money had nothing to do with my decision. I parted with the brat because I couldn't bear the sight of him any longer. The foul stench of his soiled napkins and those infernal cries waking me in the middle of the night. His birth is a mishap I am well rid of."

Brogan advanced on her. Her pupils widened, reflecting her sudden fear and the fire blazing from his own eyes. In one swift movement he reached for the front of her dressing gown and pulled her to her feet. She shrieked while somewhere on the garment a rip sounded.

"You are still my wife and you will do as I say. Give me the name of the man who has Benjamin." He bellowed the demand in her face, then clasped her by the shoulders while from beneath clenched teeth he threatened, "Tell me or I swear I shall—"

"You shall what?" Her eyes challenged him to execute the deed in his thoughts.

Once he had loved this woman for the child she gave him. Now he despised her for taking him away. Still, she was Benjamin's mother.

His hands fell from her body. Abigail smiled in victory. They both knew he would never harm a woman.

"Why are you doing this, Abigail?" She had him between wind and water, a vulnerable position if he ever hoped to see his son again. "Have mercy. Your own flesh and blood. He's an innocent child. How can you speak such evil?" He breathed deeply, ignoring her insults and fighting for control as he prayed against hope he'd find the right words to inspire some compassion. "Justify your actions as you see fit, but I cannot abandon my own son. I will not. He's all I have. If you care nothing for Ben yourself, then why deny him a father who loves him?"

Why indeed?

Today he had come hailing the greatest news of his career, but all his accomplishments and success meant nothing without Benjamin. Twenty-three years of age and he had been advanced to captain . . . captain . . . captain . . .

"Captain. Captain, wake up!"

Brogan's eyes flashed open with a start. He lay frozen and disoriented, while above him a woman's features penetrated his drowsy fog. Abigail?

He bolted upright, heart lurching, his chest heaving. At the foot of his bed a shadowy figure held a lantern aloft, blinding him with its golden glare. "Tell me where he is," Brogan rasped. "Where's Benjamin?"

"I am here," returned a child's sweet voice.

"Ben," he whispered as relief eased his racing heart.

Brogan felt a woman's touch on his arm. "Captain, are you ill? He's warm and his nightshirt is soaked with sweat," she said, brushing the hair from his forehead. "Warrick, fetch him a tumbler of water."

Eyes heavy with sleep, Brogan blinked, fighting off the stupor until he'd oriented himself to his surroundings. He took a deep breath and realized he sat within the large box-framed bed of his cabin. Moonlight shone between the damask curtains like a pearl, spreading the faintest illumination across Lorena's—not Abigail's—features as she stood beside the bed, eyeing him. Slowly he roused to the smells of new wood, clean linens, and tallow from the lantern's candle. A lantern held by his chief mate, Jabez Smith.

The sea rolled in a long, low swell, lifting the *Yankee Heart*, then carefully easing her down again. As his eyes adjusted, Brogan looked with annoyance at the gawking faces about him and suffered no small measure of self-consciousness.

Reaching down, he clutched the sheets snug about his waist.

"Mr. Smith, for what reason are you gathered in my sleeping cabin at such an hour?"

"You were moaning and cried out in your sleep," Lorena was quick to explain. "We all heard you, didn't we, Mr. Smith?"

Brogan's heart thumped wildly as Lorena's gaze found the jagged raised scar on his right shoulder. His nightshirt had twisted around him and slipped off one shoulder, he realized. He quickly covered himself, but not before he caught her pitiful wince.

As her eyes found his, she suffered embarrassment over her scrutiny and promptly retreated to stand alongside Drew, as though suddenly aware of the intimacy. In the lantern's light, her springy ginger-brown curls reflected subtle tints of auburn and gilt. They fell loose about her small face and down across her shoulders as she stared back at him, disarmed.

Brogan quickly diverted his attention to Jabez. "There was no need to come running. I am not a child."

"And yet ye have little trouble screaming like one."

His young steward Warrick let slip a snicker.

Lorena gave him a sharp look. "The water, please, Warrick."

"Yes, miss."

"I don't need water. Nor anyone's concern, thank you. It was an unpleasant dream and that is all," Brogan assured them, catching his son's eye.

Drew, who had been quietly observing by Lorena's side, laid his cloth doll on the edge of the bed. "Captain Briggs helps when I have bad dreams."

Brogan reached for the doll, recalling the day he'd presented it to Ben. Captain Briggs was to be Ben's protector while his father sailed the seas. *Just think of me when you hold Captain Briggs,* he'd told his son as he tucked him into bed, *and remember how much I love you.*

Brogan blinked the moisture from his eyes, thankful that he sat within the shadows of his corner bed. "Thank you, Ben," he said with pride welling in his breast. "I shall keep Captain Briggs with me for the rest of the night."

Ben grinned broadly, responding to the name, and for the first time Brogan sensed the son he thought he'd lost acknowledge his true identity. Not as Drew Huntley, but as Benjamin Talvis.

Lorena twittered disapprovingly and moved to take the boy by the shoulders. She pulled him to her in that mother-hen fashion she was known to employ. "Surely, Captain, you mean *Drew*."

"Aye, pardon . . . Drew. Seems I'm still quite sleepy." And before Lorena could say another word, he quickly added, "Now back to bed, all of you. Mr. Smith, I leave it to you to see them safely to their cabins."

It had been an eventful and emotional day for them all. Everyone was exhausted. And in the dead of night, who could think clearly? Or so Lorena tried to tell herself as she padded back to her cabin with Drew. Before bidding them good-night for the second time, Warrick reminded her that breakfast would be served at half past seven.

Her thoughts continued to whir as she climbed back into bed. No amount of reasoning could explain the exchange she'd witnessed between Brogan and Drew. Lorena could no longer deny there was something to their relationship other than a sea captain's kindness to a small boy. Brogan's longing looks, the interest and concern he showed for Drew seemed to indicate this was more than an unlikely pair of kindred souls brought together by happenstance. Could it be that Brogan concealed a deeper relationship with the boy, a relationship not even Drew was aware of, and yet for some reason he responded to it?

She could not dismiss Drew's remark about the papa he'd lost. He had never complained about his lot in life. He'd resigned himself to the fact that both his parents were gone and had accepted her father as his own. He'd been content, and with the exception of his attachment to Captain Briggs, Lorena never knew he longed for more.

She curled her body protectively around his on the goose feather mattress, staring wide-eyed into the darkness, every faculty alert, unable to sleep for the accelerated beating of her heart.

"Drew?" she whispered from behind. "Tonight the captain called you Ben."

"Oh, he does that sometimes."

"Don't you find that odd?"

The boy grew silent, then admitted drowsily, "I don't know."

"You've told me how much you enjoy Captain Talvis's stories. Did he ever tell you how he got that long raised scar across his shoulder?"

She felt Drew's nod. "He let me touch it."

He rolled over and told her of a battle with cannons fired and the quarterdeck shattering. A wood splinter had speared the captain in the fray. He wouldn't allow the wound to be treated until his privateer's coat had been carefully removed, no matter how much additional pain it caused to his shoulder. The garment was not to be cut off.

Lorena could find no relief from her disturbing thoughts. Why would a coat, an article of clothing, hold such import?

It was almost as though the coat were as precious to Brogan as Captain Briggs was to Drew.

She should confront Brogan for an explanation, but she was frightened of discussing a subject that might lead to the exposure of her own secret.

Lorena didn't sleep well that night. She rose late, and by the time she entered the great cabin, the men were well into their breakfast. Mr. Smith, second mate William Farragut, and Brogan all set down their coffee cups and rose to bid her a good morning.

Drew looked to be working with something on his lap. He glanced up with delight to see her and let out a belch.

Brogan scowled with disapproval. "If Mr. Huntley were here, he'd say you'd left your manners beneath your pillow." He looked embarrassed for the child's sake and offered Lorena an apologetic smile. "We were just about to leave for our duties, but please sit, Lorena, and enjoy breakfast."

His eyes twinkled at her. Lorena found him especially handsome this morning, from the amused quirk of his lips to his strong, sharp nose and longish sandy mane. Over a starched white shirt and cravat he wore a double-breasted jacket of dark olive gray with gold ornamental buttons and tails that fell below the knee. His pale yellow trousers tucked smoothly into his black leather Hessians.

She blinked, conscious she may have stared overlong and hastened to the dining table.

Brogan led her to a seat as the men resumed theirs. "Yesterday was quite an eventful day for you. You rested well, I trust?"

She'd hardly slept a wink. "My turn of fate has worked wonders for my well-being. And you, sir? How fared the remainder of your night?"

"Captain Briggs and I shared a fitful sleep."

Lorena noted the strain in his smile and wondered again what darkness haunted Brogan that would cause him to cry out in his dreams.

"Drew accompanies me each morning as I take first observation of the decks," he said. "With your permission I'd like for him to continue at my side."

From across the table, Drew's eyes shone enthusiastic and bright. "Sometimes I help Warrick fill the ship's lamps and sometimes I fetch coal for Mr. Mott. And I have been learning to tie knots." He slapped a length of halyard down on the table. "See?"

"A fair rolling hitch," Mr. Smith observed.

Warrick, to the contrary, did not look amused. "This morning I woke to find my feet bound with a reef knot."

"Oh, Drew, I hope you haven't been misbehaving this whole journey." Lorena bore her correction sternly at the boy.

"The lad is in high spirits to be back with ye, miss, and it seems the wee rascal inside that has lain quiet for missing ye is returned." Mr. Smith wiped his mouth on his napkin and, excusing himself, scrambled to his feet. "Lively now, Mr. Farragut. We've decks to wash down and ready for inspection. I'll meet ye above, Cap'n. Enjoy yer breakfast, Miss Huntley," he bid.

As the mates took their leave, Lorena helped herself to what remained of the oatmeal. "I find it remarkable the responsibility you've all shown where Drew is concerned," she told Brogan. "At first I wondered how my father could have sent him on this journey, being as young as he is, but you show the child no less care than a father would his own son. Though, after last night's exchange, I'm not entirely certain who is taking care of whom."

He seemed to grow uncomfortable under her thoughtful gaze. He pushed his plate away, making ready to depart. "Warrick will see to anything you need. At your leisure he'll escort you to the main deck. Perhaps you'd care to work on your needlework or read under the shade of the sails. Later, Drew and I shall fetch you for a proper tour of the *Yankee Heart*. I know you've seen her as she was being rigged, but she is quite another thing to behold, a living creature in her own right, fully manned and on the sea."

"If you don't mind, I think I'll visit the galley instead. I'd like to thank Mr. Mott for last night's supper and give him my compliments. And then I must seek out Edward Hicks. Edward was a friend of George's and is as saddened and disappointed as I by his actions. I promised to explain the events that befell me."

"When I see Mr. Hicks, I shall send him to you." Brogan rose. "Enjoy your morning, Lorena."

"And you also, Brogan."

Lorena followed man and boy to the door with her gaze, marveling at the pair they made. A stranger could recognize their bond. She felt pride at Drew's interest in the ship and the sacrifice he'd made last night in parting with his beloved Captain Briggs. He had accompanied Brogan on this rescue mission, a larger-than-life adventure for an imaginative child, especially one with a fondness for sea captains. Brogan had become a hero in Drew's eyes. Not a cloth doll, but a flesh-and-blood captain on whom to bestow his admiration and awe.

And yet Lorena sensed there might be more to it than that.

"Can I bring you anything, miss?" Warrick asked, interrupting her thoughts. "Hot water for your tea?"

"You can have a seat and tell me something about your captain, Warrick. What sort of man would you say he is?"

The boy looked stricken. He seemed to consider whether it was his place to answer such a personal question, but at length he lifted his chin with confidence. "Captain Talvis gave us a chance, William and I. Employment, food, and shelter when we'd nowhere to turn. My parents sent us off on our own, we being the eldest except for my brother James, who is quite sickly. We were too many at home, miss. Eleven of us and our parents were too poor to care for us all. Men were needed to sign on with the privateers, but no captain would have us because we'd no experience on the sea. None until Captain Talvis. He's a fair and generous captain. He made certain we were treated fairly." Warrick squared his thin shoulders. "It has been an honor to serve him."

Lorena felt humbled by his confession. "Thank you for sharing your story with me, Warrick. I believe I would like that hot cup of tea."

As he left to fetch the water, she pulled her silver thimble from the pocket of her gown. Lorena did believe she was falling in love with Brogan Talvis. *Love*, yes. For how else to explain this intensity of feeling that overtook her whenever she stepped into his presence?

Other than his exploits as a privateer, she knew little of his life before he'd arrived in Duxboro. And yet the more she learned, the more it confirmed the good treasure of his heart.

Unfortunately, more than treasure was buried in that heart.

Something painful and dark. And she knew, with secrets, there could be no chance for their love.

15

The *Yankee Heart* bowled along on a smart breeze under a heavy press of sail. Lorena stood at her bow, bracing the rails as she leaned into the sea. From several paces behind, Brogan watched as, unawares, she raised her face to the spray like some life-sized figurehead.

The wind blew fresh, snapping at the slightly raised hemline of her narrow, gauzy gown. Her flat sandals tied with leather straps, and the skirt's edging of white embroidered lace flirted in the breeze with her trim, delicately boned ankles. The sight entranced him, and it was here his gaze lingered.

The ocean rolled with a sound that echoed strong in his ears like the flap of the sails high above. Crew members moved busily about, and he knew Lorena had not heard his approach. As Brogan stepped up behind her, he placed his hands gently on her shoulders and cautioned in her ear, "Don't be startled."

She swallowed a sharp intake of breath and turned, only to smile when she saw it was him.

Brogan dropped his hands as she whirled about to face

him, swatting back the ginger-brown tendrils that blew across her eyes.

"I've been searching for you," he explained.

With a knowing smile she shouted above the noise and commotion. "I've been in the galley, visiting with Mr. Mott. Together we baked a lovely shortcake to be served with dinner. I could not pass up the opportunity," she tittered. "I do enjoy baking, as you well know. There's peace in the distraction of my busy hands, and I find the task silences my mind. I've muddled through many a dilemma in the kitchen. I assumed you wouldn't mind, since Drew was with you. . . ." She glanced behind him, her eyes narrowing with concern. "Where is Drew?"

He wondered why any dilemma should trouble her now when she'd been taken off the *Lady Julia* and saved from George Louder. Had she discovered something about his past? Did she suspect his relationship to Drew?

He cast the thought aside to ease her mind about the boy. "Drew is with Warrick below. If you'd like, I'll have the pair of them take you on that ship's tour I promised earlier. But first, I'm glad we have a moment, Lorena, because I have something to ask of you, and Drew might be disappointed if he knew I had plans for us tonight that do not include him."

"Oh. Plans? For us, you say. You mean for you and me?"

"Exactly."

She grinned like a child ready to receive a surprise, intrigued yet not entirely convinced it was going to be something she'd enjoy. Then, as she peered more deeply into his eyes, Brogan decided, nay. Not a child, but a woman.

"What sort of plans?" she asked.

His heart rate quickened, and he clasped his hands behind

his back to better brace himself. "Will you walk with me after supper, Lorena, once you've put Drew to bed, so that we might spend some time alone together?"

He seemed to have stunned her silent. Smiling, Brogan reached up to tame the loose spirals of hair whipping about her face. He'd removed his jacket earlier, and now the full sleeves of white shirt billowed in the wind.

"The skies predict a fine starry night," he coaxed, drawing a breath. "Are you game for standing a trick at the wheel?"

"I beg your pardon?"

Brogan explained, more softly, "Would you enjoy a lesson on manning the *Yankee Heart*'s helm this evening?"

"Oh! Why, yes. I think I should enjoy that very much," she answered within seconds, much to the delight of his impatient heart and with a radiant smile that had the blood pumping a little more freely through his veins.

He led her to where he had left Drew with Warrick and returned to the business of captaining his ship. He thought of her all day, envisioning the moment he would have Lorena's attentions all to himself.

Fortunately, this cruise was not a demanding one requiring his constant focus, for Brogan found he spent many a moment that day staring out to sea.

By nightfall, however, he'd managed to harness his energies and employ them in entertaining Drew. After their Bible reading, they took turns at a game of draughts. Drew giggled himself silly when the pieces slid off the board with a heavy roll of the ship, and on that occasion it was the lad's assignment to locate and collect them. Later, they played hide the thimble. Lorena covered Drew's eyes with her hands while Brogan hid the thimble somewhere within the great cabin.

Drew searched, aided by hints of "you are hot" or "you are freezing."

They played until Drew collapsed from exhaustion, and then Brogan carried him to bed. He was asleep before Lorena had finished tucking him in.

That done, Brogan smiled down on her, anticipating the night ahead and offered his hand to escort her on deck.

They sailed under a clear dark sky. Brogan found the wind stronger and the air crisper since he'd last stepped outside. It whistled through the rigging. Yards creaked. A slatting sail blew against the mizzenmast, where sailor John Bowne stood watch.

Brogan invited Lorena to ascend the companionway ladder to the quarterdeck before him. There stood a man at the wheel wearing a checkered shirt with a blue bandanna tied around his head. Brogan called out to him as they approached.

"Good evening, Mr. Fletcher. How is she headed?"

"Evening, Captain. She's headed right on her course, sir. West, southwest by west."

Lorena was introduced to the broad, rugged quartermaster.

"Avast your stand here," Brogan commanded. "I have a desire to take the wheel myself tonight. Break for an hour and then you may return and resume the rest of your watch."

"An hour, sir?"

"Aye." Brogan took one spoke into the clutches of his strong hand. "Have you supped yet, Mr. Fletcher? Go forward and sample Mr. Mott's fine fare for this evening. Do as you please. Mr. Smith will give you no complaint for your idleness. He knows I have taken command of the wheel and have granted you leave. Though you may remind him I do not wish to be disturbed."

"Aye, Captain. Thank you. I'll tell him, sir."

Lorena watched with rising anticipation as Brogan took full possession of the wheel, honored by his invitation to stand at the helm of his ship. He trained his eyes across the *Yankee Heart*'s vast length, where Lorena followed his gaze to the black sea. Even beneath the moon's reflection, she could detect movement only when a whitecap broke the surface.

"Be sure to take firm grasp of the spokes, for there's a good breeze and quite a sea running." He made way for her to stand before him at the wheel.

At her hesitation he urged, "Where's my willing helmsman, eh? Come, Lorena, take the wheel."

"Are you quite serious? Do you intend I should turn it by myself?" Chin held high, she shored up the corners of her mouth in a pretty, though incredulous, grin.

"You doubt your abilities?" He gave her a knowing wink. "'Behold also the ships, which though they be so great, and are driven of fierce winds, yet are they turned about with a very small helm, whithersoever the governor listeth.' Come, be my small helm. I find the wheel easily steered. And I shall man it with you, my hands alongside yours, standing behind you the whole while."

Lorena cast a discerning eye over him. "You know your verses better than you let on, sir. That was the book of James."

"Well, you've no argument with James, have you? It's possible for the mightiest to be moved by even the most humble. If Drew were awake, he'd remind you of the story of David and Goliath."

The night wind blew brisk, yet Lorena felt no chill, only a sense of refuge and peace with Brogan at her back, an acute awareness of his arms surrounding her, legs braced solidly on deck. She brought her hands to the spokes beside his and held on, waiting for direction.

A great swell raised the stern under their feet. It sent the bow plunging into a towering crest, and as the huge wave continued to roll beneath the *Yankee Heart*, it sent the ship listing to larboard. Brogan pulled upward on a spoke as they held it together, then guided her right hand to an upper spoke and, closing his fingers over hers, instructed, "Now we heave right."

Lorena put her weight into turning the wheel with him, and the stern settled with a roaring splash, plunging the *Yankee Heart* into a blanket of spray as she raced ahead into the night.

Lorena was taken with a tremendous surge of daring and excitement. She laughed, exhilarated. It was as if the stars twinkled just for her. She tilted her face up to the misty salt air and inhaled.

"It is my desire that you enjoy this journey as much as your homecoming," Brogan said at her ear.

Lorena radiated delight at the sentiment, her spirits soaring. "Then you have your desire already. For since I boarded your ship less than two days ago, my destiny, as well as my course, has been altered completely. The voyage I anticipated to endure with sadness has now become a holiday cruise."

She'd expected her words would please him, but Brogan grew silent and pensive behind her. She felt him balance with the roll of the deck. One leg braced, the other knee bent, he leaned into the ship's heel, then straightened, keeping himself steady in order that she might lean against him.

"And now our lesson," he said, speaking at her ear again. "Glance aloft, Lorena, at the sails and the stars in the sky."

Three masts towered above, the tallest reaching a height of

ninety feet. Their square sails billowed on a steady breeze, the white of the canvas in sharp contrast to the deep midnight of the sky, where stars twinkled in a scattering of white-gold light.

Lorena admired the view. "It is a lovely night, isn't it?"

"Indeed, but I have another purpose in directing your attention aloft. Tell me, which is the topgallant of the mainmast?" Brogan's breath was at her cheek, and Lorena felt her heartbeat quicken because of it.

"It is there, third sail from the top, beneath the skysail and the main royal."

His laughter rumbled in her ear. "As a shipbuilder's daughter I should hardly be surprised you're no saltwater sailor. All right, Lorena, let your gaze drift past the luff of the topgallant. Its forward edge, rather, and there I want you to focus on a single star in the sky."

Lorena obeyed, though she failed to see what this had to do with steering the ship. "Very well. I have a star in sight."

"Set your eye on that star, and as long as it remains in the same position in relation to the topgallant, the *Yankee Heart* keeps straight on her course."

"Ah, clever," she said, understanding.

"Keep her as close to the wind as possible without her sails flapping. Full and by. And if she swings too far from that star, turn the wheel a spoke or two. I'm going to keep my hands alongside yours, but I'll leave it up to you, Lorena, to decide when she needs a turn."

An excited, frightening rush of exhilaration surged through her. She had been around ships her whole life, but this was entirely different, a challenge to her mind and body, requiring the use of all her faculties. She held the wheel with fingers clenched, toes curled inside her sandals and fighting for purchase on the deck, all the while maintaining concentration on that star.

At the same time she couldn't resist wondering about the sea captain who stood behind her. Curiosity for him burned inside her.

He shared old sailing stories, several of which made her giggle. He told of his escapades during the war.

"The British had our American harbors heavily blockaded, so we adopted the practice of sailing out stern-first. That is, sailing backward so they'd think we were traveling in the other direction." He chuckled at the memory. "On one occasion, Mr. Smith and I ran the blockade in an old sloop with a load of gunpowder, hoping to make delivery to Newport. We buried it in manure, and the stench was so great the British boarding officer gave it only a cursory inspection. We managed to slip past, undetected."

The time flew by unheeded, and with it the wheel grew more difficult to control. Lorena begged relief and transferred full command of the helm to Brogan.

"You tell many fascinating and amusing tales," she said, "but I sense in you a story you have yet to share. A story you keep to yourself. One more personal and far more interesting. Quite likely painful. You jest, and yet there are times your smile does not reach your eyes."

The sea churned, running higher than it had when they'd first gained the quarterdeck less than an hour ago. His sights remained trained ahead, the corners of his eyes creasing in concentration. Lorena suspected not so much concentrating on the ship's course as on her words.

She pressed further. "I am convinced there is something

troubling your spirit. I know the look—that melancholy in your eyes, the tightening of your jaw. I've been there, Brogan. I understand what it is to be burdened by secrets. And your burden has increased since I've come aboard the *Yankee Heart*, hasn't it? Has it something to do with me? With Drew? Won't you talk to me, Brogan? What troubles you?"

"The wind shall soon be blowing a gale," he said. "I can feel its breath." He alerted her to the ship's increase in motion, the shift in pressure on the soles of their feet as the *Yankee Heart* began to rise and plunge with greater force over the waves.

With a jerk of his chin he directed her attention to the skies. "Notice that vaporish halo surrounding the moon? Foul weather is ahead. Already I can see the *Yankee Heart* beginning to labor under her heavy press of sail. I'll have to escort you below, Lorena. I need to alert Mr. Smith."

But Mr. Smith was already aware of the increase in weather. He called in the next watch to stand at the helm and met them as they descended the companionway ladder to the main deck, awaiting orders.

"Have her topgallants and courses sheeted down," Brogan commanded.

Mr. Smith removed himself to relay the order. His booming voice projected over the creaks and groans of the ship's timber and the wind as it whistled through the shrouds. Sailors leapt to their tasks, some working the ropes, others beginning the lofty climb up the ratlines.

Taking firm grasp of her hand, Brogan pulled her toward the cabins while Lorena padded behind as quickly as her feet could find purchase on the slick deck. The gauzy cotton of her gown had grown damp from the spray, and she shuddered as they entered the quiet emptiness of the great cabin.

Brogan was not going to respond to her plea. Or maybe he could not.

He rubbed his palms up and down her bare arms, trying to warm her. "You'll be all right," he assured. "It's just a chill."

She raised her face to his and trembled for another reason altogether. Candlelight flickered over the rugged planes of his handsome face. The air stirred with more than just the odor of whale oil from the lamps outside the door.

From without, chains rattled ever so faintly. Yards creaked. The *Yankee Heart* rocked slowly, port to lee, the sea lapping at her sides. Brogan took her chin in hand to tilt her face and gaze more deeply into her eyes.

Lorena's lashes fluttered closed like butterfly wings as he angled his face down over hers. At that first exquisite press of his mouth, she quivered. His lips skimmed hers with a feathery lightness, and she felt herself drawn with an ebb and flow as timeless as the tide, swept away as easily as if she were a grain of sand.

He released her. His eyes opened slowly, a deep blue.

Lorena reached up and pressed her palms to his lean cheeks, silently thanking Providence for bringing him to her so that she could experience this fullness of heart.

Brogan's stare deepened, then he turned, and with eyes closed pressed a kiss into her palm.

When he looked again, Brogan found Lorena's velvety brown eyes had taken on a vulnerable roundness. They reflected something he'd never before seen in a woman's eyes.

Never in Abigail's eyes, though he'd often searched for it. Here it was, at last. *Love*.

Brogan's chest constricted with panic. This graceful young dove terrified him. What if he were unworthy of her?

He must tell her the truth. He hated to keep putting it off, but then neither was he prepared to face the consequences of what his news might bring. Naturally a woman in Lorena's position would feel threatened by the discovery of his blood relationship to Drew. She might withdraw her affection if she thought he intended to take the boy from her. But Brogan no longer had any desire for that. He wanted only his rights as a father. He wanted to be able to watch his son grow, to offer the lad his support and guidance and participate in his upbringing.

He wanted to pursue Lorena without a child's future weighing in the balance. His feelings for her stirred a thousand doubts and fears within him, yet they grew more affectionate with each passing day. He hardly cared to jeopardize those fragile emotions before his heart had had a chance to come to terms with them.

He pulled away with a hollow laugh. "Don't look at me so, Lorena. What is there to trouble me? Look around you. I have everything a man could ask."

"Everything?" she asked. "Mr. Smith says you have not the thing you desire most. Tell me what it is you desire most, Brogan."

His gut reaction was to kiss her again. The scent of her, soft and ethereal, surrounded him like a cloud. He pressed his mouth to her petal-soft lips, more firmly this time, and as he tasted the promise of her sweetness, he felt something click into place deep within his soul.

When his lips parted from hers, it was with regret. Straightening, Brogan gazed down at her in complete surrender. "Very well. You've made your case," he said. "It is true. There is something I have not revealed to you, but until I can find the words, will you be patient with me, Lorena? We cannot speak tonight. This gale increases, and I must attend to the safety of the ship."

16

_L_orena woke to a clamor of activity on deck.

She flashed open her eyes as her body responded with alertness to the sounds overhead. Yards creaked and groaned. The wind fairly shrieked through the rigging. The *Yankee Heart* had sprung to life, and she heard urgency in the movements of her crew and their shouts.

Waves thrashed the ship's side, rocking her bed. Lorena rose onto her elbows for a deep breath, grateful for her empty stomach, which between the motion and the clamor had begun to recall its queasy upset of not so long ago from the vomit powder.

A searing flash of light shone behind the silk brocade drapery, illuminating the cabin with an ominous brightness to reveal Drew's slumbering form beside her.

A peal of thunder cracked through the cabin and they plunged back into darkness. Drew woke with a cry. The ship rose on a heavy swell, lunging leeward, tilting their bed to such an angle they were pitched, bodies and bed linens, onto the deck.

Suddenly, Lorena feared for their safety.

Her backside crashed down on the hard wooden deck. Drew landed on top of her, swooshing the air from her lungs and leaving her dazed as they slid downhill before the floor leveled back. It took a few moments for the shock to subside enough for Lorena to lift her head and check on the child.

"Drew! Sweetheart, are you all right?"

She breathed with relief at his round, sleepy face and thought he gave a bewildered nod. The cabin was murky, full of shadow. With the porthole draperies closed, only a very dull light shone beneath. "It seems we're having some weather."

Gently she rolled him off her, then climbed to hands and knees. She grasped the edge of the bed for support and then helped Drew gain his feet.

Searching about, he rose on plump bare toes and danced anxiously while Lorena dragged herself up off the floor.

"What's happened to Captain Briggs?" he whined.

"There! See, Drew. Over by the door. Hurry now and collect him. We must be busy about getting dressed. I'd like a word with the captain before he grows too busy with his duties. Where are your socks?"

She found them hidden within the lump of bed linens, a tiny pair of striped knit socks. As she rolled them in her fingers, she could not help but incline an ear outward with increasing alarm. A howling wind rattled the running rigging, and the sails could be heard slatting against the masts.

Hurriedly she donned a checked gingham work dress and emerged from the cabin with Drew to find the great parlor in sorry disarray. Dining chairs had been knocked onto their sides. Books, charts, and navigational instruments from

Brogan's desk lay scattered across the carpet. Her needlework basket was overturned. As a way of showing her gratitude, she'd taken to sewing for the crew, mending tears, replacing missing buttons, darning socks. Now their clothing lay strewn, along with her crewel embroidery and sewing notions. Her thimble, however, remained with her always, tucked deep inside a pocket.

She didn't know whether to start tidying or immediately go out in search of Brogan. The angry tempest heard raging behind the stern window's curtains left her flummoxed, and it was Drew who jumped into action by racing across the cabin to the window seats. He pushed aside the draperies to a threateningly somber sky and roiling, churning seas. Only the bleakest of light trickled in.

Behind them, the door to the outer corridor burst open, and Warrick stumbled in, breathless and drenched from head to toe, escorted by his brother William.

Warrick looked at her forlornly, his brown hair sopping wet and lying flat to his head. "I am truly sorry, Miss Huntley."

Lorena worried after his appearance. "Whatever for, Warrick?" She looked uncertainly from one to the other of them, the elder William, by all appearances, only slightly older in years. "This storm . . . did something happen?" she asked.

"Warrick's fine, miss." William removed his round top hat, and seawater dripped from its rim as he greeted her with a nod. "Not injured, except for his pride. A comber crashed over the bulwarks and swept him off his feet and into the lee scuppers. Sorry to say, it also took your breakfast tray and washed it into the sea."

"Oh, I hardly give a care about that. What's important is that Warrick was not injured."

Warrick bowed his head. "Thank you, miss."

Lorena felt for him in his embarrassment, for she was certain the loss of the breakfast tray pained him more than his fall. "You had better go quickly now and change your clothes."

"He'll have time for that later," William announced sternly, hastening toward the stern windows. "A seaman gets used to working in wet clothing, miss. Warrick, step lively and come help me close these deadlights."

Lorena's concern multiplied. "Pray, tell me of this weather we're having, Mr. Farragut."

William and his brother drew the damask curtains out of their way, allowing her a clear view of the storm for herself. Below, the ocean rolled white with foam. A greenish-gray sea lashed violently—rising, rising, then curling into a foaming, towering crest that crashed down in an explosion of spray.

Drew gasped in awe. Lorena lifted him off the seat and away from the windows.

"A mighty gale has come upon us, Miss Huntley," William explained, working quickly with Warrick to close the heavy wooden shutters. "The *Yankee Heart* rides under close-reefed sails, and the great height of her quarterdeck has been a blessing in breaking the force of the sea. Captain Talvis and Mr. Smith are presently completing a tour of inspection. The captain has asked me to inform you that he has ordered Warrick to remain inside with you and Drew. None of you are to leave the cabins until further notice."

Off in the starboard horizon a flash of white-hot light appeared just before William secured the last deadlight into place. The shutters were fitted to keep out water and the threat of broken glass, but they also blocked what little daylight shone into the cabin.

Drew shook off Lorena's embrace to approach the second mate. "But, Mr. Farragut, I must come with you. The captain needs me to help shorten sail—"

The cabin rattled with a deafening boom, cutting him off and startling Lorena, regardless that she'd known thunder was coming.

Lorena felt hard pressed to contain her smile, as it seemed did William. "You heard Mr. Farragut. You'll not be going anywhere," she told the boy. "Off to your cabin, Warrick. Quickly now, and change into something dry. Here, Mr. Farragut, allow me to help you close the draperies over these deadlights. Do you think there's any chance I might be able to speak with Captain Talvis?"

As young Warrick excused himself and made for his cabin, his brother turned to her in earnest. "I cannot go against the captain's orders and allow you on deck, but I will let him know you have asked for him. Please understand he is quite busy battling this gale and keeping a wary eye out for any shift in weather. And if I may ask, Miss Huntley, please help keep my brother safe indoors. He wants to do his share with the rest of us, but I expect Warrick to follow your direction. He does not look the part, but he has a much determined will."

Lorena swallowed her disappointment that she'd not be able to see Brogan. "Of course I shall look out for your brother, Mr. Farragut. Is there anything more I can do?"

He scanned the disorder of the great cabin with a thoughtful expression. "Yes, miss. For your safety, extinguish the lanterns. Have Warrick secure all moveable objects by storing them in the lockers under the cushions of the stern window seats. Then wedge yourselves into a place where you shall be less likely to be tossed about. Other than that, there's nothing more to be done but watch and ride out this gale. Warrick knows where to find a store of ship's biscuits until the galley fires can be restarted and we're able to bring you something more to eat."

William returned to his duties, and Lorena sought out her small companion, who had begun to snoop through the charts and instruments scattered on the carpet. "You heard Mr. Farragut, Drew. Help me get the captain's things into the storage lockers."

"Are you scared?" he asked.

It was impossible to ignore the roll and pitch of the ship or dismiss its groans, its strain and labor. "No. Are you?"

Drew shook his head. He'd never admit to feeling frightened if she were not.

His brave front bolstered her confidence. "All shall be well."

"But when will the captain come?"

"As soon as he can. Once he's navigated the ship safely through this storm, he'll come. He's brought ships through much worse, I'm certain. Now let's get busy putting the cabin in safe order."

Warrick appeared in a fresh pair of high-waisted white trousers, an oversized red waistcoat, faded and frayed and quite likely handed down, and a dark navy neckerchief, which Lorena suspected of being the finest article he owned. His brown hair was damp and mussed, she assumed from a hasty towel drying.

He joined them in dousing the lantern flames and securing all loose items. At his suggestion they huddled on the settee together in the dark and gloomy cabin.

Warrick and Drew shared the tin of ship's biscuit and the last of the maple sugar fudge. Lorena had no appetite for either. Her thoughts were with Brogan out in the gale. She'd seen the look of concern on William Farragut's face when he'd asked her to look out for his brother. She understood the grave danger of working a ship in heavy weather. Even the heartiest and most seasoned sailors were not invulnerable to the mountainous swells that could snatch a man from the safety of the deck and drag him into the sea.

Life was precious. It could be altered in an instant or someone dear lost in one stroke of fate. Having survived her mother's passing, and more recently the events of these past weeks, Lorena had never believed this to be more true. Whatever Brogan had to tell her, whatever secret he revealed, it wouldn't change the way she felt about him. *Just, please, let him return safely.*

She listened to the commotion from without and realized it had begun to rain.

The *Yankee Heart* gave a pitch, nearly tossing them off the settee. The tin flew from Drew's fingers, crashing to the Brussels carpet, where it rolled among a shower of dry biscuit crumbs. Upended dining chairs shifted to leeward. They'd been diligent in tucking away even the smallest of articles, but one overlooked item glided toward them, delivered as if by Providence.

A cracked and worn brown leather volume, tied closed by a thin leather strap.

Dark clouds descended over the *Yankee Heart* in an unearthly haze of deep violet stirring into black. Lightning played back and forth in the distance, and thunder rent the air with the report of a cannon shot, echoing until Brogan felt its vibration in the quarterdeck beneath his Hessians.

A hard rain pounded the decks and lashed in windswept fury against his face and chest. "Hard-a-lee," he shouted to Josiah Carter, manning the wheel.

Quartermaster Cyrus Fletcher had been sent below for some much needed rest. Brogan had relieved Jabez as well, the mate having worked tirelessly through the night, and asked that he check on Lorena and Drew before grabbing some winks.

Mr. Carter put down the wheel and turned the ship's head. Brogan followed the circuit of the *Yankee Heart*'s bowsprit as she came round, then snapped his gaze to the sails as she picked up the wind from her other quarter. Gusts wailed through the rigging with a shrill loud enough to curl an old salt's toes.

As the ship swung past the eye of the wind, his trained and discerning eye took measure. She still carried too much sail.

"Reef the main upper topsail, Mr. Farragut," Brogan ordered into the squall, where his second mate manned the waist with several of the crew.

The wind carried back the faint echo of William's "Aye, sir!"

The agile youth took two seamen with him into the rigging. The wind whipped around them with evil ferocity as they made the slick, dangerous ascent. It filled the sails, turning them into snapping sheets of unforgiving canvas, heavy and wet with spray. Twenty . . . forty . . . sixty feet and upward they continued to scale the mainmast. Reducing sail was tricky business in fair weather. In a gale like this, such a feat could seem near impossible. It was a precarious hold on those lofty, wet footropes, balancing against the roll and pitch of the sea, but Brogan had complete faith in the skill of his men.

And yet something disquieted him. Uneasiness churned in his gut. Something was amiss. A sense of danger surrounded him like a shark circling its prey, and Brogan searched frantically for the reason.

A broken spar hurtled up through the air on a violent gust. He yelled out a warning that was quickly lost in the deafening report of the snapping mainsail. The projectile struck Gideon Hale on the thigh and knocked him off the ratlines.

Brogan could do nothing but watch his man helplessly drop over eighty feet to the deck.

His heart plunged along with Gideon, and he felt the impact as though it were he who'd fallen. He recognized the stillness of death in Gideon's prone form. Anguished, he dashed down the companion ladder and, upon reaching the main deck, hailed assistance from the starboard watch. It required a good bit of strength and time to walk aft against the screaming winds, and even with his own height and weight it was difficult for Brogan to stand erect.

He was first to reach the mainmast and Gideon's body. The loss of his crewman engulfed him as the *Yankee Heart*'s bow rose on a swell. She rode the wave, then went down by the head. A wind blew across her beam, and as the vessel pitched to starboard, a pillar of frothing green seawater burst over the lee rail.

Brogan braced himself, but the turbulent stream struck with force. It knocked him flat, propelling both his and Gideon's bodies across the deck. They scudded along and crashed into the bulwarks, where Gideon's body washed over the rails. In the blink of an eye, a man was lost. The sea had buried a friend and shipmate.

Grabbing on to the first rope he could find, Brogan prayed it was secure and held fast as the surge flowed over him.

The rush of sea crushed his chest, so dense it immersed him in its watery depths. Like a drowning man his lungs burned, and as he felt himself grow faint, he thought of Drew and Lorena. *You may have taken my man, but you won't have me! I won't let you have me! Not until I've secured their safety and the lives of every other man on this ship. Not until my son knows his father!*

Brogan tightened his grip, but the hemp inched through his fingers, taking with it little bits of flesh. His hands burned as though on fire, yet he continued to bear down on the slimy, wet halyard. He felt his blood on its roughened fibers.

As the last of the deluge flushed away and the ship righted, the *Yankee Heart* shook herself free. Brogan hoisted himself to his feet and took a deep, fortifying breath, no sooner releasing it when a cry of "Man overboard!" sounded.

The two hands from the watch rushed to the weather side and leaned over the rail, where another of their fellows had fallen. Shock hit Brogan like a physical blow to his body. His heart crushed under a heavy weight of grief. *Who? Who's fallen?* And who now remained alone in the rigging? He bounded to the mainmast, searching aloft through the blur of driving rain, but the mainsail thrashed over the yard, obscuring his view.

He searched helplessly up into the swirling blue-black heavens. A rescue launch would be overturned within moments in this running sea, if not dashed to splinters. Yet Brogan would row out himself before surrendering another of his men to the deep.

He was fighting his best to save the ship, his men, and the loved ones below, but now it felt as though control was slipping away from him.

In desperation he realized he couldn't do this all on his own and cried out to the Almighty.

"Their soul is melted because of trouble. They reel to and fro, and stagger like a drunken man, and are at their wit's end.

"Then they cry unto the Lord in their trouble, and he bringeth them out of their distresses."

The psalm he had read to Drew on Lorena's first night aboard echoed through his consciousness, and Brogan turned with renewed hope to the sailors at the rail.

They sadly shook their heads.

Gone.

Injustice and disappointment festered inside him, a tempest as angry as the one that raged against the *Yankee Heart*. Brogan yanked off his Hessians and leapt into the rigging, climbing up the ratlines to reduce sail before any more lives were lost.

Against howling winds, flapping sails, and sharp rain, he scaled the heights of the mainmast and spotted John Bowne further aloft, balancing on the yardarm of the lower main topsail.

William, then. Willie Farragut . . . *dead*! Brogan plummeted into a dark abyss of despair. Willie, who from that first day that he'd come under Brogan's command never failed to give the vessel his best efforts. Who at the age of sixteen, being a bright lad, however green, had petitioned Brogan to sign articles with the privateer *Black Eagle*. Brogan promised himself he'd look out for the Farragut lads, and he thought he'd succeeded.

Until today.

How was he going to tell Warrick his brother was dead?

Before he could conceive of an answer, he climbed past

the main yard and scaled the maintop, where to his great amazement he found something stretched across the platform.

Someone, rather.

It was the prone figure of William.

Brogan blinked, astonished. His prayer had been answered, and suddenly he understood. The Lord had shown him who was in control. Not Brogan, but *Him*.

He was humbled as he gave the second mate's shoulder a good shake. "Mr. Farragut! Are you well? Wake up, man, and explain. We thought you gone."

William shrugged off his stupor and climbed to all fours. "I was knocked from the yard and thought for certain I was done, but the next I knew, I landed here."

"Nothing broken?"

"No, sir."

"Well, on deck with you. Lively now, and send up Mr. Partridge and Mr. Beckett to haul in this mainsail. Mr. Bowne and I will reef the topsails." Brogan was not about to risk another fright from William before delivering him safely to his brother.

William jumped to the order, the horror and embarrassment on his face clear indication he believed his captain was displeased with him, when in reality Brogan felt such joy he wanted to shout praises to the Almighty from the crosstrees.

He'd been certain he had lost another of his valued crew, but God had been merciful. The realization sobered him, and right there, balancing on the main yard, eighty feet above a violently swaying deck, Brogan counted his blessings.

The squall quieted to a calm wind and showers by late afternoon, when Brogan stepped out of the weather for the first time since he'd escorted Lorena to her cabin the previous evening. Exhaustion weighed on every muscle as he trekked the dark corridor to the great cabin.

He opened the door and entered the parlor, leaving concern for crew and ship out in the rain.

One glance at the precious child seated between Lorena and Warrick on the settee and everything else ceased to exist. He stood on the Brussels carpet, dripping wet, while Drew stared back with astute blue eyes, wise beyond their years.

The boy scooted off the settee and rushed forward into his arms.

As he held his son, Brogan thought then that Jabez had been wise in his opinions. Five years old was too young for a life at sea. Drew needed more. Even his father needed more.

He met Lorena's gaze over the boy's pale blond head as she stepped forward in a gingham work dress with Warrick, her jumbled mass of tight ringlets loosed from their pins to overwhelm her slender face.

Brogan stared, entranced by her beauty, yearning to say all the things that remained unspoken between them.

She smiled sweetly, and he realized that with this voyage, his heart had expanded to include someone besides his son. Someone just as precious and just as loved, though in a different way.

He wanted to marry Lorena. He never expected he would feel this way, but Brogan wanted to settle down in quiet little Duxborotown with a wife and his son . . . if Lorena would have him, if she'd forgive him, once she learned the truth of his identity.

With a grin Brogan crooked a finger beneath Drew's chin and gave it a nudge. "Have you missed me?"

The boy's head bobbed in a vigorous nod.

"And I missed you," Brogan said, rising. "Both of you." He turned from Lorena to his steward Warrick and, reaching out, gave the young man's shoulder an affectionate pat. "Go to your brother in the fo'c'sle and be with him. William has an amazing tale to share of God's goodness."

Drew peered up at Brogan, craning his neck. "I want to hear, too."

"And you shall. At dinner. Fred Mott is starting up the galley fires, and soon I promise you something hot to eat. But first there is another story I need to tell." His faith had been stirred with William's sparing, and this time Brogan felt armed with courage for what he knew he must do. "I'm going to change from these wet clothes," he said, lifting his gaze to Lorena, "and then I have a confession to make."

17

Brogan's sentimental mood had Lorena baffled. What happened out in the storm to open his eyes to God's goodness? What amazing tale did William have to share? She felt as anxious as Drew for news, but was she prepared for Brogan's confession? She'd encouraged him to open up, and now that she'd soon have her desire, Lorena fretted his revelation would alter the tender, developing relationship between them.

With the release of a latch, the mahogany door to the sleeping cabin opened and Brogan emerged in a fresh pair of buff trousers and the blue military cutaway coat of his privateer uniform. She found the formality odd until she remembered the coat was part of the puzzle. His damp, longish hair he'd neatly combed, and the stark look accentuated Brogan's rugged features. She noted shadows beneath his eyes, and when he smiled it did little to ease the severity of his expression.

His attention went directly to the boy. "Drew, fetch Captain Briggs for me, would you, and bring him here?"

Drew dashed off as though in anticipation of some sort of game.

Lorena knew this was no game, and her heart raced because of it.

"I'll open wide the draperies and let in some light, shall I?" Suddenly she remembered the deadlights protecting the rain-splattered panes of the stern windows. At her hesitation Brogan stepped up behind her to draw aside the curtains and unlatch the shutters. As he folded them out of the way, soft gray light filtered down from the cloudy skies into the cabin, as solemn as the expression on his face.

Lorena studied him. "I've not seen fear in your eyes before. Yet you wait here for Drew as though he were returning with some powerful adversary and not a cloth doll. Whatever you have to tell us, Brogan, I know it does not come easy for you."

As he took her hands, she felt the ragged sores crossing his palms. "You've been injured." She examined his hands, wincing at the torn, raw flesh. "I should dress those wounds and perhaps apply a salve—"

"Later," he said impatiently, jerking out of her grasp.

He took a breath, then started again, staring her full in the face with a wry grin. "I know you are confused, but in a moment all shall be explained. Forgive me for not speaking up sooner. You have to understand, I have been waiting three years for this moment, hoping the opportunity would arrive, rehearsing what I should say over and over again. And still, I feel . . . unprepared."

The robust, masculine timbre of his voice thickened with each word, and there, in the midst of that dear, beloved face, Lorena saw his intense blue eyes fill from beneath his lashes. She ran her gaze over his crisp lapels with their red facings and the column of shiny brass buttons. Identical to the coat Captain Briggs wore in miniature.

Drew returned, and Brogan bid them sit together on the settee while he stood before them holding Drew's doll.

"Do you remember the tale I told that day of our picnic on Captain's Hill? I told of how Captain Briggs came to be crafted."

"Yes, of course." Lorena remembered the tale well for its curious nature, but it was Drew whom Brogan addressed.

"Sailmaker Thomas Pinney, being crafty with a needle, was asked to sew a doll in the likeness of a privateer captain. This is the doll he made," he explained again. "Captain Briggs. The doll your papa gave you. Do you . . . remember?"

Drew's eyes rounded at the mention of his papa. "When I was still a babe," he said in a soft voice, "I had a papa."

Satisfied, Brogan smiled and included Lorena with his gaze before continuing. "When I learned I was to be promoted to captain, I commissioned Thomas to stitch me a military coat. Thomas's father had been a tailor, you see, and he trained his son well in his profession. But when the old man died, Thomas decided he would rather go to sea and fight for his country than pursue a clothier's trade. So he signed on as a sailmaker for the *Wild Pilgrim*." Brogan opened his arms. "And this is the coat Thomas made."

As he paused, Lorena caught a shimmer in his eyes. She didn't understand. What was he implying?

"When I saw the fine job Thomas had made of my coat," he continued, "I commissioned him to make a doll in my likeness as a gift to my young son, so he'd not forget me while I was away on the *Black Eagle*. I told my son that whenever he felt lonely, he was to hold Captain Briggs and remember how much his papa loved him, and to know that nothing would stop his papa from coming back for him."

Brogan stared intently at Drew, tears in his eyes, while Drew gaped back in fascination.

"My son's name was Benjamin," he said.

Lorena gasped as realization struck.

"My papa died at sea," Drew said.

"Lorena and your papa Huntley surely believed I had died, for I sailed into battle. It was a dangerous war and many men did die. But not I. I've been searching for you these three years we've been apart. The reason I've waited until now to tell you who I am was because I wanted to let you get to know me first."

Lorena didn't know why she didn't say anything, other than the fact she was dumbfounded . . . and as entranced by the story as was Drew. She didn't know what she'd been expecting Brogan to reveal, but never this.

"I love you, Ben," Brogan told the boy. "I made you a promise that no matter how long or whatever it took, I would return. I left you Captain Briggs as a symbol of that promise, and when I saw that you carried him still"—Brogan touched a finger to the child's heart—"I knew some small part of you had to remember. Else why would you still cling to this doll after all these years and after you were told I was gone?"

A grin spread across the boy's face as if suddenly it all made sense. "Papa?"

"Aye, son."

As the child went voluntarily into his arms, Brogan softly cried. Drew clutched the man tightly, afraid to let go.

Lorena slipped into a state of numbed shock. And really, what protest could she voice, watching Drew's joy at being reunited with the papa he'd never forgotten, the man they'd thought long dead?

He had not perished in battle as they'd been led to believe, but had survived the war. Uncle Stephen had lied.

And now to be confronted with her family's secret, to hear Brogan confess to being baby Benjamin's father . . . it weighted her heart with heaviness knowing the circumstances, learning her captain had once been married to that Boston twice-widowed woman . . . no, not a widow for a second time, as Lorena now knew, but Mrs. Abigail Talvis. They'd never learned her married name. Papa had agreed to collect the babe and depart—no questions asked, no names given, no pleasantries exchanged.

Lorena swallowed a lump in her throat. That Brogan loved the child and had pursued the boy despite the great injustice done him was more than her mind could grasp.

For years now, she and her father had been sheltering Drew from his past so that he might have a new future, never suspecting that all along there'd been someone out there working just as diligently to restore Drew to his origins.

Lorena supposed she should feel outrage at Brogan for keeping his identity hidden, but knowing what she did of matters, this revelation shed an even brighter light on the goodness of his heart, and her love for him increased tenfold. His melancholy looks and fatherly concern now made perfect sense.

He was quite the unusual man, this Captain Brogan Talvis. Truly remarkable.

She lifted her gaze to his and saw all he'd suffered in his eyes. He was churning with questions for her, questions that, for the moment, would have to remain unanswered. They could not speak in front of Drew. But what about when Brogan got her alone?

What would she tell him then?

Lorena wondered as much all through dinner and the tale of William's near brush with death. When Drew could no longer keep his eyes open after such an exciting day, Brogan carried him off to bed. She watched from the doorway as he tucked the coverlet around the boy, then Captain Briggs in beside him with a poignancy that made it easy to imagine his doing so countless times before. He brushed the curls off Drew's forehead and kissed him good-night.

Brogan lingered a moment longer. When she saw him straighten, Lorena backed away from the doorway to allow him entrance into the great cabin. He closed Drew's door softly behind him.

Brogan was frank with her. He shared his earliest memories of the orphan asylum and his first days at sea. He told of lean times before the war, when he and Jabez and countless other unemployed sailors crowded the docks of Boston Harbor. The despair, the hunger, the boredom, until one day he caught the eye of a wealthy widow, several years older than himself.

Within weeks they were married in a civil service by a justice of the peace. Brogan found positions for himself and Jabez with the *Wild Pilgrim* and left his bride for a four-month term aboard the privateer. When he returned he learned she was with child.

Good fortune had found him at last, he believed. He was young and naive in that, until then, he'd spent his life at sea far from female society. He fancied himself in love. Or perhaps he only imagined he loved Abigail for the son she gave him.

"Abigail was not the most attentive of mothers, but I was more than willing to make up the difference so that Benjamin never felt unloved or neglected. We were the closest to a family I'd ever known, but two years after his birth, on the eve of my departure to take command of the *Black Eagle*, she informed me she had sent him away. She refused to reveal where."

"She presented herself as a widow," Lorena explained in her own defense.

"And yet my existence does not come as a shock to you. You understand who I am? You believe me?"

Lorena gazed at his proud, earnest expression with eyes of compassion. "I believe you. I'm sorry for all you've suffered, but to our minds you were a nameless casualty of the war."

A worried crease appeared between his brows. "Who told you I was a casualty?"

"My . . . my uncle Stephen."

"Stephen Huntley? The man suspected of fleeing from the fire that took Abigail? Then the rumors were true? Stephen was there the night Abigail died? They were acquainted?" Turning from her, Brogan began to pace anxiously. "More than acquainted, I'm beginning to suspect. It seems while I was at sea, she sought the attentions of a rich companion. A benefactor. Could that be why my promotion meant nothing to her? It does make perfect sense. She hoped to rid herself of her husband, and our son stood in her way. Is this true? Am I correct?"

"Yes, I believe so," Lorena acknowledged, hoping to put an end to his torturous, racing thoughts. "She wanted Ben to disappear. They both did. As far as my father and I understood, Ben had no one. No one who cared for him. We gave him a loving home when we thought he had none."

"And changed his name."

"To shield him from his past. To raise him as one of our own. As a Huntley."

"Your uncle's family refused to see me. Their attorney warned me away with the assurance that none of them had any knowledge of an Abigail Talvis or her child."

"They spoke the truth. They never knew anything of my uncle's association with your wife," she told him.

"In all my inquiries, it was as though Benjamin never existed. Duxboro was my last hope . . . a hope that I might learn something, anything, some small bit of history about Stephen Huntley that could produce a lead. I came for information. Instead, I discovered my son. Not in hiding but living for all the world to see as Drew Huntley."

Lorena swallowed uncomfortably. "You must have suffered quite the shock."

Irony rumbled through Brogan's laugh. "Obviously he'd been well cared for, but all I could think of was getting him back. All the charity in the world cannot replace the bond of blood. One's own family. And so I devised a plan. I commissioned a ship, biding my time until she was complete, when I could sail away in her . . . with my son."

Lorena found herself at a loss while she absorbed this knowledge. Brogan had planned to steal Drew out of Duxboro. In the very ship her father had so painstakingly built him. All this happening while George had been purchasing vomit powder for the purpose of entrapping her. If Brogan had followed through with his scheme, Papa would have lost both his children.

She felt a jumble of turmoil, caught between fear of what might have been and relief it hadn't. "But you didn't leave with Drew," she reminded herself aloud. He had come to her rescue instead.

"The boy loves you like the mother he never truly had. I could no sooner take that from him than I could bear the thought of you in danger."

Lorena breathed slowly, forcing her emotions to calm and her thoughts to clear. "And now?" she asked expectantly. "What now, Brogan?"

He searched her face with china blue eyes full of earnest. "Can you forgive me? I thought I had no alternative but to abduct Ben. Your father never would have given him up. Not to me, a stranger. Nor to anyone. Jabez tried to reason with me, but it was you, Lorena, who opened my eyes. I always had another choice, yet I deliberately ignored the right one. A choice for the good of all concerned, not just for myself. Because no matter where or with whom Ben lives, I shall always be his father. I shall be a part of his life, and he will know a father's love. But what I still don't understand is, why? Why did another man's child matter so much to your father? Why Benjamin?"

When she made no immediate reply—for indeed, Lorena hesitated to make any sudden revelations—he studied her with a hard, contemplative stare.

"It's my belief there was more behind your father's charity than good Christian kindness," he said. "I don't know what, but something else transpired between the Huntley brothers and Abigail. For why else would a man of your father's strong moral character help his brother carry on an affair with a married woman? And while Stephen was married with a family of his own? What influence did Abigail have over them that both brothers should act so extensively on her behalf and in her favor? Your father knows the answer. And perhaps even you, Lorena."

As much as she'd like to unburden the ugly truth, Lorena could not bring herself to utter the words. Brogan was destined to find out eventually, but with his renewed faith she yearned to shield him with the same care she'd been protecting Drew, or Ben, these last three years.

If only she could. She needed Papa's counsel in this. She had to get to him before Brogan did.

Lorena tilted her face to look at him. "That, Brogan, is a question for my father. I can't tell you any more than I already have. Papa's a wise and understanding man who believes in your integrity or he would not have sent you for me. He would not have entrusted Drew to your care or asked you to join in his shipping enterprise. Explain to him what you've just told me. You can trust he'll be honest and forthcoming."

He responded with a reluctant nod. "Fair enough. I will have that conversation with your father. And I will find out the truth. You can depend upon it." Though disappointed, he did not push her further.

His good humor returned in a smile. "And now I have another confession to make," he announced. "I've fallen in love with you, Lorena Huntley. These past months I have never felt more content. Every sense alive, every moment precious, as though for the first time I am experiencing life at its fullest. And I know the reason for this has to do with more than my reunion with my son. It's you, Lorena. I want us to be a family. You already love Ben and he loves you. Do you think you can forgive and love his father, as well?"

Her heart filled with fierce emotion—love, happiness, compassion. Tears in her eyes, a lump in her throat, the best

Lorena could manage was a nod. Forgive Brogan for possessing such faithfulness and devotion he could not let go of a precious loved one? Yes. He was a man not unlike her father, a man with good treasure stored in his heart, a man committed to family. The man she'd been destined to love.

He took hold of her hands. "Will you have me, Lorena? Will you marry me? Don't give me your answer yet. I must first speak to your father and convince him I am worthy of you. For should you give me the honor of agreeing to be my wife, I should want his blessing."

Lorena suspected he knew her answer already, if only because of the tears shining happily in her eyes. Her smile, however, was bittersweet with worry, not so much of her father withholding his blessing as for whether Brogan would feel the same after speaking with Papa.

Brogan's love had brought promise and joy to her life, but was it strong enough to endure once he learned of the secret surrounding Drew?

18

The *Yankee Heart* approached the forest-dense southern shores of Massachusetts ten days later, where it entered the Bluefish River.

A slight delay was owing to the fact there'd been no work for the crew the day following the storm. Jabez conducted a memorial service for Gideon Hale on the main deck. Brogan read Scripture aloud, then gave thanks to the Lord for sparing William and for the safe passage of the ship. He prayed for the protection of those still aboard her. Jabez's music books were pulled off the shelves, Frederick Mott brought out his fiddle, and the crew joined in singing hymns.

Brogan did not push Lorena further for answers about her father's relationship with Abigail, though instinct assured him she knew more than she was willing to let on. He trusted she had good reason for directing him to her father. Actually he preferred news of Abigail come directly from Huntley. Still, it troubled him, this aura of mystery.

Why did Lorena feel she must hold something back from him? Did she not trust him?

He stood on the *Yankee Heart*'s quarterdeck under the shadow of darkening heavens. Humidity wavered in the air, blurring the sighting of land with an ashen haze. Brogan raised his telescope, adjusting the lens and bringing into focus the fitting wharf with its outbuildings and then the stately home beyond.

Somewhere inside that large black-and-white Federal house, Nathaniel Huntley awaited. Brogan waited, too. He waited for his questions to be answered, for three years of agonizing speculation to be over. But what harsh realties lay hidden behind the truth of Abigail's scheme?

Lowering the glass, he snapped it closed. Brogan lifted his hat to swipe his shirtsleeve across his perspiring brow. He could not stave off the apprehension and hardened himself for what lie ahead. He had deceived the shipbuilder and now must confess to him that the man he'd entrusted with the safe return of his daughter had at one time been plotting to abduct another child from his home.

Lorena emerged onto the deck below, catching his eye in a becoming apricot gown. She looked all sweetness and femininity, from her springy head of ginger curls to the toes inside her flat leather sandals.

Glancing upward, she gave him a wave, and Brogan thought never was there a smile more beautiful than that of his beloved.

His heart flooded with love for her; his eyes filled with adoration. She radiated serene elegance, and her goodness cast a glow about her like that of an angel, an angel who had pulled his soul from bitterness.

Mounting the companionway, she joined him on the quarterdeck. Brogan greeted her with a smile and extended his hand. "Come. Stand beside me, where the welcome party ashore can see you."

She slipped her much smaller hand in his, and he drew her to his side before the rails. The *Yankee Heart* was drawing attention, and Huntley yard workers and Duxboro townsfolk had now begun to assemble all along the lengthy fitting wharf.

Happiness glittered in her eyes and her smile grew. "Oh, let me fetch Drew. He'll want to see this, too."

Brogan detained her with a squeeze of his hand. "In a moment." Selfish of him perhaps, but he'd had little opportunity to be alone with Lorena and was hungry to steal what moments they could. Especially this moment.

Lorena lifted her gaze to Brogan's and what she found in his eyes reflected the same uncertainty gnawing at her. She smiled reassuringly. What words could adequately convey her love? What deed? She fully intended to accept his proposal and promise to stand by his side through the worst. She'd do anything for him, but oh—if only she could spare him this. Still, the past must be put to rights before they could move forward with their future. Brogan understood or he wouldn't have asked her to hold off with her answer.

Lorena held tight to his hand, drawing on his bulwark strength and remembering her faith as she turned her attention to familiar sights on shore.

Soon their feet would touch Duxboro soil, but given recent events, *home* had taken on quite a different meaning. Home was not so much a location as it was she, Brogan, and Drew being together.

Owning to the shallowness of the Bluefish River and the

imposing hull size of the *Yankee Heart*, soon they could venture no closer to shore. Brogan gave the order to moor the merchantman and lower the boats.

He sat in the stern directly across from her, Drew fidgeting restlessly at her side, and paused before taking up the oars. In his eyes was a look of love and longing.

"You're nearly home now," he told them.

"Will you come live with us?" Drew asked.

"We'll settle all that later. But wherever I do live, I shall always be nearby, and we'll see each other whenever we like, agreed?"

The child released a breath. "Yes, sir."

"You promised, remember, not to say anything about me being your father until after I've had a chance to speak with your papa Huntley. Do you think you can keep our secret for a bit?"

"Uh-huh."

"Good lad." Brogan's grin widened, a grin he quickly turned on Lorena as though seeking her consent. "Ready, then?"

She nodded. "Ready."

Gripping the oars, he squared his shoulders and put his back into rowing. Lorena ran her gaze up the *Yankee Heart*'s great towering side and continued to watch in admiration as they sailed beneath the projecting spar of the bowsprit and the shadow of the jib boom's sail.

"I wonder why I don't see Papa among any of the figures on the wharf," she puzzled as they drew closer to land. "Oh, but there is Temperance and Mrs. Culliford." Lorena reached up and waved excitedly, catching a glimpse of Edward Hicks's wife beckoning to her husband in the longboat behind them.

Under Mr. Smith's command, it carried several of the crew as well as Lorena's and Drew's trunks.

Brogan dragged the boat up the beach and lifted them out in turn onto the warm, soft beach sand. While he secured the boat, Drew scrambled up the dunes into Mrs. Culliford's arms. She stooped to receive him, rocking him in a hug and showering his face with kisses.

Lorena followed unsteadily on sea legs while Temperance ambled down the dune to her assistance, her voice carrying over the echoing surf and screeching gulls. "Is it really you, Lorena? We missed you so much! Your father has even purchased a fine porcelain tub for you. It waits up in your room. And there are soaps and bath salts of every fragrance imaginable."

"I missed you too, Temperance." Lorena hooked an arm with her sweet young friend. Sand sifted into her sandals and between her toes as together they climbed to where Mrs. Culliford and Drew awaited. They reunited in a huddle of kisses, tears, and hugs. Mrs. Culliford drew her close with an arm wrapped about Lorena's waist, then tenderly tucked a stray curl behind Lorena's ear. There were questions about that fateful day, questions about George and what had happened, which for the moment would have to remain unanswered, as shipwrights, workmen, their families, and other townsfolk gathered around to welcome her home.

"Everyone, please," she called as Brogan strode up the path to join them. "This is a happy occasion indeed, but your good wishes belong to the hero who has made my safe return to Duxboro possible." Lorena brought her hands together in applause, and all those fine citizens present lifted their faces to Brogan and joined her.

Shouts of "Hurrah" rose up. Drew broke away from the onlookers and ran proudly to his papa's side. Grinning, Brogan reached down and hoisted the boy into his arms. As he continued with Drew up the dune, Mrs. Culliford separated herself to approach him.

She took his hand reverently between both her own. "On behalf of Mr. Huntley, Captain, bless you for bringing his children safely home. We are truly indebted to you."

"You are most welcome, Mrs. Culliford." Brogan lowered Drew to the ground and cast his gaze warily over the spectators gathered. "Tell me, where is Mr. Huntley, and why is he not here with you?"

The petite housekeeper spared a glance behind with a smile for Lorena, emotion misting her eyes. "I found him to be in such a state of loneliness and worry that I convinced him to continue with his business trips. Work seems to be the only thing that consoles him. He left for Boston shortly before the *Yankee Heart* was sighted in the bay."

Mrs. Culliford addressed Brogan once again. "I sent word immediately after him, Captain, and expect him to arrive shortly. In time, no doubt, to join you in the meal Temperance and I have been busily preparing. Not that Mr. Mott is not an able cook, but we thought you might be hungry for a taste of Yankee home cooking. Mr. Smith is most welcome, as well," she was quick to assure him.

"Mr. Smith will be pleased to hear it. Thank you kindly, Mrs. Culliford. I cannot imagine an occasion when we would decline your home cooking."

Brogan appreciated the woman's excitement at having her household restored. She blushed shyly under his thoughtful gaze and offered him a smile of gratitude, eyes bright.

She turned next to Drew, sifting her fingers through his long, baby-fine curls. "Your hair has grown since I saw you last. A quick trim would tidy you up nicely before Papa Huntley arrives. Would you let me cut your hair, Drew?"

The lad turned his face, ducking from her reach. He looked to Brogan instead. "I think I need a nap first."

Temperance scoffed. "Don't believe him, Mother. He never wants to nap."

Brogan rested a hand atop his son's head and chuckled, for he understood the lad's reluctance. *Why must I get a trim when my own papa's hair is so long?* he imagined the boy thinking. Brogan's hair had now grown to where it skimmed the top of his shoulders.

Observing them, Mrs. Culliford blushed with horror. "Oh, Captain, I did not mean to imply—"

"Please, don't apologize, Mrs. Culliford. I agree with you; Drew could do with a haircut. Though, clearly, I do not set the best example on that score."

Mrs. Culliford set her chin proudly. "Well, in that case, Captain, you are most welcome to join us. I've often been told I have talent with a pair of shears."

Shears. The image sent a coldness racing through him.

Even though twenty years had passed since he'd last seen that nightmare of an orphan asylum, moisture formed on Brogan's brow. The sharp clip of the steel blades rang in his memory. The cruel, ragged chopping of his hair, meant to disfigure and humiliate. A much-dreaded, oft-repeated punishment and a warning to any other child who dared defy authority.

He had been signaled out as rebellious, punished for his inability to succumb to the despair of his ill birth, for the fire in his heart that raged against injustice, and sometimes to the extent of a bleeding scalp.

Never since had Brogan allowed anyone near his head with a sharp instrument. Whenever his hair became too ungainly, he would lop off an inch or two by his own hand.

"I promise it won't hurt a bit, Captain," Mrs. Culliford encouraged sweetly.

Brogan reminded himself he had nothing to fear from this petite, gentle housekeeper. And a respectable appearance couldn't hurt his meeting with Nathaniel Huntley. If his little mite of a son could survive a hair trim, so could he. They were bred of the same stock.

Today he'd put the ugliness of the past to rest. Abigail. The orphan asylum. Painful memories. They couldn't hurt him.

Chuckling, he gave the lad's head a tousle. "We'll do this together, aye? Get a trimming and make a good showing for Mr. Huntley." Then to the housekeeper he said, "Thank you, Mrs. Culliford. I would be pleased to join you."

She smiled as though delighted to be able to do this small kindness for him.

The dear woman had no idea how great a kindness.

A platter of crisped bacon and sausages balanced in her hands, Lorena bid farewell to Brogan's shaggy blond mane as she watched him push the breadboard table off to one side, transforming the summer kitchen into a barber shop.

Such a dashing fellow could well afford to wear his hair in any style he chose, and if he preferred a more fashionable length—well, all the good for it.

And convenient, because this meant that Brogan would

be otherwise occupied when her father arrived. She had to prepare Papa. Her stomach twisted awaiting his arrival, knowing what damage could be wrought from the truth. Brogan deserved nothing less, but the man she had come to know and love was not likely to walk away from such a confrontation with her father unscathed.

Lorena shuddered, departing with her platter to the main house. Temperance arranged the fare on the sideboard while Lorena laid the table, until an unmistakable commotion in the front hall caused her to drop what she was doing.

"Children!" her father called. "Children, I'm here. Lorena? Drew? Where are you?"

Lorena hurried from the room to join him in the foyer. Papa stood on the Oriental rug before the opened black-lacquered door, through which could be seen a vista of the bay and Brogan's three-masted *Yankee Heart*. He appeared dusty from his travels, even fatigued from the heat. His buff-colored beaver hat tipped precariously to one side, and as he reached up to remove it, his eyes shone with tears.

"Oh, my darling child."

Lorena rushed into his outstretched arms. He pressed his cheek to hers, and she felt a little girl again, hungry for her papa's embrace, comforted by the quiet strength of his voice and the soft brush of graying whiskers that grew low in front of his ears.

"Are you well? Were you harmed?" Papa stepped back, holding her at arm's length and assessing her with a long, loving stare.

Lorena smiled, blinking back tears. "I'm well. Very well. Better than when I left, in fact."

"I've been lost without you, Lorena. I've paced the wharf

every day, watching and waiting for your return." He frowned in a despairing way that Lorena found endearing. Tell me, how did it happen, you getting stuck on that brig? And the letter from George. I don't understand."

Lorena explained.

"Vomit powder! Why, if I am not the biggest fool to ever breathe sea air. And to think I trusted George. I trained and encouraged him. He grew into a superb architect. I was proud. I knew of his feelings for you, even gave him my blessing. All the while I never suspected what harm . . ."

Papa shook his head as though to clear the direction of his thoughts. "Well, you are home safe now, thanks be to God and the decency of Captain Talvis." He searched the hallway toward the back of the house. "Where is he? And where is Drew, that little rascal? Wait till he sees the collection of stones I've been gathering for him."

She'd no chance to respond, for by then a noisy procession could be heard at the back of the house. Lorena grabbed her father's arm.

"I haven't time for long explanations, Papa, but be fore-warned. Brogan is going to ask to speak to you in confidence, and when he does, he will make a shocking confession. You'll be surprised to learn he is the one person we never expected to surface when we brought Drew into our home. The widow's husband was underestimated by us all, for as it turns out, she was not a widow at all."

"What?" Papa's eyes held many questions, but with a squeeze of his forearm, Lorena halted them and continued on. "Brogan is true and fiercely faithful to those he cares about." She smiled in reflection. "You were wise to put your confidence in him. Still, you'll be angry when he tells you his reason for coming to Duxboro. But, remember, he was a victim as much as Drew. Be compassionate. Drew loves him. And so do I, Papa. I hope to marry him."

"Marry?" Papa sputtered under his breath, his expression a mask of shock and confusion, before his attention was claimed by Drew's squeal of joy.

As Papa turned, Lorena glanced down the hall to where Brogan strode hand in hand with the child. Drew had retained his crown of fat buttercream curls, except now they lay closer to his head in respectable fashion. Brogan's shaggy hair had been trimmed to the nape, parted slightly off-center and combed forward to frame his lean cheeks and long side whiskers.

She took a careful look at him.

He wore a pair of gray broadcloth trousers with a strap passing under the heel of his black boots. His crisp linen shirt was not tied with either cravat or neckcloth. Instead, ruffles of an even finer linen adorned the front of the shirt as well as his wrists. The effect made for a stark contrast. Soft ruffles on a thoroughly masculine man. White fabric against his darkened skin. Tender blue eyes shining out a rugged face.

As Lorena held him in her admiring gaze, they exchanged smiles.

Drew meanwhile broke away from Brogan and jumped into her father's arms, where he proceeded to bend Papa's ear with embellished yarns of their adventures.

Papa stepped forward, Drew clinging to his coattails, and offered Brogan his hand. "God bless you, good fellow. I sincerely cannot thank you enough. I had every confidence you'd bring my children safely back to me and you have."

As they exchanged a handshake, Lorena caught Brogan's wink. "As it turns out, sir," he said, "it was my pleasure."

Papa beamed with pride and pleasure. "Captain, I insist on housing your entire crew in one of my boardinghouses for the duration of your stay. This evening a celebration supper shall be served them in the dining hall. As for yourself and Mr. Smith, you will dine with my family and me and shall spend the night as honored guests in my home. Mrs. Culliford, please see to their rooms at your first opportunity."

The housekeeper smiled warmly. "Sir, from the day you first informed me of your wishes, all these details were arranged, awaiting only the arrival of the *Yankee Heart*. Now that she has arrived, Temperance and I have anticipated your desire to gather at the table with your children and hear of their adventure. So, before the meal we've prepared grows any colder, may I suggest you continue this conversation in the dining room?"

Papa's eyes crinkled at their corners, shining with the warmth of his smile. "Excellent. A cup of tea would be most welcome. I can tell you, Mrs. Culliford, I am prepared to allow plenty of time for family in the future, devoting myself less to business and even abandoning my plans for a shipping enterprise, if necessary. How well I have learned the importance of that, suffering as I have without my children."

He glanced again at Lorena and Drew, almost as if he found it impossible to believe they were actually sharing the same space.

Lorena felt Brogan's eyes upon her and turned. A lump caught in her throat. Despite the gravity of the confession before him, his expression shone with the hope and repentance he carried in his heart. A man of justice and honor and loyalty, he stood prepared to humble himself before her father with the truth.

She slipped a hand into the pocket of her apricot gown and closed her fingers around the silver thimble he had given her. Smiling her love, she gave him a nod of encouragement.

"Sir, before I accept further of your generosity, it is imperative I share a private word with you," Brogan announced. "There is much you don't know about me, and it cannot wait any longer to be revealed."

Papa sobered at that. He looked shaken, uncertain what to expect. "My daughter informs me you have something to discuss, Captain. Come, let us retire to my study. Excuse us," he apologized to all. "Don't wait on us, Lorena. Take Drew and eat while the food is warm."

"Yes, Papa." Lorena knew she would not be able to swallow a morsel herself, but for the child's sake she turned to him and said, "Mmm, is that molasses bread I smell? How long has it been since we've squashed gooseberries in a bread and butter sandwich?"

She led Drew into the dining room, one ear harkening to the sound of her father's study door as it closed shut.

19

After years of agonizing why his son had been taken from him—bitter, angry, haunted by imagination and secrecy—Brogan took heart. At last he'd be granted the peace of mind in knowing what had happened to Benjamin three years ago. Finally, he would get answers. Huntley would deal with him honestly, as Abigail never had.

The shipbuilder closed the door behind them and gestured to a pair of winged chairs on an Oriental rug before the fireplace. They were tall, handsome pieces, jacquard-upholstered in vibrant red.

Brogan declined the seat and paced across the wide-plank pine floor to an east-facing window on the opposite side of Huntley's desk, a desk littered with architectural drawings and drafting implements. He gazed out the panes to a sweeping view of land and sea. Hundreds of questions sprang to mind, yet before he could voice a single one, he must disclose his relationship to Ben.

Mustering his courage, Brogan turned from the window. "Mr. Huntley, you should know that I am privy to the true identity of the boy you call Drew. I have known from the beginning, in fact, because *Benjamin* was my reason for coming to you."

"Oh." Except for a slight paleness of complexion, Nathaniel Huntley's face disclosed nothing. "I hope you won't mind, Captain, but I believe I shall have a seat." He lumbered to a wing chair and eased his burden down onto its cushioned seat, gripping the armrests for support. "And here I was convinced you came to me for a ship."

He heard betrayal in the man's tone and reminded himself Nathaniel Huntley had good reason to feel wronged, though Brogan himself had also been wronged. Brogan was well aware he was not perfect; he had made mistakes, but in his heart he sought forgiveness and to please God.

He squared his shoulders. "I came for my son. I am the boy's natural father. I am the husband of the late woman who surrendered Benjamin to you. Abigail Russell Talvis. We were a family, or so I thought, until the day she sent our son away and refused to tell me where."

"The widow. Not a widow at all, as it turns out," Huntley said in a tone laced with distaste. It was the first time he'd acknowledged acquaintance with Abigail in Brogan's presence. "And now it seems my own daughter has fallen in love with you." Crooking his neck, Huntley began to massage the base of his skull as though to ease an ache. "You did not exaggerate, Captain. This is all most revealing. But I would like to know why you didn't come to me when you first arrived in Duxboro. What were your intentions that you chose to keep your identity hidden?"

Brogan stepped forward and took the chair opposite Huntley's. Poised on the edge of his seat, he explained everything just as he had to Lorena, beginning with his meeting Abigail along Boston Harbor. He told of Benjamin's birth and the joy and purpose it brought to his life. He made clear his resolve to be a good father and provider, and how, to his mind, he had been growing successful at both—until Abigail snatched it all away.

Huntley made no attempt to interrupt, but listened quietly. Brogan detailed his search and how he finally came to discover the whereabouts of his son. He explained his desperate plan to commission the *Yankee Heart* and then sail off with Ben.

"My intentions might not have been honorable," he admitted, "but at the time all that concerned me was my son. Abigail swore I'd never find him. Soon after, she perished in a blaze that destroyed our home, and I knew, even if I were to locate Benjamin, there was no one to speak for my paternity."

Huntley's pensive silence grew unbearable. When at last he spoke, Brogan thought he glimpsed perspiration on the fellow's brow. "Then tell me why, when you had the opportunity, did you not depart with Drew as planned? Why instead did you go after Lorena?"

"Because, sir, I understand how it feels to have a child you love suddenly snatched away. How far would a father go to save his child? Would he launch a ship after her?"

Huntley blinked, his eyes moist, at which point Brogan sprang off his seat and strode to the mantel. His eyes landed on an oil painting hanging above. Likely an ancestral portrait, for its somber-faced gentleman subject bore a strong resemblance to Nathaniel Huntley.

Impatient for answers of his own, yet knowing he had more to confess, Brogan whirled about to face the man. "When I realized I would need to spend time with Lorena if I were to get anywhere near my son, I had no idea I would fall in love with her or that her love would so change my heart. It is my great desire to wed your daughter, sir. I understand how disturbing this news must be for you, but believe me when I say things have worked themselves out to the benefit of all. Lorena, Drew . . . that is, Ben, and I have been happy together on the *Yankee Heart*. I am prepared to do all in my power to give them the bright future they deserve. If that necessitates first proving my character to you, then so be it. I am determined. Lorena has forgiven me, and now I beg your forgiveness, as well. If not for you, my son would have perished alongside Abigail. I don't know how it came to be that he was placed in your home, but clearly he has thrived and been well loved here. For that, I shall remain forever in your debt. But as I've explained to Lorena, all the charity in the world cannot replace the bond of blood. I shall remain a part of my son's life, and he shall know a father's love. However, it is my hope you should give us your blessing, sir, to be a family."

As Brogan waited impatiently for an answer, he noticed Huntley's hand begin to tremble. What vile thing had Abigail done that, even dead, she could cause a man of Huntley's sophistication to be distraught over a discussion of her?

Huntley leveled his gaze with Brogan's and, leaning back, folded his hands over his rounded belly. "I shall not withhold my forgiveness, Captain, nor my blessing. Your character is proven in faithfulness and deed. Further, it would seem I owe you an apology, for I never doubted my brother when he told me you were dead. Indeed, I never gave you a second thought. You were a complete unknown. The child was the only innocent. Now here you have resurfaced, alive and hale, a hero to your country and a hero within my own home. You are worthy of my daughter's hand."

At those words Brogan felt more happiness than his heart could contain. He thought of Lorena and Ben, of their beautiful faces and the way they smiled at him with adoration and trust. His burden lifted. Joy exploded inside him, the future dawning brighter than he could ever have imagined. "Thank you, Mr. Huntley, sir."

He could scarcely believe his good fortune. There remained just one final matter to put his mind at rest. "And now I feel I deserve some answers of my own. Lorena directed me to you as the one who should give them. What was your relationship to my wife that you should have aided her in her scheme?"

Huntley rose to address him. "Lorena was wise in sending you to me. You've traveled a long, difficult road searching for the truth, and I am the only person alive who can give it to you."

Turning, Nathaniel Huntley crossed the room to a Chippendale secretary and idly skimmed his fingertips over its opened cherrywood desktop. As he glanced up, the sadness in his eyes unnerved Brogan.

"My brother Stephen and I had little in common as far as siblings go," Huntley said. "Stephen followed his own path and at a young age married into the Bainbridge family of Boston. You've heard the name, I take it?"

"Aye." Every Bostonian had, but Brogan failed to see what Stephen Huntley's marriage had to do with either himself or his son. Before he could voice his impatience, however, Huntley raised a hand to silence him.

"Indulge me, Captain. Please. For without the whole story, you might not believe me."

Brogan nodded. The whole story. At last.

"The Bainbridges are one of Boston's oldest and most respected families, merchants by trade, and Stephen's marriage to Ellen Bainbridge assured him the highest possible social standing and great prosperity. The couple enjoyed prominence in Boston society and produced five beautiful children. Stephen had wealth, power, and family, but like many men of affluence, all was not enough. He kept a mistress."

Brogan made the connection and found he was hardly surprised. "Abigail?"

Nathaniel Huntley's forlorn expression confirmed it. "With time, Stephen's marriage began to suffer. He did not hide his infidelity as well as he believed. His good name was threatened, not to mention what effect a scandal would have on his wife and children. To make matters worse, this mistress, a widow who for years believed she was barren, conceived."

A cold tremor rocked Brogan to his very bones. What was Huntley implying? He searched the shipbuilder's eyes, eyes so gravely serious they spoke louder than words.

"Abigail was with no other man at the time she was with me," Brogan asserted. "I know this for a fact."

"No, Captain, she was with child before she met you and deliberately led you to believe you were her baby's father. I regret I must inform you that you have been the victim of a cruel deceit. Drew . . . *Benjamin* is not your son. He is the offspring of my brother Stephen. My nephew. But not even he, poor child, knows this. Lorena and I have allowed him to believe his father perished at sea."

Brogan struggled against accepting such a possibility. He couldn't think. He felt numb. Abashed. With all he had endured for his son's sake . . . no, it could not be true. It was inconceivable.

"I would have thought it beneath you to concoct such a wretched lie in order to keep my son," he fired out, though in his heart Brogan knew Nathaniel Huntley was not a man to speak falsely.

Huntley's cheeks paled between a set of ginger-brown side whiskers tinged with gray. "Sadly, it is the truth, Captain." The man's brow creased as he stepped away from the secretary to draw closer to Brogan. "My brother welcomed the prospect of an ill-born son as much as he did the tainting of his good name. Marriage was out of the question, and his mistress—your wife—was unwilling to release her hold over one of the richest, most powerful men in Boston society. She held a strange power over Stephen, but they decided they would not see each other for a short time. Meanwhile, she was to marry and pass her pregnancy off on another man."

Brogan stalked the room like a caged animal, as if by pacing he could walk off the pain and humiliation that filled every pore of his being. He thought back, recalling the day he first set eyes on Abigail as she passed over the cobblestones in her chaise. He recalled the interest in her smile. She returned to that same waterfront locale by the shops, seemingly innocent but hoping to meet him again as though by chance.

Brogan knew all along she had been singling him out, and it had flattered him. No ordinary seaman would dare approach such a fine lady, but Brogan had been just bold enough to open the millinery shop door for her. Abigail was equally bold enough to inquire after his name.

In his vanity he let himself believe she truly loved him, for why else would she have married him? He was but a common sailor in want of employment.

Here he thought himself clever in outwitting her and recovering their son, but she would have the last word again, reaching beyond the grave to deliver this final, crushing blow.

The truth hit him with such force, Brogan could scarcely breathe. It took a moment to realize Huntley was still speaking.

". . . grew increasingly jealous of his lover's husband. Stephen desired to resume the affair, but one person stood in his way. A seafaring youth caught in the middle of his treachery, whom I now discover was you, Captain."

Brogan quit pacing to grab on to the mantel for support. The yellow cream walls closed in on him, and it was all he could do to remain in the same room with Huntley and listen to the rest of his sordid tale.

"Aside from the knowledge my brother kept a mistress, I was unaware of what had been going on, or even of Benjamin's existence, until Stephen appealed to me just weeks before I took custody of the boy. Stephen confessed to having used his influence to secure Abigail's young sailor a position with a privateer sailing out of Bristol, Rhode Island. He later made arrangements to finance a privateer schooner, secretly arranging for this sailor to be promoted to captain and sent on a dangerous mission with a sloppy crew and little experience in commanding them. A certain death. He swore you were gone, never to return for the boy. Benjamin was alone in the world, I believed. But it seems Stephen grossly underestimated you."

Brogan felt as though he were drowning in a sinking black hole, listening to Huntley's voice from underwater.

His greatest accomplishments had been a lie, from his marriage to his placement among the crew of the *Black Eagle* to his captaincy on the *Wild Pilgrim*. Most important, his son did not belong to him! Abigail and her lover had stripped him of all pride, and hate for them overwhelmed him. His wrath demanded to be vented, but on whom? Both his enemies were dead.

"Stephen admitted things had gone awry," Huntley was saying. "He said he should have sent the woman away to have his child, then disposed of him in an orphanage. By the grace of God, Stephen came to me instead. He knew I would never turn my nephew away. I was outraged at my brother's behavior, but I kept his secret, for I knew exposure could only bring suffering to my brother's family, not to mention the damage to Benjamin. With me, the boy would be loved and cared for, free from the scorn of his illegitimacy. I took legal action to assure he carried the Huntley name and would become heir to all that entailed."

Nathaniel Huntley frowned with deep regret. "My sympathies, Captain, but you should know Benjamin did not forget you. When he first came to us, he cried for his papa in his sleep. You see now why we continued to let him believe his father did not leave him, but died at sea."

A great pang wracked Brogan's chest in the form of tears he could not shed. Until he'd come along, the lad rightfully believed both his parents were dead. The truth would break his heart.

Brogan had one final question. "The fire that took Abigail. Your brother was rumored to have been seen near the blaze. Was Stephen with her that night?"

Huntley nodded, his expression grave. "I ministered to my

brother on his deathbed and entreated him to ask forgiveness for his sins. It was then Stephen made another shocking confession to me. He had wanted to end their relationship, but your wife would not hear of it. She flew into a rage, threatening to go to his family. Stephen abandoned the notion of discontinuing their affair until one wintry evening . . . their last together, he knocked over a candlestick, quite by accident, while she lay sleeping. He told me he watched it burn up the carpet, an idea forming. The flames crept to the draperies, and before he knew it, the room was ablaze. He had barely enough time to steal off in his nightshirt. He slipped away quietly on his horse, leaving the poor woman to die. He kept to alleys and back roads, riding through the snowfall, then walked across his own fields to wait in his stable for one of his servants to retrieve dry clothing from the house. He got away with murder, and all the while his wife, Ellen, thought he was at his club. The irony was, in making his escape, Stephen caught pneumonia and set in motion his own demise."

It was a wicked tale, and Brogan could not bear another moment of it. He made for the door and flung it wide, his emotions ready to explode from the grief and anger swelling inside him.

Upon his exit he nearly collided with Lorena, who was standing just outside. She stared up at him, uncertain, her small face lost in a thick cloud of spicy-brown ringlets, her soft brown eyes larger than ever. She must think him the biggest fool. She'd known the truth and yet had allowed him to believe they could be a family.

Brogan stormed past her, down the hallway, and out the front door. Outside, the smell of salt and sea mulled about in the humidity. Clouds had begun to move in again. He heard Lorena calling for him as he ran toward the beach.

He pushed the jolly boat into the surf, then climbed in and grabbed the oars.

And started rowing.

20

*L*orena chased Brogan out onto the front stoop. She called to him as he sprinted down the brick walkway, past the flower beds and box elder toward Squire Huntley Road. He was headed for the shore, and as she lifted her hemline to follow, her father halted her.

"Let him go. He's suffered a great shock and needs time alone. You must give him that time, Lorena, for if you intrude upon his grief before he's had a chance to face it on his own, he may say hurtful things you'll both regret later. Only the captain knows the extent of his pain, but once he's accepted facts, he will return to you."

A sob arose from deep within her throat.

She had yet to accept Brogan's offer of marriage. She yearned to tell him she loved him. He needed to know the indispensable place he held in both her and Drew's lives. Brogan wasn't alone in his pain. She felt it, too.

She'd never forget the haunted, stricken look in his eyes as he opened the door to her father's study. Lorena lifted her face toward the wharf and, through a blur of tears, watched Brogan shove the jolly boat into the bay.

"What did you say to him, Papa? Did you give him your blessing?" Lorena asked of the man she'd always turned to in times of trouble. This time her papa could not make it all better. "Tell me everything you said to him."

Her father wrapped her in his arms. "I'll tell you what you want to know, Lorena, but understand this. Nothing any of us could have done would have made the news any easier for the captain to bear. What happens next is entirely up to him. We can offer our comfort, but in the end he has to make his own choices."

"I can't not reach out to him, Papa. I need to do something."

"The captain's desire was to give a father's love, and now he feels that dream is lost. He believes he is alone in his grief. You and I know that's not true, Lorena. We know God loves him, but before Captain Talvis will hear our words of encouragement, he needs to experience a father's love for himself. The love of his heavenly Father."

"How, Papa? How can I convince Brogan of a heavenly Father who loves him at a time like this? How can I help him if I cannot speak to him?"

"Pray, Lorena. Pray the Lord makes His will known to all of us who care for the captain."

A tear streaked down her cheek as her father pressed a kiss to her temple. Lorena wished she could remain strong, but at Papa's tenderness she sobbed. Her hopes drained. It tore at her, not being able to help someone she loved.

From within the house came the patter of feet, quickly headed their way. Drew called out as he bounded over the threshold, and Lorena pulled from her father's embrace to dab at her eyes.

The boy halted at the sight of her swollen eyes, confused. He followed her gaze toward the bay. Together they watched Brogan's boat grow smaller and smaller with each pull of the oars that rowed him farther away.

"Papa?" he moaned in a weak, small voice.

He glanced up, alarmed. "Where is he going, Lorena?"

"The captain needs to return to his crew," her father explained. "Come, Drew. Join me for a taste of that fine meal Mrs. Culliford has prepared." He reached for the child's hand, but Drew had already sensed something to be terribly wrong and leapt out of reach.

He took off in the direction of the fitting wharf, shouting for his papa.

A light rain fell that afternoon. Daylight waned, until twilight lingered over the Huntley estate in that intermediate moment between sunset and the encompassing fall of darkness.

Lorena waited at the windows, yet Brogan did not return to the house for supper. A much bewildered Mr. Smith did call, however, concerned as to what ailed his captain. Brogan had returned to the *Yankee Heart*, wearing the ghastly look of one whose spirit had been crushed.

She was a barren merchantman that now sat in the Cowyard waters of Duxboro Bay, Mr. Smith explained. Nothing but the creaking of the yards echoing across a vast, lonely deck. No cargo filled her hold, no seamen kept her watch, for Brogan had ordered all to partake of her father's generous offer. The crew was currently making merry in one of his boardinghouses, feasting on one of the grandest meals they'd ever been treated to in their seafaring careers. Comfortable beds awaited them at the end of the evening.

The *Yankee Heart* had turned into a mournful, empty shell of a ship, with her captain locked away in her bowels, refusing to speak to anyone, not even Mr. Smith.

Brogan had never been one to sulk, the mate confessed. This silent despair made little sense after the welcoming and grateful reception they'd all received earlier. Were harsh words exchanged between Brogan and Mr. Huntley? He decided to row over and find out for himself.

But Mr. Smith was encouraged to stay and dine with the family, which he did.

There seemed little point in keeping the truth from Brogan's closest and dearest friend. The mate bore the news gravely and agreed with her father that she should not accompany him back to the *Yankee Heart* to try to speak with Brogan.

Lorena reminded herself to take heart, but found she could not sleep for worrying. Her bedroom lay at the rear of the house and the call of crickets waxed strong, yet she could clearly distinguish the gentle roll of the surf as she sat on the sill of her opened window.

She searched the murky, blackened sky for stars, remembering the night Brogan had taught her the trick of manning the ship's wheel. *"Be my small helm,"* he'd said. *"It's possible for the mightiest to be moved by even the most humble."*

Lorena never suspected the day was soon approaching she would need to be exactly that for Brogan. His small helm. Could she move him to faith in his dark hour? For even if he did come to her and was willing to hear her out, what words could adequately convince him of the good that had come from this terrible deceit?

Did he lie awake at this very moment, blinded by grief and lost in hopeless thoughts?

She might not be able to see Brogan for herself or speak to him personally, but she could look upon his ship. She could steal another glimpse of the *Yankee Heart* and assure herself he was aboard. She could send her prayers out to him over the waves.

Before venturing anywhere, Lorena checked in on Drew and found him whining in his sleep.

"Papa . . . papa . . . papa . . . nooo!"

"Wake up, Drew."

Lorena pulled him into her arms. "Shush," she told him. "It's all right, sweetheart. I'm here." She stroked the curls off his forehead and rocked him in her arms as he slowly began to wake.

He sat up suddenly. "Papa?"

"The captain is on his ship, in bed, like you . . . sleeping, as you should be." She wiped his face and produced his doll from behind her back. "Look, I've brought you Captain Briggs."

He scowled and wrenched the doll from her hands, tossing it to the floor. Lorena understood. He didn't want a doll made to look like his papa. He wanted the man he truly believed to be his father.

"Why did Mr. Smith come to say good night and not Papa?" he asked. For the first time since Drew had sailed on the *Yankee Heart*, Brogan had not tucked him into bed or wished him pleasant dreams. Lorena ached for the child in his confusion.

She retrieved the doll off the floor, then removed her sandals and slipped her feet under the coverlet to join him in bed.

She patted the pillow and he laid his head down beside her.

"The captain needs time alone with God," she said. "Like David did, when David ran into the wilderness to hide from Saul. Right now, the captain feels he is in the wilderness. A bit like the way I felt when I was aboard the *Lady Julia*, being carried farther and farther away from those I loved."

She could see that the soft tone of her voice soothed him. Drew's eyelids grew heavy.

"Why?" he whispered.

Lorena gave his nose a tweak. "Why does the captain feel God has deserted him? Because, Drew, he does not know the truth. All the while David was lamenting in his psalms, God had a plan that he be ordained king. Just as, all the while I despaired, there was a plan in motion to rescue me. And God has a plan for the captain, too. Only he doesn't know it . . . *yet*."

Something occurred to her with those words, and as Drew drifted off to sleep, Lorena lay in the darkness, thinking up a plan of her own.

Eventide had fallen like a dark curtain over the long day, and nothing, save a faint sliver of moonlight, dispelled the blackness of the great cabin.

Brogan welcomed the loneliness of the night, the darkness that engulfed him, as he listened to the rhythmic lapping of the sea against the *Yankee Heart*'s hull.

Grief had drained him. His tears were spent. Like so much dead weight, Brogan sat hunched in a wing chair, his ship's Bible clutched in his hands. He'd taken neither food nor drink the entire day, and now the emptiness inside him extended to even the pit of his stomach.

Perhaps he never saw through Abigail's trickery because he had not wanted to see. He'd wanted marriage and a family. Benjamin's birth meant that at last he was related to someone by blood, and he'd been prepared to do everything in his power to love and protect his own.

All he had left was anger—a frustrated rage that consumed him the tighter he clutched the Bible, until Brogan felt the blood vessels in his hands might burst.

It was told the Bible's message was one of love for God's children. But what of children born outside the church? As early as memory served he had been taught that God would not listen to the prayers of a bad orphan like himself.

Jabez proclaimed different. The blessed Savior loved all sinners. And when Lorena Huntley entered his life, Brogan very nearly believed it was true. Her gentle spirit and kindness had seeped into his soul and opened his heart. All he'd ever wanted was to be part of a family. Lorena represented the steadfast core of her family. She was all goodness. The woman they looked to for direction and reassurance, Brogan included. He had believed that if she could love him, then he must be worthy. She'd made him feel so.

He mourned his love for her, for the life together he had hoped they'd share. No more, though. Everything had changed. All of it gone. Oh, how he wished he could open this Good Book and find comfort, but its words, its promises, had not been written for the likes of him.

Why had this happened to him? What had the lonely orphan boy ever done that the Almighty should punish him? What except long for family life with an ache that tore at his soul. As a man, had he been too confident in his abilities, too arrogant in his actions, that he had invited the wrath of a God who would put an end to everything precious in his life?

He was done . . . exhausted . . . finished.

Rising, Brogan flung the Bible across the room. It hit the doorframe, missing Jabez's head by inches as the mate opened the door.

Jabez froze, his beefy torso illuminated behind the golden glow of a lantern. As he raised it higher, an eerie pattern of flickering light spilled across the Brussels carpet and furnishings to reveal the discarded Bible, lying facedown and opened.

Brogan squinted into the brightness and turned away. He didn't want anyone looking upon his pain or seeing the humiliation on his face.

He felt as vulnerable now as he had as a runaway orphan. A boy of six years, hungry and filthy, huddled in a Boston dockside alley, alone and at the end of his wits.

"I told you I wanted to be left alone," he barked.

Jabez stepped deeper inside the cabin. "Ye look like ye could use a friend."

Some twenty years ago, the mate had uttered those very same words to him. The unexpected compassion had torn down Brogan's defenses then and produced nearly the same effect now. "I need a moment to myself is all."

"Yer moment has extended over an entire day."

"Aye . . . well . . . so it has."

Lantern light bounced off the cabin's rich mahogany paneling, reaching for the darkened corners as Jabez filled the room with his bulk. "I've been to see Nathaniel Huntley. I am sorry, truly, but ye must not allow yerself to grieve for long. It will accomplish no good purpose, and besides yer enemies are long dead."

Brogan quickly blinked the mist from his eyes. Indeed, his enemies were gone, but oh, what he wouldn't give to confront Abigail one last time. As for Stephen Huntley, he'd never met the man, had never set eyes upon his face. Did Drew favor him in looks? Seemed foolish now, but Brogan had always been of the opinion that he and the boy shared a strong likeness.

He raked his fingers through his recently shorn hair. "From the first, Abigail played me false. My captaincy was not earned by merit but planned for my demise. Yet what I find most contemptible is that she used an innocent child. Her own flesh and blood. Do I tell Drew the man he calls papa bears no relation to him at all? Do I break his heart when he is so thrilled to discover he is not an orphan? Do I tell him his true parents never wanted him and died in shame? Of course I cannot! And if you've spoken with Mr. Huntley, then you know well enough I have no authority to make any decision concerning Drew. The ground has been hauled out from under me, Mr. Smith, and I've nothing solid left to stand upon."

Jabez hung the lantern on the nearest wall hook and bent to retrieve the discarded Bible. "Ye can stand upon this," he declared with all the conviction of his powerful voice.

Brogan dragged himself from his pit of inner turmoil to set his gaze upon his old friend. "Very well, Mr. Smith, ask that Book, what shall I do? Shall I go forward with a shrug of my shoulders as though events of these past weeks never occurred? Forget I ever believed I had a son and came to Duxboro? Come morning, shall we sail off to trade with southern markets or venture to Russia for Huntley's manila hemp? When I was a child I ran to the sea to escape the horror and loneliness I faced on land. Perhaps that is my lot in life."

He could flee, but this time there would be no escape. He

loved Lorena Huntley with an ardor he had never known and could hardly contain. And he loved Drew still, like his own. In his heart that had not changed. Yet every time he would look upon the son that was not his, Brogan would be reminded of the indignity his wife and Stephen Huntley had wrought on his life. How could he be a husband to a woman who pitied him, so much so Lorena felt she could not be candid for want of protecting him? Was it love or sympathy she felt?

She deserved better.

"The *Yankee Heart* sails on the morrow," Brogan announced. "I will speak with Lorena and her father in the morning, and then we shall leave the Huntley family in peace, to continue on as they should have been before I intruded in their lives."

"Don't be so hasty to make a decision tonight." Jabez unhooked his lantern and prepared to exit. "Trust God to steer ye on the right course. Ye can start by having a glance outside yer windows. Seems someone's been trying to send ye a signal."

Curious, Brogan peered between the curtains dressing the stern windows. From across the still, black waters of Duxboro Bay he saw Huntley's fitting dock aglow with a row of small twinkling lights.

Lorena breathed in the clean night air. Only the gentlest of breezes blew off the bay, while deep in the Cowyard waters Brogan's lovely merchantman sat illuminated by the reflection of her watch lights.

She admired the ship from her father's wharf, where Lorena had lit every lantern she and Temperance could gather.

They burned brightly all about her, a visible symbol of the hope that glowed in her heart and called to the *Yankee Heart*.

Lorena prayed silently as she waited . . . and waited . . . and waited.

She grew drowsy, and several times her bleary eyes focused on what she thought to be movement. But, no. Each time it turned out to be nothing but her imagination. Nothing until a tiny speck of illumination appeared. Lorena blinked, uncertain, then saw a light bob on the water. Several minutes later she could actually discern a shape. As she continued watching, that shape took form as a boat, and very soon she could see a man sitting at the oars, rowing toward her.

Stars twinkled from the heavens, and Lorena lifted a smile to them in expression of her thankfulness.

As Brogan beached the boat, Lorena ran down the wharf to greet him. He carried a lantern, its light looming brighter the closer he got, until she could distinguish him clearly. The grass crunched beneath his Hessians.

She sensed reserve in his posture and yearned to run to him, but remembering what her father had told her, Lorena slowed. She halted her steps. She would wait for Brogan to reach her.

He came to stand before her, and knowing he'd have no patience for idle talk, Lorena got straight to the point. "I love you. Your future is here with Drew and me. He is not my natural child either, yet I could not love him more had I birthed him myself."

"I do love you, Lorena. That has not changed or diminished," he insisted. "Neither has my love for the lad. I want you, but Abigail and your uncle Stephen have stripped me of my dignity, my accomplishments . . . my very soul. I've nothing left to offer. I no longer feel worthy of your love."

His voice sounded so somber, so devoid of hope, Lorena shuddered.

"Nothing could be further from the truth, Brogan. You are worthy to be called Drew's father. And I truly believe you need to be his papa as much as he wants you to be."

He did not deny or affirm her words but said nothing.

It was all the encouragement Lorena needed. "This challenge you face . . . it's not a matter of what you believe has been stolen from you. It's to do with your thinking and in the way you perceive things should have been. It is hopeless thinking that prevents you from seeing the whole picture. Self-pity has blinded you."

Brogan's careworn face contorted into a painfully bitter sneer. "Self-pity?"

She certainly had his attention now. Lorena had prepared herself for just such a response.

"You had it all planned," she said. "But, as you've admitted even to yourself, the way you intended to get Drew back was wrong. Surrender your plan, Brogan. Surrender your dreams to God, and let Him show you His plan for your life."

He scoffed. "I see what you're trying to do, Lorena. You think to fill me with silly hope, because you feel sorry for me, but all the sympathy in the world won't alter the past. The truth remains. I came here to deceive you. I know the plan for my life. I have never belonged anywhere . . . except on the sea. And the only thing I have ever received of the Almighty is indifference."

Lorena shook her head. "Think back, Brogan, and you'll see how untrue that statement is. God has had His hand on your life. Even when you refused to acknowledge Him, He was there. You told me the story, remember, of how Mr. Smith found you as he was off-loading cargo in Boston Harbor? Two huge wharves with the capacity to handle about five hundred ships, countless sailors and dock workers passing by every minute, and it just so happens that you caught the eye of a rare man with Christ in his heart, who reached out to help you. Do you think it was coincidence? Had anyone ever offered to help you before Mr. Smith came along? It was God's grace, I say. Abigail and Uncle Stephen meant to see you killed, yet you were protected during the war. A few inches more and that splinter from the cannon shot of a British corvette would have struck you in the chest instead of your shoulder."

At his look of confusion, Lorena explained, "Drew told me the story. Brogan, you not only survived but returned a hero to your country and made your fortune. Best of all, you were brought into the life of a child who desperately needed someone looking out for him. I believe God ordained that you should be Drew's guardian in the same way Mr. Smith has been yours. For who better than you to understand the love an unwanted child would need? God has seen the good treasure of your heart, even though you've made mistakes. He has taken what others meant for evil and turned it around to your advantage."

Though Brogan reacted with no more than a hard, thoughtful stare, something in his eyes told Lorena he was struggling with a way to overcome his prideful nature, a way to turn his cheek from the wrongs he'd been dealt and still maintain his self-respect as a man.

"Angst and anger fester inside me with no one alive on

whom I can vent my wrath," he admitted. "They will not give me peace."

"There is a cure. It's called forgiveness. If you can receive God's mercy for the mistakes you've made and forgive others for the hurts they've inflicted on you—"

"Forgive! How am I to forgive?"

Moving closer, Lorena touched her fingertips to the front of Brogan's full white shirt, and when he didn't resist, she pressed her palm over his heart. She felt it beating and knew he needed encouragement to take that heroic step. To forgive.

"My father is of the opinion, and I agree, that revealing Drew's natural parentage would serve no good purpose. You have earned the right to be his father. You dreamed of a son, and now God wants to bless you with a family. There is no one to stand in the way of our happiness. We can go on with our lives as planned. Marry, and raise other sons and daughters besides. Abigail and Uncle Stephen cannot stop us, unless you remain unwilling to lay aside the past."

He searched her face as though willing himself to believe. "You make it sound so simple," he said.

"Simple? Certainly not. Only a courageous man could be so forgiving."

At her challenge a mischievous gleam sparked in his eyes. "Ask any of my men. You'll not find a braver soul anywhere in New England."

"Oh, I've no need to ask," she acknowledged dutifully, "as I am quite certain it is the truth."

"And not to boast, for that would be a sin, but in all truth I do make an exceptional papa."

"Indeed. Save for my own father, I have never met a man

more loving and patient. So, you see, you stand in excellent company."

Brogan's nod was one of immense satisfaction. "Did I hear you mention something about more sons and daughters? Are you saying, Lorena, you accept my proposal of marriage?"

Lorena felt a warm blush of happiness rise to her cheeks. "Yes, I will marry you, Captain Brogan Talvis. Gladly."

His grin widened to a full-fledged smile, but as his gaze continued to bore deep into hers, his expression sobered. He lowered his face to hers, and Lorena closed her eyes, feeling the touch of his breath and then his lips as he pressed them upon hers and kissed her.

When at length he released her, Lorena feared her bones had turned to dust. She stood shakily, her senses clouded by love.

Brogan sighed. "How easily you make me forget everything except that which is most important."

"Pray tell, what is most important to you, sir?"

Lorena placed her hand in Brogan's offered palm, and he clasped it tightly. He raised her fingers to his lips, all the while holding her in the warmth of his gaze.

"God and family. I promise to let nothing come between us. I love you, Lorena. More than any obstacle, any test of life. I love you with my very soul."

Then Brogan kissed her again, and Lorena knew in her heart he was letting her know he would forever remain faithful to that promise.

Epilogue

Duxboro, Massachusetts, 1817

Brogan Talvis could not care less that he was slowly amassing a fortune from his partnership interest in the Huntley-Talvis merchant fleet. There were plans to construct more vessels. Warehouses and a counting house had been built at the wharf, but he gave them not a thought.

Neither did he care that he lived in an enormous manor house of Federal architecture, built to the east of his father-in-law's estate, and set on five acres of Duxboro's finest tree-studded soil. A brick wall overgrown with shrubbery fronted the property and contained its own special door, opening to a multilayered garden spanning two of those charmed acres. A brick path wove through the foliage and blooms and led to a lavish rose garden planted for the enjoyment of his wife.

When he heard an infant's wail, he bounded up the manor's grand staircase to the second floor with no thought to the luxury he lived in, caring only for the health of his young wife and what wonder he would find upon reaching the source of that squalling.

He took his steps two at a time. His son and father-in-law followed behind as Brogan dashed down the hallway to the closed double doors of the master bedroom. He would have thrown them open himself, but the latch turned and out stepped the midwife. Brogan saw only the blood on her apron. He could still hear a baby's cry from inside.

"You may go in now, Captain, and meet your new son," she said.

Drew plowed into the back of Brogan's legs, where he came to an abrupt halt. "I have a brother?"

"Did I hear a son?" Nathaniel Huntley called as he joined them.

Brogan swept past the midwife and strode to the foot of his bed, taking in the scene.

The room was dimly lit and toasty warm. The newborn, thoroughly bundled and hidden from view in Mrs. Culliford's arms, had quieted. In the bed, Lorena lay quiet and still amid a mound of quilts and blankets, and for a moment Brogan panicked.

Please, Lord. Her face looked so very pale, her eyelids heavily closed. If anything were to happen to her, if she had been injured . . .

They had been married before family, friends, and crew on the main deck of the *Yankee Heart*, which was anchored in Duxboro Bay and had been festooned for the ceremony. Afterward, a wedding breakfast had been served at his father-in-law's house, but before that, more decorations and refreshments awaited in the great cabin, including a tall white wedding cake, studded with gilded almonds and adorned with flowers and laurel.

It had transpired on a Tuesday morning, nearly two years ago. The most extraordinary day of his life. Until today.

"Lorena?" he rasped.

Her eyes sprang open, arresting him in their intensity and flooding him with relief, until the infant's gurgle drew her attention away. He followed the stare of her beautiful brown eyes to Mrs. Culliford, who stood by the fire cooing to the curious thing in her arms.

She smiled and his breath caught in his throat. His vision blurred.

"Would you like to see your son?"

Tears pricked at his eyes. Brogan walked over to her side of the bed, leaned down and pressed a soft kiss to her forehead. "I need to be assured that you are well, my love."

She lifted a hand out to him from under the coverings, and he clutched it like a lifeline.

"I'm quite well. And very happy." She motioned to Mrs. Culliford to bring her the babe. She gazed up at Brogan, her own eyes glistening with unshed tears, then turned to Drew and Mr. Huntley, who stood in the doorway. "I hope you all know how very much I love you."

"If it is one-tenth of the love and gratitude we have for you, Lorena, then we are blessed indeed," Brogan responded on behalf of them all.

"Look, Captain," Mrs. Culliford urged, stepping forward with the bundle. "Look at your son. He is exceptionally beautiful, I daresay."

Brogan drank in the sight as she approached and laid the newborn on the bed beside Lorena, then loosened the blankets. He saw a tiny red face, an amazing face with a thick crop of hair, gingery brown like his mother's. Brogan gazed at Lorena, astonished.

As Drew and Mr. Huntley moved closer, he touched one of the babe's hands. Brogan spread the miniature fingers and they curled around one of his own. His breath caught in his throat.

A tear slid down his cheek. He looked again at the babe, then back at Lorena. "Thank you."

His wife smiled sweetly, and Brogan used his free arm to embrace Drew. This beautiful boy of seven years was also his son.

At seven years, Brogan had been a dirty, scrawny orphan on the run with nowhere to go, living off the streets. As a man, he now possessed the means and wealth to assure his children would be afforded every opportunity he'd been denied. Not only that, but this incredible woman, his wife, had borne him a flesh-and-blood son. Though he'd not love this new child any more or less, it felt good to know his blood was bonded to a family. His family.

With thanks and glory to God, Brogan took stock of these and all his blessings, which at the moment seemed too numerous to count.

He took Lorena's hand in his, unable to believe what treasure he beheld. A prize indeed.

Acknowledgments

Although writing is a lonely pursuit, in reality, *Prize of My Heart* would not be here today without some very special folks who have seen me through the journeys of both writing and publishing.

For the inspiration and creativity I know comes from Him, to God be the glory.

Special thanks to my family, Carrie, Dick, Cheryl and Chaka, Rich and Karen Norato, for their love and encouragement.

Thanks to Lisa Diaz for her friendship and prayers across the miles and over the years, to my brainstorming buddies Annette Blair and Jeanine Spikes, to Amy Stratton for giving the manuscript a final read, and to Dante Giammarco for research help and support during the workweek. To all, thanks for your continuing encouragement.

Thanks to my agent, Mary Sue Seymour, for her faith in me and for handling my career with class and understanding.

Thanks to everyone at Bethany House for all the creative and marketing input that has gone into making *Prize of My Heart* a publishing reality, especially editors David Long and Luke Hinrichs—two considerate and creative gentlemen I feel blessed to be working with.

A lifelong New Englander, **Lisa Norato** lives in a historic village with homes and churches dating as far back as the eighteenth century. She balances writing with a career as a legal assistant specializing in corporate law. When not writing, she enjoys precious time with family and her dog, cooking, reading and television, especially British comedy and historical dramas. You can visit Lisa's website at *www.lisanorato.com* or follow her on Facebook.

If You Enjoyed *Prize of My Heart,* You May Also Like…